"Um...good afternoon. Or is it morning?"

Leafa § Kirito's adoptive sister.
She logs in to the Underworld using Super-
Account 03, the Earth Goddess, Terraria.

"Sorry it took so long, Asuna."

Sinon § A sniper who logs in to the Underworld using Super-Account 02, the Sun Goddess, Solus.

"...Looks like...your skill with the blade isn't much to write home about...Your Majesty."

Bercouli § Wielder of the Time-Splitting Sword. Commander of the Integrity Knights, the cornerstone of the Human Guardian Army.

"I grow tired of this...Begone."

Vecta § Supreme commander of the Dark Army and god of darkness in search of Alice, the Priestess of Light.

"Subtilizer...why are *you* here?"

"...I fought against you in a *Gun Gale Online* event, didn't I? ...To think we'd run into each other again here."

Subtilizer § The *Gun Gale Online* avatar of Gabriel Miller, who is logged in to the Underworld with Super-Account 04, Vecta, the god of darkness.

Battle for the Underworld Status Map

Final Stress Test, Day T

Eastern Gate

Integrity Knight
Fanatio

Orc Battalion
Chief Lilpilin

Pugilists Guild
Champion Iskahn

Emperor's
Regiment

Dark God
Vecta

Integrity Knight
Deusolbert

Ravine
Created by
Asuna

Asuna

Human Army Decoy Force

Ruins

Integrity Knight
Bercouli

Integrity Knight
Alice

Deceased

Human Guardian Army

Integrity Knight
Eldrie

Integrity Knight
Renly

Integrity Knight
Sheyta

Dark Territory Army

Mountain Goblin
Kosogi

Giant
Sigurosig

Flatland Goblin
Shibori

Dark Mages
Guild Chancellor
Dee Eye Ell

Student
Ronie

Student
Tiese

Other

Dark Knight
Vassago

Kirito
(Empty)

World's End Altar

Illustration: Tatsuya K

SWORD ART ONLINE

ALICIZATION AWAKENING

VOLUME 17

Reki Kawahara

abec

bee-pee

YEN ON

NEW YORK

SWORD ART ONLINE, Volume 17: ALICIZATION AWAKENING
REKI KAWAHARA

Translation by Stephen Paul
Cover art by abec

SWORD ART ONLINE Vol.17
©REKI KAWAHARA 2016
First published in Japan in 2016 by KADOKAWA CORPORATION, Tokyo.
English translation rights arranged with KADOKAWA CORPORATION, Tokyo, through Tuttle-Mori Agency, Inc., Tokyo.

English translation © 2019 by Yen Press, LLC

Yen On
150 30th Street, 19th Floor
New York, NY 10001

Visit us at yenpress.com
facebook.com/yenpress
twitter.com/yenpress
yenpress.tumblr.com
instagram.com/yenpress

First Yen On Edition: October 2019

Yen On is an imprint of Yen Press, LLC.
The Yen On name and logo are trademarks of Yen Press, LLC.

Library of Congress Cataloging-in-Publication Data
Names: Kawahara, Reki, author. | Abec, 1985– illustrator. | Paul, Stephen, translator.
Title: Sword art online / Reki Kawahara, abec ; translation, Stephen Paul.
Description: First Yen On edition. | New York, NY : Yen On, 2014–
Identifiers: LCCN 2014001175 | ISBN 9780316371247 (v. 1 : pbk.) |
    ISBN 9780316376815 (v. 2 : pbk.) | ISBN 9780316296427 (v. 3 : pbk.) |
    ISBN 9780316296434 (v. 4 : pbk.) | ISBN 9780316296441 (v. 5 : pbk.) |
    ISBN 9780316296458 (v. 6 : pbk.) | ISBN 9780316390408 (v. 7 : pbk.) |
    ISBN 9780316390415 (v. 8 : pbk.) | ISBN 9780316390422 (v. 9 : pbk.) |
    ISBN 9780316390439 (v. 10 : pbk.) | ISBN 9780316390446 (v. 11 : pbk.) |
    ISBN 9780316390453 (v. 12 : pbk.) | ISBN 9780316390460 (v. 13 : pbk.) |
    ISBN 9780316390484 (v. 14 : pbk.) | ISBN 9780316390491 (v. 15 : pbk.) |
    ISBN 9781975304188 (v. 16 : pbk.) | ISBN 9781975356972 (v. 17 : pbk.)
Subjects: CYAC: Science fiction. | BISAC: FICTION / Science Fiction / Adventure.
Classification: pz7.K1755Ain 2014 | DDC [Fic]—dc23
LC record available at https://lccn.loc.gov/2014001175

ISBNs: 978-1-9753-5697-2 (paperback)
       978-1-9753-5698-9 (ebook)

10 9 8 7 6 5 4 3 2 1

LSC-C

Printed in the United States of America

"THIS MIGHT BE A GAME, BUT IT'S NOT SOMETHING YOU PLAY."

—Akihiko Kayaba, *Sword Art Online* programmer

SWORD ART ONLINE
Alicization Awakening

Reki Kawahara

abec

bee-pee

CHAPTER TWENTY

1

It was five o'clock in the morning in the city of Alne.

At the center of the virtual world *ALfheim Online*, in the massive dome that lay beneath the roots of the world tree, a motley collection of over three thousand players had gathered.

The winged monsters that had once guarded the gate that stood at the pinnacle of the dome were long gone, and the dome itself was now used as a public event space—an appropriate venue for meetings and negotiations between leaders of the nine fairy races.

Today, just four players spoke to the unprecedented assembly of three thousand. They were Agil the gigantic gnome, Klein the salamander samurai, Silica the cait sith beast-tamer, and Lisbeth the leprechaun blacksmith—the companions of Kirito the Black Swordsman, who had still not awakened from a dive into the Underworld.

At the time that the companions began sending out messages to everyone on their friends lists, it was 4:20 AM, and of the various territorial lords of *ALO*, only three had been online. But with their help—delegating tasks to subordinate officers, and even practicing the forbidden art of contacting people offline—they succeeded in summoning this massive gathering in the span of only forty minutes.

Over a quarter of the players currently standing or hovering in the half-dome space were newly generated characters—but they were not VRMMO newbies. These were all veteran players of the Seed ecosystem, and they'd shown up at the behest of their friends and guildmates with *ALO* accounts.

So these three thousand players in the World Tree's dome were the cream of the crop of Japan's VRMMO players. And they were the last and best hope of Yui, the top-down AI, the only force that could save the Underworld's Human Guardian Army.

In the hush, Lisbeth the leprechaun's magically amplified voice addressed the crowd.

"…This is not a joke or a scam! A research organization based in Japan has built a special Seed-based virtual world with government funding, and very soon, thousands of American players are about to dive in without understanding what it really is—and slaughter all the residents of the Underworld!"

As she spoke, Lisbeth felt pangs of guilt and shame that she was propounding a kind of gaming-based nationalist sentiment, but the desperate stakes of the situation left her with little else she could use to make her case.

"The people in the Underworld are no mere NPCs! They're real artificial intelligences built from the data harvested from all the VRMMO worlds we enjoy! They have the same souls, the same emotional depth, that we flesh-and-blood people do! I beg of you, help us protect them! We're asking you to convert your character data to the Underworld!"

At the end of her five-minute speech, she surveyed the crowd, her eyes pleading, praying. The fairies in the dome looked confused and unsure. She knew it was the kind of story that couldn't be fully appreciated when it appeared out of the blue like this. Even Lisbeth wasn't fully clear on all the inner workings of the Underworld and its artificial fluctlight residents, as far as Yui had explained it to her.

Among the skeptical, murmuring crowd, one player raised a

long, graceful arm. It was Sakuya, lady of the sylphs, her slender form clad in a green gown.

"Lisbeth, I know you and your friends, and I do not take you for the kind of people who would do this as a prank. And as Kirito has not logged in to the game in nearly ten days, I would indeed assume that something is wrong. However…"

Her smooth, calm voice wavered with indecision. "In all honesty…I have difficulty believing this. An AI with the soul of a human being—and the American military attempting to invade and steal it…? Neither of these things sound believable in the slightest. Although I feel certain that we will be able to confirm them upon logging in to this 'Underworld'…you mentioned a number of potential issues when logging in? Would you explain this to us?"

Well, the time has come.

Lisbeth took a deep breath and let her eyelids close.

This was it. If she failed to make the proper case now, no one would come to help.

She opened her eyes again and surveyed Sakuya, the other lords and ladies, and the thousands of *ALO* players behind them.

"That's right," Lisbeth said, loud and clear. "The Underworld isn't operated the way an ordinary VRMMO is. There will be a number of problems upon diving in. First, the Underworld does not have a player UI that can be manipulated. That means that there is no voluntary logging out."

The murmuring in the background grew louder.

No voluntary logging out. It was a phrase that inevitably brought the infamous and deadly *Sword Art Online* to mind. *ALO* and all the other Seed-based games allowed players to log out with both menu buttons and spoken commands.

"The only way to log out is to 'die' within the simulation. But that brings us to the second problem. The Underworld does not have a pain-absorber function. If you suffer enough damage to reduce your HP to zero, it will come with a considerable amount of virtual pain."

At this, the players began to stir uncomfortably. Shutting out pain signals was a mandatory part of the VRMMO experience. In a virtual world without it, a slash from a sword or burn damage would feel essentially as painful as it did in real life. That kind of signal, once sent to the brain, could even cause the player's actual skin to swell temporarily.

But the potential concerns didn't end there. Lisbeth waited for the murmuring to die down a bit before she continued to the third and biggest sacrifice of all.

"Lastly, the Underworld is currently in a state in which even its developers are unable to operate it fully. Meaning there is no guarantee that if you convert your character data…it will be able to convert back to your original game. That means there is a good chance that your character might be lost forever."

There was a moment of stunned silence—and then the dome erupted into angry shouting.

Lisbeth, Silica, Agil, and Klein—with Yui on his shoulder in pixie form—stood silent in the center of the open floor, letting the waves of outraged voices wash over them from all directions.

It was exactly what they'd expected to happen.

These were three thousand of the best players in the nation, and they had spent countless hours and immeasurable energy building up their characters. In *ALO*, an entire hour of hard, constant work fighting monsters might earn you a single point of skill efficiency. Building these characters up was akin to emptying a lake with a single bucket.

No one who had put that kind of effort in would be fine with the suggestion that their painstaking work might be lost forever.

"S-screw this!!"

One player flew forth from the crowd, jabbing a finger at Lisbeth. He was a salamander decked out in crimson plate armor with a battle-ax strapped to his back. This was Lord Mortimer, the second-ranking commander of the salamanders after General Eugene.

The salamander lifted his helmet visor to reveal eyes burning with rage. He spun around to the vast gathering behind and shouted with enough force to quiet them all.

"You're crazy enough to wake everyone up at this hour and suggest that we should go dive into some sketchy server, and now you say we might lose our characters?! Are you putting up some kind of collateral if we get wiped out?! Or is this just some kind of trap to weaken the other fairy races?!"

"...!"

Klein was all set to shout back, but Lisbeth held him back with a hand on his shoulder. She tried to remain as calm as she could.

"I'm sorry, but I cannot offer you any guarantee against damages. I know that the characters you've created and nurtured can't be replaced with money. That's why we're asking you for help... Please, lend us your strength in saving our friends who are fighting to protect the Underworld against the American players."

She didn't have to raise her voice for it to carry to every inch of the dome. The salamander was initially taken aback, but he found his voice and his fury again momentarily.

"And I'm guessing those 'friends' of yours are more *SAO* survivors, who go around acting like they're special among all VRMMO players! We all know that you former *SAO* folks secretly look down on everyone else who didn't go through all that!!"

Now it was Lisbeth's turn to be at a loss for words.

She had never consciously recognized that kind of mentality within herself until the salamander pointed it out—and now she felt that, in fact, she couldn't say with all certainty that there was nothing like that in her mind. After all, she had made her player home not in the city on the surface, but in the floating New Aincrad, and she had spent all her time interacting with her old companions, rarely ever mingling with the general population below.

The salamander sensed he'd struck a nerve with that comment and continued mercilessly, "Invasions, artificial intelligence, souls—why should I care?! Don't bring your real-life crap into VRMMOs and tell us what we should do about it! You got a problem? Handle it yourselves! With your little club of celebrated survivors!!"

Other voices in the background echoed his sentiments, telling them to step off or mind their own business.

It didn't work. I completely failed to convince them, Lisbeth thought as she fought back tears. She sent pleading glances to those *ALO* power brokers whom she'd had good interactions with in the past: Sakuya, lady of the sylphs; General Eugene of the salamanders; Alicia Rue, lady of the cait siths.

But they did not say anything when she met their gazes. They just stared at her, their eyes cold. It was as if they were demanding that she *show* them how serious she was.

Lisbeth took a deep breath and closed her eyes once again. She thought of her friends fighting in that far-off otherworld—Asuna, injured Kirito, and Leafa and Sinon, who had left for the Underworld earlier.

Even if I transfer over, I don't have the strength to fight the way that Asuna and the others can. But I know there must be something I can do. This moment, right here and now, is my battlefield.

Her eyes shot open. She wiped away the tears.

"Yes...this is a real-life problem," she repeated. "And like you said, we *SAO* survivors might be guilty of blending real life and virtual life together. But I assure you, none of us think of ourselves as heroes."

She reached over to her right and grabbed the hand of Silica, who was tearfully silent.

"She and I? We go to a school that only the survivors attend. Our original schools treated us like dropouts, so we didn't have any other choice. Once a month, every student at the returnee school must undergo a counseling session. They monitor our brain waves in the AmuSphere and ask us unpleasant questions like 'Do you ever feel like things aren't real? Do you ever want to harm others?' Some of the kids have to take medications against their will. To the government, we're all just potential criminals who need to be monitored."

The waves of anger subsided, leaving only a tense silence filling the dome. Even the salamander who'd been shouting at her looked stunned.

No one knew exactly where she was going with this, least of all Lisbeth. All she could do was put her pent-up feelings and thoughts into words.

"But the truth is, the students at the returnee school aren't the only ones being treated like that. Every VRMMO player is subjected to that kind of thinking to some degree. That we're dead weight dragging down society or cowards who hide from reality and don't pay taxes or social security...Some people even debate if they should reinstate the draft and force us to do something productive for society."

The tension in the room grew thicker and hotter. One little pinprick might lead to an even greater eruption of outrage than before.

Undaunted, Lisbeth pressed her hand to her chest and shouted, "But I know how it is! I have faith! That what we have here *is* real!!"

She lifted that hand to point at the dome of the World Tree—and all of Alfheim beyond it.

"This world, and all the many virtual worlds connected to it, aren't just some empty escapes from life! To me, it's reality, where I have a real life, real friends, real encounters and emotions! And that's true for all of you, too, isn't it?! You put all your effort into playing because it's another kind of reality for you! But if this is just a game...if this is all just a virtual fake to you, then what *is* real to us anyway?!"

At last, the tears burst from Lisbeth's eyes. She didn't bother to wipe them away. Not until she had said what she needed to say.

"The many virtual worlds we've all nurtured as a group have come together, firm and tall, like this World Tree, which has finally bloomed the flower that is the Underworld! And I want to protect that precious flower! Please...please give us your help!!"

She thrust her hands up to the ceiling of the dome.

Through vision blurred by tears, the motes of light trickling from the wings of thousands of fairies glittered and sparkled.

—ᘯᘮᘯ—

Light glittered in an arc across the silvery dawn sky.

A second later, that thick rope cracked drily and split in the middle, both ends whipping and writhing in the air like black snakes. Dozens of soldiers clinging to the rope screamed as they plummeted into the bottomless ravine. Meanwhile, the Double-Winged Blade that cut the rope did a sharp turn and fit back into the hand of its master, the Integrity Knight Renly Synthesis Twenty-Seven.

Of the ten ropes the Dark Army had stretched across the ravine, Renly had already severed five, but there wasn't a single shred of pride or accomplishment on his face. If anything, he seemed anguished to have cut the literal lifelines of those enemy soldiers who'd bravely carried out death-defying feats on cruel orders.

The same could be said of Asuna, who watched at his side, clutching the reins of her horse.

By the time that Asuna, Renly, Alice Synthesis Thirty, Sheyta Synthesis Twelve, and Integrity Knight Commander Bercouli Synthesis One rode up to the ravine, hundreds of enemy soldiers had already crossed it and launched desperate attacks to protect the ropes. Nearly all of them succumbed to the attacks of Bercouli, Sheyta, and Alice, but a few came around to flank Renly, forcing Asuna to draw her rapier and defend him during his task.

The Underworld virtual realm used the Seed program as its foundation, which meant that she could utilize the sword skills and horse-riding techniques she'd learned back in *SAO*.

And because Asuna was in the super-account for Stacia, Goddess of Creation, her statistics were essentially at maximum values. Plus, her rapier Radiant Light was even more powerful than the divine weapons the Integrity Knights possessed. Even the basic

Linear Thrust skill was enough to pierce the thick armor of the dark knights and hardy flesh of the pugilists in one go.

However, the fresh blood that spurted from the enemies' wounds, the howls of agony and hatred that erupted from them, and the life that was lost were all real.

The people who lived in the Underworld, human side or dark side, all had souls—fluctlights—that were fundamentally no different from Asuna's own. They were real people, and these video-game statistics and superpowered weapons meant that she could kill them with a single blow. It was wrong; it was an unbearable agony for her.

And the knights and pugilists who leaped at her with grim determination were not even doing so of their own free will.

As artificial fluctlights, they were incapable of disobeying a direct order from a higher being. They'd been ordered to attack her, knowing that it was pointless and would lead to certain death, on the command of another real-world human who was using the equally powerful super-account for Vecta, the god of darkness. From another perspective, they, too, were victims of a real-world battle over cutting-edge technology.

Asuna had to use every last ounce of willpower to cast such thoughts out of her head. The overall priority at this moment had to be protecting Alice, the Priestess of Light, from Vecta's grasp—as well as Kirito in the base camp behind her.

She'd been told that the only forces left in the Dark Army under Vecta's command were the pugilists and the dark knights. If they used the opportunity of the enemy's suicidal rush across the ravine to wipe out their numbers, the enemy would have no moves left to play.

"Let's go for the sixth one!!" shouted Commander Bercouli, bringing Asuna back to her senses. Alice, Sheyta, and Renly responded immediately, with Asuna just a moment or two later.

As soon as she turned her horse to move west, a bright, loud horn sounded behind her. She spun around to see, on the hilltop a portion of a mile away, the orderly rows of the men-at-arms in the Human

Guardian Army's decoy force rushing toward them. They'd armed themselves and gotten into formation just fifteen minutes after the knights and charged out of the camp area.

"Psh...They don't know when to quit," Bercouli muttered, eyeing the guardsmen, but with about five hundred enemy troops already across the ravine, backup forces were a welcome development. If they could help keep the enemy soldiers at bay, it shouldn't be too hard to sever the other five ropes.

It looks like we've won this round, Vecta, she thought. But no sooner had the sentiment crossed her mind than she caught sight of something odd.

Against a dawn sky the shade of dark blood, something rather eerie descended onto the battlefield.

There were lines that shone red, a lighter shade than the sky. Many lines, in fact. Dozens...hundreds.

Perhaps thousands.

The countless descending lines appeared to be made of strings of fine pixels. But if she squinted, she could make out that the individual dots were actually a number or letter. The unidentified strings of text fell silently to a range of a mile or so east of the battle, on this side of the ravine.

Before long, it wasn't just Asuna stopping to watch, but the other Integrity Knights, and even the dark knights and pugilists from the Dark Territory side.

When the first string met the dried, dusty earth, it writhed and massed into an amorphous clump.

It was only a matter of seconds before it assumed a human form.

———

Iskahn, head of the pugilists guild, forgot the fury that boiled within him, if only for an instant.

What is that?

On the far bank of the ravine, five hundred denizens of the dark lands prepared to take on the four Integrity Knights. But they suddenly came to a stop and looked away from the battle-field in disbelief.

When Iskahn looked in the same direction, he witnessed a crimson rain descending upon a location about two kilors east.

It was a stream of many red lines, falling from the sky and emitting strange vibrations. When the streams reached the ground, they expanded, eventually taking human shape.

They were warriors, armed with longswords, battle-axes, and spears and clad in reddish-black armor. Color aside, the armor was very similar in form to the kind the dark knights wore. At first, Iskahn thought that Emperor Vecta had used his godly powers to send reinforcements.

But it was only moments until he was hit by an eerie sense of wrongness about this.

The red soldiers carried on without a care for order or discipline in a way that was utterly unbecoming of any knight trained by the late General Shasta. They gestured broadly, spoke with nearby soldiers, sat on the ground, or drew and swung their weapons without being ordered.

But the main thing was their number.

When the strange rain ended, the group of soldiers that it brought had ballooned to a number that Iskahn could scarcely believe. It was easily over ten thousand at a glance, if not twenty…and possibly thirty. If the dark knighthood actually had this much supplementary manpower, the ten-lords system would have been obsolete long ago, with Shasta reigning as the true ruler in the world of darkness.

And the dark knights on this side of the ravine waiting their turn to cross the ropes exclaimed in shock, too. They did not recognize this mystery force any more than he did.

That meant these red soldiers must be true forces of darkness, summoned through some arcane method from the depths of the earth by Emperor Vecta's godly powers.

And that recognition turned Iskahn's shock into deep, indignant fury.

If he could summon such a tremendous force, why had he not done so earlier? Why, it made it seem as though the pugilists and knights that had given their lives in this reckless, mad attempt to cross the ropes were nothing more than a decoy, a ploy to lure the enemy's forces into the open.

In fact...perhaps it was true.

Had the emperor ordered them to cross the ropes, begging the enemy to kill them, just to get those enemies to engage them out in the open?

...Not quite.

It wasn't just this time. From the moment the attack against the Eastern Gate began, the damage suffered by the army of darkness was needlessly severe. The emperor had ordered the goblins, giants, ogres, orcs, and dark mages guild to their deaths, and he had barely even batted an eye, much less mourned the loss.

From the very start, the fifty thousand members of the Dark Army were just sacrificial pawns to Emperor Vecta.

Until this moment, young Iskahn, head of the pugilists guild, held an interest only in further improving his own physical discipline and technique and in the advancement of his people. Now, for the very first time, he was in a position to view all of the Underworld, both the dark side and the human side. And this perspective created an unresolvable dilemma within him.

Emperor Vecta was supremely powerful. The powerful must be followed.

But.

But...

"Hrrgh—!"

A terrible pain shot through Iskahn's right eye; he pressed his palm to it, staggered, and then fell to a knee. The head of the pugilists guild watched as thirty thousand warriors in crimson red began running, speaking words he'd never heard before.

They headed for where the thousand Human Guardian Army forces were descending the hill to join the Integrity Knights and prepare to fight them off.

In between the two sides, five hundred pugilists and dark knights stood bewildered, unsure of what to do.

No matter how merciless Emperor Vecta's orders might be, this could at least signal that those five hundred lives were saved, Iskahn thought as he clutched his stinging eye.

But even at this late point in time, he was underestimating the callousness of Vecta's thinking. The thirty thousand warriors rushed not for the human army, but straight at the Dark Territory's five hundred.

All of those raised swords, axes, and spears caught the red light of dawn, glinting cruelly—and then swung downward with bloodthirsty roars, right at the men and women that were supposedly on their side.

———⁓———

"Wha…? Who are they?!" cried Bercouli.

Asuna had no answer to his question. It was clear that the thirty thousand soldiers who had suddenly descended—no, dived—to the east had been called here by Emperor Vecta.

But where had he summoned a force of this size from, exactly?

Did he generate NPC warriors like monsters and throw them into battle? But the Underworld control panel in the *Ocean Turtle*'s main control room was locked down and couldn't be operated without admin access. They wouldn't be able to do anything but designate coordinates and dive in themselves, like Asuna did, and on Vecta's side, they had only two Soul Translators available to them.

The momentary confusion was thawed when the red warriors drew within a few hundred yards, and she could actually hear them speak.

"Charge ahead!!"

"Give 'em hell!!"

It was English.

They were people from the real world, and based on the accent,

Americans. But how was that possible? This was supposed to be a closed-off VR world, unconnected to any other system.

Except.

No...

Through the STL, the Underworld was a true alternate world, more real than reality, thanks to its Mnemonic Visualizer. But the development of that system was done on top of The Seed, the universal VRMMO development package. In other words, if you had an AmuSphere, you could dive into that world...and the *Ocean Turtle* had a massive satellite connection pipeline.

So with a simple hacked-together client program distributed on the Net in the real world...you could bring tens, if not hundreds of thousands, of people to the Underworld.

It was what the red warriors did that gave credence to Asuna's stunned suspicion. Their first move was to set upon the knights and pugilists of the Dark Army, who were ostensibly on their own side, swinging their swords and axes without hesitation or mercy.

"Wh-what are you...?!"

"I thought you were on our side...!"

Shocked, the knights attempted to deflect these attacks, but the numbers were against them. And the red soldiers' weapons and armor were apparently superior to those of the Dark Army, as the swords and shields raised in defense quickly broke and shattered. Screams and blood began to issue from where the armies met.

"Dude, this is awesome!!"

"Sweet! Gore!!"

The elated real-worlders seemed to have no idea what was actually happening here. They'd probably been convinced to dive into what they believed was an open beta test for a new, unannounced VRMMO.

The American players couldn't have any natural hostility to the Underworlders. They just saw the Dark Army before them and assumed they were enemy NPCs to be targeted. In fact, if there was enough time to explain what the Underworld was, and how artificial fluctlights worked, maybe even the majority of them would agree to log out.

But there was no way to do any of that now. If Asuna rushed in and tried to speak to them in English, they would assume she was just another NPC delivering her programmed lines. And if they thought that defeating enough targets in the beta might give them some kind of exclusive bonus item when the game officially launched, Japanese players would do the exact same thing.

Convincing them with words would be impossible.

The people the Americans were trying to kill weren't NPCs, but artificial fluctlights with real souls. If they slaughtered all the Dark Territory forces, they would come after the Human Guardian Army's decoy force next. In that case, she was the only one present with a temporary life, not a permanent one. She had to fight.

Resolute, Asuna lifted her rapier and spoke a quick command.

"System Call! Create Field Object!!"

A rainbow aurora appeared around the rapier. She would not be creating a bottomless ravine like she did last night. There was nothing to be gained by cutting off the human army's escape route.

Instead, she swung the sword hard, imagining huge, jutting rocks as sharp as spears.

Laaaaaaa! There was a booming, heavenly sound effect. Rainbow light shot from the tip of the rapier, jabbing just a bit before the collision point of the Americans and the Underworlders.

The ground there shook, and a gray rock split the surface. It erupted to a height of a hundred feet, hurling the red warriors around it into the air.

Four more boulders appeared after it, doing the same. The earth quaked, sending hundreds of suits of crimson armor skyward. They screamed and swore, some crushed to a pulp by the rocks, others dashed against the ground. Blood and guts flew everywhere.

Asuna had no time to consider how they might have perceived

their deaths. She was instantly inflicted with a searing pain in the center of her head, and she slumped over the neck of her horse.

Silver sparks burst in her eyes, and she gasped for breath. The agony was far worse than what she'd felt when creating the ravine last night. It was the lurid sensation of her very fluctlight being spent as so much terrain data passed through it.

But I can't stop here.

If she suffered the same injuries as Kirito, so be it. She set her jaw, gritted her teeth, and rose in the saddle.

Her efforts seemed to have slowed the rush of the American players from the east. But the five jutting rocks spanned a width of only five hundred yards or so. The tens of thousands of players would quickly rush around them.

She'd have to make another wall of rocks on the south side and allow the human army to escape from behind it. Her breathing was ragged, and she raised her sword high again.

But a golden gauntlet grabbed her arm this time.

"Alice…?!" she gasped when she saw who it was.

Alice the Integrity Knight, her beautiful features hard with resolve, quickly shook her head. "Don't push it, Asuna. Let the Integrity Knights handle the rest."

"B-but…those soldiers in red are from the real world…They're enemies from where we came from!"

"Even still. Thousands or not, if they are blindly lusting for blood and swing their swords with abandon, there is no reason for us to fear them."

"That is true," Bercouli said with a grin, following up Alice's sentiment. "Let us have a moment to shine."

Their boldness in the face of such desperate circumstances was laudable, but Asuna could sense that they were more determined than ever.

The red tsunami of foes outnumbered their forces thirty to one, however. This was not a situation in which grit and determination would reign supreme.

The knight commander raised his polished blade, however, and barked, "Gather up!! All forces, tight formation!! We're breaking out of here!!"

———ᨆᨆ———

"A…aah, ah…"

It was a guttural cry from Iskahn's throat, more growl than words.

"Aaa…aaaaaaaaaah!!"

He clenched his fists so hard that blood oozed and dripped from his palms. The young gladiator wasn't even aware of the pain, however; he just howled like a wild beast. Nearby, his second-in-command, Dampa, hung his head, sharing in the anguish Iskahn felt.

They were dying. Dying.

His fellow combatants, with no orders or guidance, and no ability to fight, fell prey to the swarm of cruel, murderous blades.

And yet, the soldiers making their way across the five intact ropes were not stopping. The emperor's order that they cross to the other side was still active. As their master bade them, they scrambled along the ropes, only to promptly be surrounded by the hordes of red soldiers and their deadly swords.

Why wasn't Emperor Vecta calling off the ravine-crossing strategy for the pugilists and dark knights, and why wasn't he forbidding these red soldiers from attacking the other members of the Dark Territory forces?

At this rate, Iskahn's fellow tribesmen were not even decoys. They were just blood sacrifices for the army the emperor had summoned.

"I…I must…"

Report. I must beseech the emperor to call off this strategy.

Through the rage, despair, and agony of his right eye, Iskahn took a step toward the dragon tank at the rear of their position. Dampa lifted his head, sensing his chieftain's intent, and made to say something.

But just then, a huge shadow of something overhead passed them. Iskahn and Dampa looked to the sky automatically.

A dragon.

On the back of the creature, fine pelt cape and long golden hair flowing behind him, was Emperor Vecta himself.

"Aa…aaah!!"

Perhaps he heard Iskahn's unconscious shout. From the saddle of the dragon, the emperor glanced down at the surface.

There was no emotion in his eyes. Not a single shred of mercy or pity for the soldiers of his own army as they died. Not even a bit of interest. Those orbs were ice.

Emperor Vecta looked away from Iskahn and flew the dragon toward the far side of the ravine.

That was a god. That was a ruler.

But if he was the ruler…if he had absolute strength that none could hope to match—shouldn't there be a corresponding sense of duty to wield it?

A ruler ought to command his army and lead his people to greater prosperity. No man who sacrificed hundreds, thousands of lives for nothing, and showed no emotion about it, ought to be emperor… My eye…Don't call yourself…My eye hurts…No right to…

"Uah…aaah…aaaaah!!"

Iskahn thrust his fist into the air.

He curved his fingers like claws.

Then stuck them against his right eye, the source of the agony that burned at his mind.

"Ch…Chief!! What are you doing?!"

Dampa rushed over, but Iskahn pushed him off with his left hand and uttered a brief shriek as he tore out his own eyeball. The white orb still glowed red in his palm, but it vanished when he crushed the soft organ with his grip.

At this point, Iskahn had not actually reached the spontaneous unlocking of the right-eye seal, Code 871, that Alice and Eugeo had accomplished. So he was unable to manifest any direct rebellion against the emperor, and his two outstanding orders, carrying out the ravine-crossing plan and staying back on this side of the gorge, were still active.

Instead, the young pugilist forced through a means of avoiding those orders at such a level that it was tantamount to rebellion.

Iskahn turned slowly to look up at the shocked Dampa and said quietly, "The emperor didn't give us any orders relating to those red soldiers. Am I wrong about that?"

"N...no, you're not wrong."

"Then us killin' all of them has nothin' to do with the emperor."

"...Champion..."

Dampa fell silent. Iskahn glared at him with his one remaining eye and ordered, "Listen to me...if we get a bridge across the valley, take all the troops over there. Save our people on the far bank, no matter what you do."

"Huh...?! B-bridge? H-how...?"

"I don't know. Just ask whoever can do it," Iskahn growled quietly, facing the abyss.

Soon, red flames engulfed his powerful legs. He began to spring toward the yawning ravine, leaving behind footprints that smoldered in the dark ground.

If I'm not allowed to cross the ropes...then I'll just have to jump across myself!!

Iskahn bounded off the earth just before the hundred-mel-wide portal to hell.

Jumping was one of the physical skills that pugilists trained in. They started with safe long jumps on gravel ground, until graduating up to leaping over rows of blades and boiling oil, all in pursuit of absolute faith in their jumping abilities. In other words, to utilize the mental power of Incarnation.

A top-level pugilist could jump a span of twenty mels. Given that any flight utilizing sacred or dark arts was forbidden in this world, it represented the maximum possibility of flesh and blood.

But Iskahn was hurtling himself over a bottomless abyss five times the length of his maximum jump distance. He stared straight ahead, pumping his feet against the air, leaving fiery traces in the space behind him.

Ten mels. Twenty mels. His body continued to rise.

Thirty mels. Thirty-five. Powerful winds pushing up from the canyon below buffeted him upward, as though on invisible wings.

Forty mels.

A little farther—just one more push…and then he could coast to the far side on momentum alone.

But…

Cruelly, the wind stopped right before he was about to reach the middle of the ravine. His body jolted, losing forward propulsion. The curve of his leap hit a peak and began to sink downward.

I'm five mels short.

"Raaaah!!"

He bellowed, reaching as though to grab on to something. But there was no purchase for his hands or feet. The only thing that brushed his body was the cold of the approaching darkness below.

"Champiooooon!!"

A rumbling roar struck Iskahn's ears.

He glanced over his shoulder to see his second, Dampa, going into a throwing motion holding a boulder many times the size of his head. Iskahn instantly knew what his longtime faithful assistant was going to do. But it was not possible for humans to hurl a rock of that size over fifty mels…

Dampa's arm suddenly bulged. The muscles rippled and tensed, popping veins, as though all of his entire body's strength was converging in that arm.

"Aaaaah!!"

The massive man ran a few steps and then swung.

The boulder shot forward, shaking the air, like some kind of catapult—and Dampa's arm burst apart into a shower of blood and meat. Iskahn gritted his teeth at the sight of his slumping second-in-command, then focused on the boulder hurtling straight for him.

"...Oraaaaa!!" He screamed and bounded off the rock with the sole of a single foot.

The rock exploded into pieces, jolting Iskahn forward and giving him a fresh source of acceleration. The sight of the soldiers fighting on the far bank of the ravine rushed closer and closer.

"*Damn!!*" swore the American player before Asuna pulled her rapier from his lifeless body. She gasped for breath atop her horse.

There was no mental pressure weighing on her now, the way that she felt when fighting against the Underworlders. She had already defeated over ten of the red warriors, using the ultrafast combination skills that had earned her the nicknames of the Flash and the Berserk Healer.

But there were just too many of them.

Asuna wasn't the only one fighting. The men-at-arms of the human army and especially the four Integrity Knights fought like madmen. They stood at the head of the tight formation and produced mountains of bodies as they tried to cut out an open path to the south.

But they couldn't overwhelm the waves of red soldiers who continued to flood around the rocky mountains that Asuna had created. At best, they could stop only enough of them to produce a stalemate.

Eventually they were going to notice that the enemies they were cutting down vanished without bodies—or even a bloodstain. They would realize that they were fighting a phantom army without true lives of their own.

"Aaah...no! Aaaah!!" a voice screamed, causing Asuna to glance behind her.

Part of the line of guards had broken, and warriors dressed in red were spilling through. They set upon the human army's guards, hollering and screaming gamer slang, surrounding them and slicing them to pieces. Blood and flesh flew, and the shrieks of panic turned to death screams.

The red soldiers mobbed their next targets, seemingly driven to greater heights of bloodlust by the sheer realism of the deaths they brought.

"Stop...stop...!!" cried Asuna.

This was the time to ignore the few losses they would suffer and focus only on pushing to the south, she knew. But her body ignored her mind and leaped off her horse.

"Stoppppp!!" she screamed, feeling her throat go raw, standing alone against the deluge of red.

The Americans had no malice. They were only being manipulated by the invaders. But that understanding alone could not withstand the flood of raw, surging emotion.

Zukakakaow!!

Her right hand flashed, sending a Radiant Light through red visors. Four soldiers suffered critical hits to the head. Dropping their swords, they slumped to the ground with a groan. Based on their reactions, it was clear that although they dived through their AmuSpheres, the pain absorber wasn't functioning. Sensing that it was likely the case, Asuna had been trying to pierce them quickly through the heart to log them out instantly, but that idea now fell by the wayside.

Her rapier, an item of the highest priority level, spun and danced, thrusting through armor, slicing, and occasionally even severing the enemy's weapons.

The Americans were seeing polygonal in-engine models, with blood spray modeled as a visual effect of damage. But to Asuna, who was diving through The Soul Translator, they were flesh-and-blood people, their blood warm and pungent with the stench of iron.

It began to pool on the ground around them, and her right foot slipped. She lost her balance and toppled over, right as she saw a large warrior step up to her.

"*Take this!!*" he roared, swinging his battle-ax down at her. Asuna rolled to the right, but she couldn't get all the way free. The thick blade caught her left arm.

Chunk.

It severed her forearm below the elbow. The loose part flew into the air.

"…Aaah…!!"

Her vision flickered white. The breath caught in her throat. Her entire body seized up with pain.

Asuna bent over, clutching the arm that gushed blood like a geyser. Through a sudden rush of tears, she saw four or five shadows surrounding her, raising their weapons.

Suddenly, the head of the man with the battle-ax appeared to explode.

There were more dull impacts. Each of the soldiers trying to finish off Asuna split to pieces in turn, vanishing out of view.

"Heh…They're all soft."

Through her agony, Asuna managed to straighten up and see a hardy young man with bold features, hair red as fire, and darkened skin.

He's from the Dark Territory!

For a moment, she forgot her pain and sucked in a breath. The color of his skin and the single leather belt on his upper half made it clear that this was one of the Dark Army's pugilists. But why would one of Emperor Vecta's own troops attack the red soldiers that Vecta had summoned? It was as if he'd just saved her life.

He had only one eye looking down at her. There was a grisly, bloody wound where his right eye had been, as though it had been gouged out. A dried trail of red-black blood ran down his cheek.

Then he turned that eye on the Americans pressing in on them again and raised a fist high. The hard, bony hand began to burn with bright flames.

"*Raaaaah!!*" he roared, his voice splitting the air as he slammed his fist into the ground.

A shock wave like a wall of fire burst outward, hurtling all the soldiers before them into oblivion without a trace.

What incredible power!

Asuna was stunned. If she fought him now, she would lose…

But the pugilist reached out without a word and grabbed her armor. He stood her up and stared closely at her with that one good eye.

"…Let's make a deal," he said in a voice that was young but heavy with anguish. At first, Asuna didn't understand what he meant.

"A…deal?"

"That's right. You're the one who split the earth and made those huge rocky outcroppings, yeah? I want you to put a firm bridge over that ravine behind us—doesn't matter if it's skinny. Then my four thousand pugilists can come over and help you until all of these soldiers in red are crushed into nothing."

The Dark Army…fighting with us?!

Was that possible? The people of the dark lands, like everyone else in this world, couldn't disobey direct orders from above, thanks to the seal of the right eye, Code 871. She glanced at the wound on his head.

Was it the mark of him removing the seal all on his own? Had he, like Alice, evolved into a fluctlight that had surpassed its own limitations?

But last night, Alice had claimed that if a person fought against Code 871 long enough, the "eyeball itself explodes without a trace." And the ugly injury to the pugilist's eye socket looked more like it had been gouged out with fingers than burst from within. How should she interpret his offer? What should she do?

Her answer came from a voice that was calm and quiet, despite the extreme danger of the circumstances.

"I don't think he's lying."

That was the gray Integrity Knight, Sheyta Synthesis Twelve, who spoke as she easily severed the head of an enemy warrior with a sword that was surprisingly thin, wavy, and black.

The pugilist looked at Sheyta and grinned, equal parts confidence and what might actually be shyness. He grunted in agreement.

In that moment, Asuna made up her mind. *I'll trust him.*

This was probably the last time she'd be able to use the land-altering powers of the Stacia account. It wouldn't be bad to have that last burst be used to create something, rather than simply destroy.

"…All right. I will place a bridge over the ravine."

She let go of her weeping arm, grabbed her pearl-white rapier, and raised it to the sky.

Laaaaaaa!

Another heavenly chorus boomed around them, and a rainbow aurora descended onto the wasteland. It plunged straight to the north and reached the far side of the ravine. The earth shook violently. Pillars of stone jutted out from either cliff, reaching toward the middle. When they met in the center of the open space, they melded together into a firm, thick bridge.

"Ooh-raaah!!"

The roaring of four thousand pugilists drowned out the rumbling of the shifting earth. The hardy fighters began to rush across the stone bridge, led by a one-armed giant of a man.

Asuna squeezed her rapier, feeling like she might pass out from the cost of using her godly powers—the sensation of a burning spear jabbed into the center of her brain.

Alice should have been at the forefront of the Human Guardian Army, carving a path ahead with blood, but she was no longer visible. Asuna could only pray that she was all right…and that, as the red-haired boy claimed, the pugilists would help them fight against the common enemy.

I'm coming for you, Kirito, she said to herself. It felt as though the pain eased just a bit.

About a minute before that, Alice the Integrity Knight was losing count of the number of red soldiers she had cut down. There seemed to be no end to them.

They're...abnormal.

There was no military discipline to them. They screamed words she couldn't understand and stepped all over their comrades' bodies to attack. It was as though they didn't care about the lives or deaths of their companions—or even themselves.

If these were people from the real world...then Asuna was right. It was certainly no sacred land of the gods.

The endless slaughter and continuous arrival of the enemies had a numbing effect on Alice's mind.

I hate this. This is no battle.

She wanted to cut through their line and break free from the circle around them.

"Move...out of the way!!" she screamed, swiping the Osmanthus Blade in a flat line. Enemy heads and arms came loose, flying through the air.

"System Call!!"

With the initiation for a sacred art complete, she generated ten flame elements. She followed that with the command to fuse them together into a long, narrow shape: a spear of flames for her left hand.

"Discharge!!"

Kabooom!!

Though it wasn't as powerful as Deusolbert's Conflagration Bow, the burning line pierced the enemy crowd, blasting nearly a dozen of them off their feet and gouging a hole in their blockade.

And through it—she saw black earth and a rising hill.

She would run up that hill, use all the tremendous spatial sacred power spilled by the battle to produce a reflective cohesion beam art, and burn all those damned red soldiers.

"Out of the waaaay!!" she shrieked, launching herself forward.

"...Little Miss!!" she heard Commander Bercouli call out after her.

But she never heard him say, "Don't rush ahead."

I can get through. I'm almost there.

She cut down the last one in her way without slowing down, finally broke through the seemingly endless ranks of enemies, and raced into empty space. Her abused sword went back into its sheath; she took in a deep breath of fresh air that didn't stink of blood for once, and she ran for all she was worth.

Suddenly, the world darkened.

At first, she thought it was simply clouds blocking the morning sun.

Then a tremendous force buffeted Alice's back. By the time she realized that a dragon had descended and grabbed her from behind, its claws were already pulling off the ground again. Immediately, she raised the Osmanthus Blade and made to activate her Perfect Weapon Control art.

But before she could chant the command, her vision went dark, and she felt a terrible chill envelop her. The dragon's rider must've been using dark arts—but wait, that wasn't it. Alice felt her very mind plunging into what felt like a bottomless hole.

This was the enemy's Incarnation. Not like Commander Bercouli's hardy Incarnation, like polished steel; nor like Administrator's piercing Incarnation, like a bolt of lightning that burned everything in existence. This was an Incarnation like an endless void, swallowing and seizing all in its clutches…

It was the last conscious thought she had.

—◆◆◆—

To Gabriel Miller, also known as Emperor Vecta, this was a gamble.

But he was certain that if the tens of thousands of American players brought into the battlefield surrounded the Human Guardian Army, Alice would separate from her forces, either alone or in a small group, to perform that huge laser attack again.

Gabriel sat astride the black dragon belonging to the dark knighthood, hovering high over the battlefield, and waited. This period of time felt like the longest he'd experienced since diving into the Underworld.

At last, a small golden light escaped from the swarm of red army ants surrounding the group and started moving toward the hill to the south of the area.

"Alice...Alicia," Gabriel murmured, wearing a rare, heartfelt smile on his lips. He snapped the reins, commanding the dragon to descend.

Gabriel possessed an overwhelmingly powerful, if empty, sense of imagination—in other words, Incarnation. It had totally consumed the AI of the proud dragon, leaving the beast totally under his control. In one fell swoop, the dragon folded its wings and plummeted down, reached out with its right claw, and seized the golden knight as she ran. The huge creature beat its wings and began to ascend once again.

Gabriel never gave a single thought to the bloody battle that he had orchestrated. At this point, he did not care at all what happened to the Dark Territory forces, the Human Guardian Army, or the real-worlders he'd summoned.

All he had left to do was fly south, to the nearest system console, the World's End Altar. There, he would eject Alice's soul into the real world and log out.

He glanced down and spotted the unconscious woman his dragon held, her golden hair trailing in the wind.

I want to touch it. I want to taste her body, her soul, until I am content.

It would be a long trip to the console—several days, even with the dragon unit's speed. Perhaps a good way to pass the time would be to enjoy Alice while she still had the flesh of the Underworld.

He felt a sweet thrill of anticipation run up his spine. The ends of his mouth curled upward again.

———∕∿∕———

Who could have guessed that he would sacrifice the Dark Army of fifty thousand and a new summoned infantry of thirty thousand, all to kidnap one girl?

Bercouli Synthesis One, commander of the Integrity Knights and the oldest of all humans in the world, had been maximally cautious of the enemy's strategy from the moment he became aware of Vecta's empty Incarnation. But it was only once Alice was captured that he realized he had completely missed what Vecta was really after.

When the black dragon seized Alice just a few dozen mels away, Bercouli did something that he hadn't done in decades, as far as he could remember.

He shouted with true rage, right from the gut.

"What are you doing to my disciple?!"

The very air around him shook, and sparks of white lightning burst and flickered. But Emperor Vecta did not even turn to face him. He began flying directly to the south with his prize in tow.

Bercouli squeezed the Time-Splitting Sword and made to run after the dragon, but the hole that Alice's sacred art had burned through the enemy lines was already closed. More of the crimson soldiers were barging in at him, hollering their strange battle cries.

"Get...out..."

But before he could finish his demand, a brilliant-white flash raced overhead.

It was a pair of throwing blades, whistling high and pure as they spun: Renly's Double-Winged Blades. Behind him, the young Integrity Knight shouted, "Release Recollection!!"

The throwing blades briefly flashed and joined as one in midair. Now a cross-shaped set of wings, the weapon hurtled forward with a mind of its own, spinning madly as it stopped the enemy soldiers dead along its path.

"Go after her, Commander!!" shouted Renly.

Without turning, Bercouli replied, "Thanks! Hold it down back here!"

He crouched, then pushed off the ground with his right foot. Instantly, the knight commander in his Eastern-style clothes became a blue blur. He was speedy enough to break through the new gap in the enemy army in an instant—it was even quicker than the sprinting speed of the Dark Territory's pugilists, which required a lengthy combat dance first.

Emperor Vecta's dragon was already just a tiny black dot against the sky. As he ran, Bercouli put his left hand to his mouth and whistled sharply.

Seconds later, a silver dragon leaped off the ground from behind a hill ahead—Bercouli's mount, Hoshigami. But that was not the only dragon to respond to the whistle. Following it was Alice's dragon, Amayori, and then Takiguri, who had belonged to Eldrie before the knight had perished at the Eastern Gate.

"All of you…?"

Bercouli's first instinct was to give the latter two an order to remain in place, but it caught in his throat. Hoshigami swept low and fast toward him, then spun so that it thrust a leg in his direction.

The commander grabbed its talon with his free hand and swung himself up onto the dragon's back, straddling the saddle with his legs and swinging his sword in one smooth motion.

"Go!!"

Hoshigami, Amayori, and Takiguri beat their wings in unison, lifting themselves up into the purple sky of dawn. The three dragons formed a wedge as they flew, and far ahead in the distance, a little glimmer of gold flashed briefly at the legs of the black dragon.

—⁓—

Four thousand pugilists raced across the stone bridge Asuna had created, and they rejoined the two hundred who had barely survived the slaughter. Then they rushed past the human army and smashed into the center of the red force like a giant hammer.

Ten of them formed a tight sideways line, pulling back their right fists and making a battle pose in perfect unison.

"Ooh-rah!"

Ten united voices, ten thrusting fists. They broke the swords of the red soldiers and smashed through their armor. Over twenty of the soldiers screamed and flew backward, spraying blood.

When the battle-aura-infused punches finished following through, the ten pugilists spread apart so that the next ten right behind them could jump through and form a fresh line in tight formation.

"Ooh-rah-rah!!"

This time, they were forward kicks, again in perfect synchronization. Another swarm of enemies was blasted into the air as though by a cannonball explosion.

"…Incredible," Asuna murmured, in the middle of chanting the healing arts commands she'd memorized just last night to heal her wounded left arm. Though Sheyta casually drank water nearby, there was subtle admiration in her eyes.

The pugilists' rotating tactic was similar to the "switch" concept used against bosses in *Sword Art Online*, except much more refined. They formed many different hundred-strong groups, ten lines of ten each, and mowed down the undisciplined enemy with all the strength and efficiency of heavy industrial equipment. It was frightening to behold.

"You shouldn't be standing around impressed. If you get through them to the south, what then? Even we might have trouble eliminating such a huge number of enemies," said their red-haired chieftain, standing next to Asuna with his arms crossed.

It was true that pugilists seemed invincible when charging forward, but as the red army many times their number attacked from all directions, some of the formations were beginning to collapse already. There were still easily over twenty thousand American players on the battlefield.

"…If we break through the enemy to go south, keep rushing

forward and put distance between yourselves and them. I will create another rift in the earth to separate us," Asuna said, her throat ragged.

Could she do it? She'd nearly passed out just from making that small stone bridge. If she performed the manipulations to make another massive ravine as far as the eye could see, she would either be forced to log out for good or perhaps even suffer some kind of physical brain damage…

But she bit her lip and pushed those concerns from her mind. She had to do it. The summoning of the American players had to be Emperor Vecta's last play. If they put a stop to that, then there was no way they could get Alice, even if doing so knocked Asuna off the map.

That was when one man-at-arms rushed up toward Asuna and Sheyta from the south.

"Message!! A message!!"

Half of the man's face was bloodied, injured on the way to get to them at the north end of the battlefield. He slumped to his knees before Asuna and shouted, "I have a message from Renly!! Integrity Knight Alice has been captured by the enemy general's dragon! The dragon seems to have flown to the south with her!!"

"Wha…?"

Asuna could barely speak. Could…could all of this have been a ploy to lure Alice away from the rest of the army alone?!

"The emperor…flew away?" croaked not Asuna, nor Sheyta, but the chief of the pugilists. His one good eye bulged with shock, the iris fiery red. "Then, when he got onto the dragon…he wasn't just surveying the battle…? Hey! Woman!!"

He turned, fixing that baleful red eye on Asuna. "Alice is the name of the Priestess of Light, isn't it?! Why does the emperor want her so badly?!" he demanded. "What's going to happen when he gets the Priestess of Light?!"

"The world…will collapse," Asuna said simply. The pugilist's eye widened even farther. "When the god of darkness, Vecta, seizes the Priestess of Light, Alice, and takes her to the World's

End Altar…then this world—both the human realm and the Dark Territory—and all those who live in it will be returned to nothingness."

Part of Asuna's mind was aware that the things she was saying sounded just like the main plot of a fantasy role-playing game.

Yet, it was absolutely true. Now that Emperor Vecta had Alice, the assault team attacking the *Ocean Turtle* would almost certainly destroy the Lightcube Cluster that contained the fluct-lights of all the people in the Underworld.

What can I do? The Stacia account doesn't have flying abilities. How am I supposed to go after Emperor Vecta when he's on a flying dragon…?

The answer to her question came from Sheyta, the gray knight. The woman placed her empty water sack on her belt and said coolly, "Dragons cannot fly forever. Half a day is the longest they can go without stopping."

The chieftain of the pugilists, after stealing a quick glance at Sheyta, smacked a fist against his palm. "Then you'll just have to follow him with sheer willpower!!" he shouted, his face youthful.

"Follow him…? You can't be serious…," Asuna said, aghast. "You're in the Dark Army, right? Why would you suggest that we…?"

The enemy officer snorted and spat, "Emperor Vecta stood before the ten lords of darkness and told us that the Priestess of Light was his only objective, and once he had her, the rest of it didn't matter to him. The moment he flew off with her, his goal was met…meaning that all of our orders are finished. So whatever we want to do now is up to us…up to and including working with the human army to steal that priestess back from the emperor!!"

What an incredible stretch. Asuna stared at him, aghast. But contrary to his bold and determined words, there was only mourning in his left eye. He looked directly at her and said, "I…*we* can't disobey the emperor directly. His power is all-consuming… Dark General Shasta was maybe even stronger than me, and the emperor killed him without lifting a finger. If he orders me to kill all of you, I will not be able to resist that order. So we'll hold off the red soldiers here. You and the other humans go after the emperor. And…and then you can…"

He stopped there, screwing up his face as though feeling pain from the right eye that was no longer there.

"Then you can tell him something for us—that we're not his toys."

There was an even higher-pitched roar from the pugilists at that moment, coming from the south. The lead wedge of the group had broken through the circle of the red infantry and proceeded out into the open wilderness.

"Here we go…"

The young leader stomped his foot hard on the ground and bellowed with incredible force, "Hold that breach, people!!"

Then he looked back to Asuna and commanded, "You people, get out of here, too! It won't last that long!!"

Asuna sucked in a deep breath and nodded.

He's human, too.

His fluctlight might be artificial, but his soul is as hardy and proud as anyone else's. We mercilessly cut the ropes that his people were desperate to cross, and we cut down over a hundred pugilists. He must be full of hatred and want to crush us.

"…Thank you," she managed to say, turning on her heel.

At her back, Sheyta said, "I will remain here, too."

Asuna had a feeling that the woman would say that. She looked over her shoulder and favored the gray knight with a little smile.

"Very well. Please be the rear guard and aid our retreat."

—⁓—

The mysterious lady knight with the chestnut-brown hair and the seven hundred remaining members of her Human Guardian Army rushed through the breach in the red army that Iskahn's tribe held open along the east and west.

He looked away from the dust cloud of their passage and glanced at the gray Integrity Knight at his side.

"…Are you sure about this, woman?"

"I already told you my name," she said, glaring.

"Are you sure, Sheyta?" he corrected with a shrug. "You don't know if you'll get back alive."

The slender knight shrugged back, her brand-new armor rattling. "I will be the one to slice you. They cannot have you."

"Heh. I'd like to see you try."

This time, Iskahn cracked a bright smile.

He wanted to save his people from an ignoble death. That was all he wanted, and yet, now he had his entire tribe of pugilists risking their lives to protect the Human Guardian Army from the red soldiers. It was a strange feeling, but something within him felt satisfied and lightened by the choice.

Hey, this ain't a bad way to die.

His father and brothers and sisters back home would understand. That he did it to protect the entire world.

"All right, people!! Put some spirit into it!!"

The pugilists promptly replied with an "Ooh-rah!!"

"Circular formation!! Defense all around!! Destroy every last fool who tries to attack us!!"

"You're blazing, Champion," said Dampa, who had silently returned to his usual position behind Iskahn. He clenched his bloodied left fist to crack the joints.

—⁂—

As she crossed the southern hill and retreated to the forest where the supply team was waiting, Asuna learned from young Renly that Commander Bercouli had taken three dragons off in pursuit of Emperor Vecta.

"…Do you think he'll catch up?" she asked.

Renly's youthful face put on an uncharacteristically hard

Integrity Knight
Fanatio

Eastern Gate

Orc Battalion
Chief Lilpilin

Emperor's
Main Force

Ravine
Created by
Asuna

Integrity Knight
Deusolbert

Asuna

Pugilists Guild
Champion Iskahn

Attack

American
Players as
Dark Knights

Teaming Up

Human Army
Decoy Force

Dark God
Vecta

Integrity Knight
Alice

Ruins

Chasing
Vecta

**To the
World's End Altar**

Integrity Knight
Bercouli

Integrity Knight
Renly

Integrity Knight
Sheyta

Student
Ronie

Student
Tiese

Kirito
(Empty)

World's End Altar

Illustration: Tatsuya Kurusu

expression. "To be honest, it's tough to say. As a general rule, dragons all have the same flight speed and need to rest after the same length of time…but because Emperor Vecta's dragon is carrying Alice, too, it should have a slightly increased wear on its life value. And the commander can switch between riding each of the three dragons to minimize the weight burden on each, which should gradually allow him to close the gap, but…"

That meant all they could do was pray that the commander caught up to Vecta before he reached the World's End Altar.

But even if he did manage to catch up, could Commander Bercouli actually defeat Vecta, the god of darkness, in a one-on-one fight?

Asuna had failed to predict that their attackers would also use a super-account to log in, so she never got an explanation of what Vecta could do. But if he had powers on the same level as Stacia's terrain-altering ability, then even the leader of the Integrity Knights, a man as powerful as a thousand, would surely have a very difficult time winning in a solo fight, she assumed.

Renly said crisply, "If he does catch up, the commander *will* take back Lady Alice. He is the most powerful swordsman in the world."

"…Yes, I know," Asuna replied, nodding firmly.

At this point, faith was all they had. And she had just witnessed for herself how strong the willpower of the Underworlders was. "Then we should head south as a group. Fortunately, the terrain seems to be flat ahead. We won't catch up to Bercouli, but we might be able to help him somehow."

"Very well, Lady Asuna. I'll tell them all to get ready to move out!" Renly stated, picking up speed and vanishing into the woods.

As she watched him go, Asuna told herself that she had to protect Kirito and the girl he tried to protect, Alice, and all of the rest of the people of the Underworld. No matter how many scars she suffered. No matter how much pain she felt.

—〰—

And while she did that...

In the main control room of the *Ocean Turtle* marine research megafloat in the Pacific, the assault team's cyber-warfare expert, Critter, was preparing to introduce a second wave of twenty thousand American players to the Underworld.

This time, he adjusted the coordinates to follow Gabriel Miller's current location, about six miles south of the entry point for the first wave.

2

"…!!"

Vassago Casals sucked in a sharp breath and bolted upright.

He shook his long ponytail out and took a quick survey of his surroundings.

Dully reflective metal walls. Floors with a special resin finish to prevent slippage. Many, many monitors and indicator lights, glowing dimly in the darkness.

Only when he saw the tall, skinny bald man sitting in the chair in front of him did Vassago finally process that he was in the main control room of the *Ocean Turtle*.

The bald man, Critter, snorted and said in a high-pitched voice, "Well, well, rise and shine, sleeping beauty. Thought your brain cells had been fried already."

"…Shut the fuck up."

Vassago looked down at his own body. He was lying on a thin mattress along the wall, with a jacket draped lazily over his stomach. He shook his head hard to drive out the cobwebs, wondering what was going on, but felt a sharp pain in the middle of his skull.

He swore again, then called out to the circle of men engaged in a game of cards on the other side of the room. "Hey, someone get me some aspirin."

One of the soldiers, the grizzled Brigg, dug in his pocket and tossed over a small plastic pill bottle. Vassago caught it in one hand, twisted off the cap, poured several pills into his mouth, and chewed them.

The tongue-numbing bitterness finally brought his hazy memories back into clarity.

"That's right...I fell into that bottomless hole...," he murmured.

Critter smirked. "How'd you die over there, huh? You were knocked out for eight damn hours."

"E-eight hours?!" Vassago repeated, forgetting his headache and jumping up. The G-Shock on his left wrist said it was six thirty in the morning, Japan time. That meant they had only twelve hours left until the time limit was up, when the *Nagato* cruiser full of armed sailors would rush the *Ocean Turtle* to restore order.

But more importantly—if he'd been passed out for eight whole hours, then months must have passed in the Underworld, with the way its time was accelerated. What had happened in the battle between the two armies...and the mission to capture Alice?

Critter seemed to know what Vassago was worried about already. He clucked his tongue and lectured, "Don't bug your eyes out at me. At the point you died in there, the acceleration ratio was already one-to-one."

"What...? One-to-one?"

So that meant things couldn't have changed that much on the inside. But in fact, that was a major problem on its own...

"Hey, Four-Eyes, you know what that means?! Those JSDF troops are gonna come charging in here in just twelve hours!" Vassago said, briskly rubbing the man's bald head.

Critter slapped him away with annoyance. "Yeah, no shit. This is all on Captain Miller's orders."

He went on to explain the plan, which stunned even Vassago, the veteran VRMMO player.

The assault team's leader, Gabriel Miller, had given Critter secret orders through the system console in the capital city of Obsidia in the Dark Territory before he had to travel away from the palace.

He'd told Critter to set up a simple client program and a teaser site for the beta test for a new "hardcore VRMMO" that would ignore all the legal regulations of other games—meaning the Underworld, of course. He wanted the acceleration rate slowly lowered to real time by around midnight of July 7th and for Critter to go onto the Internet to rustle up beta testers among American sites.

"...With the console locked down the way it is, all I know is your coordinates and some vague unit placements. All of this was just some insurance in case the Human Empire's resistance was fiercer than anticipated."

Critter's long fingers danced over the keyboard, bringing up a map of the Underworld on the screen. The world was like a triangle with rounded corners. Two red lines ran from the east edge toward the west.

"This is the movement history for you and the captain. So you wandered around the Eastern Gate of the empire, and here's where your dumb ass died."

One of the red lines moved south from the Eastern Gate until it ended in an X.

"But the captain went farther south, past the location of your death. All alone, in fact, leaving the rest of the Dark Army behind to the north. As for what this could mean..."

"Either he's chasing Alice, or he's already caught her," Vassago growled.

Critter nodded. "The original plan said that if we got down to eight hours left or wiped out the entire Human Empire, we'd put the time-acceleration ratio back to a thousand to one. That would be an entire year inside the simulation. Bumping the acceleration back up would log out all the American players, but as long as we win the war, it's all good."

"Why don't you boost the acceleration back up, then? There's barely any forces left in the Human Guardian Army."

"It's not that simple. Take a look at this." Critter tapped a key to expand a portion of the map.

A few miles south of the Eastern Gate, which separated the human lands and the dark lands, there were stripes of flatland, hills, and forest, stacked vertically. The human army was in hiding in the forest…where Vassago had died.

But at some point, a massive fissure had opened up running east to west, between the forest and flatland, stretching at least thirty miles. Along the edges, tiny clumps of colored dots were split into red, white, and black groups.

"The ones in red are the US players we guided into the Underworld. Still about twenty thousand of them down there, though it used to be a lot more. The black dots half surrounded by the red ones are the Dark Army. About four thousand, I think."

"H-hey…why does it look like the red ones are attacking the black?"

"All I wrote on the fake beta test promotion was that you could kill all the hyperrealistic NPCs you want. The people diving from the States have no idea what the difference between the two sides is. But I will say…the black dots are holding up longer than I expected. It doesn't make sense, because the Dark Army's completely subservient to the emperor, so they shouldn't be resisting against the American players that he summoned."

"I bet those players are just having the time of their lives killing 'em."

"Well, let's assume those four thousand black dots will get wiped out eventually. The problem is you've got a little white group right there."

Critter moved the cursor. Sure enough, behind Miller in his southward movement, a small group of white dots was in pursuit.

"That's the human army. They look small on the map, but there's seven hundred of 'em. We don't want 'em causing trouble if they catch up to the captain, so we need to stop 'em somehow."

"Stop them…how, exactly?" Vassago asked.

Rather than answer him, Critter just giggled and hit some more keys. A new window opened on the map. On it, a huge red cloud swarmed and writhed against a black background.

"This is the second wave of US players, who didn't make it in time for the first batch. Once it reaches twenty thousand, I'm gonna dump these guys onto the human army's coordinates. That's twenty-eight soldiers for every one of theirs. Complete slaughter. We can wait until after that to bump the acceleration up to a thousand, and that should leave plenty of time for the captain to catch Alice and get down to the system console at the south end."

"...Let's hope it goes that well," grunted Vassago, rubbing his chin. "The human side's army is tougher than you'd think. Those Integrity Knights are crazy, man. They wiped out the entire front lines of the Dark Army. That was the only reason I got killed... so...bad..."

He trailed off midsentence.

Vassago finally recalled who killed him—and how it happened.

He sucked in a sharp breath, his eyes wide. Flooding into the back of his mind came the image of a goddess staring down at him from a great height in the sky. Without realizing it, Vassago spoke in Japanese, rather than English.

"The Flash...!! That's right...I know it was her, no question about it!!"

"Huh? What'd you say?" Critter wondered.

Vassago grabbed his bald head and switched back to English. "Hey, geek! Rath's doin' the same goddamn thing we are in the second control room!! There are Japanese VRMMO players on the human army's side!!"

"What?!" Critter looked skeptical.

Vassago ignored him and let a fierce smile curl one cheek. "If Asuna the Flash is here, then *he* might be in a dive, too...Damn, I can't be wasting my time here...Hey, get me back in there! Drop me on the white dots with those twenty thousand players!!"

"You wanna go back? We don't have that dark knight account you wasted anymore. But I can give you one of the basic soldier accounts like the other guys."

"Oh, I've got an account...One I've been saving for a rainy day."

Vassago chuckled from deep in his throat and picked up an empty energy-bar wrapper off the console desk. He yanked the pen out of Critter's chest pocket.

"Here, use this ID and password to log in to Japan's Seed Nexus portal and convert the character I've got saved in there to the Underworld. I'll dive in with that one."

He took a few quick steps toward the door to the STL room—but came to a stop just as quickly.

When he turned around, Vassago wore a smile so cold, cruel, and vicious that Critter, a hardened cybercriminal, felt his skin crawl. It was as though the vulgar, cheerful, boisterous mercenary was only one persona that this man wore.

Vassago returned to the console with the silent prowl of a cat and whispered a short extra command into Critter's ear. A few seconds later, Vassago disappeared through the STL room doorway for good, leaving the stunned hacker alone with just a small piece of paper in his hand.

It contained three capital letters and an eight-digit number. Critter did not know what *S-A-O* or the numbers signified.

—⁓—

When Asuna rushed for the supply wagon through the crowd of men-at-arms preparing to leave, she found a metal wheelchair on its side, its black-clad rider feebly waving his left hand, and hovering over him, two girls.

Ronie looked up at the sound of footsteps, her cheeks tear streaked, and when she recognized Asuna, broke into a shout. "A…Asuna! Kirito…he keeps trying to leave…"

Asuna nodded, biting her lip. She knelt down and squeezed his left hand with the only hand she had left. "Yes…Alice…was abducted by the enemy emperor. I think Kirito must have sensed that."

"What—Miss Alice?!" yelped Tiese. Her already white cheeks went even paler.

The only thing that broke the resulting silence was a weak, wordless grunt from Kirito.

"Ah...aa..."

His hand moved, trying to touch Asuna's wounded arm.

"Kirito...are you...worried about me?" she mumbled. When Ronie noticed her injured arm, she shrieked.

"M-Miss Asuna! Your arm—!!"

"I'm all right. This is really only a kind of temporary wound for me," she said, lifting the arm, which was severed a bit below the elbow.

Rath's Takeru Higa had given her a broad explanation of the technology behind the Mnemonic Visualizer that gave shape to the Underworld. Every object was generated by the Seed program, just like in *ALO*, but to Alice and Kirito, who were diving through The Soul Translator, and to the artificial fluctlights like the girls here, everything in the world was a kind of "shared memory" loaded from the simulation's Main Visualizer. It was another reality, materialized with the power of imagination.

The life (hit points) given to the Stacia super-account was vast. It was practically at the maximum number that could be designated, so not even a hundred swords piercing her with normal attacks would reduce her life to nothing.

But when the red soldier had hit her arm with that huge battle-ax, Asuna had felt true, pure terror. She'd imagined that massive ax easily chopping her arm off, and her imagination had turned it into reality.

Kirito's right arm was the same thing. His numerical life had recovered already, but the arm wasn't restored. It was because Kirito continued to punish himself.

Asuna put her good hand over the place where her bandaged left arm was severed. She focused her mind on it, internally chanting.

I will not be afraid again. I will not give in to anything...not until I've protected Kirito and the rest of this world.

A little glow appeared inside her wound. The warm light extended silently in front of her, re-creating her lost left arm. She smiled at the girls, who stared at her with the wonder of having witnessed a miracle. Asuna caressed Kirito's head with her new hand.

She whispered to her paramour, "See? I'm fine. I'm sure we'll rescue Alice, too. So when you're ready…you don't have to blame yourself anymore…"

She didn't know if he understood her, but she could feel the tension in his skinny body begin to ease, bit by bit. She hugged him again, stronger this time, and lifted her head.

"We're going to chase after the enemy emperor. Bercouli is in pursuit of the dragons now, so I'm sure he'll catch up at some point. Until then…take good care of Kirito, Ronie and Tiese."

"W-we will!"

"Don't worry, Miss Asuna!"

She smiled at the girls, then left Kirito to Ronie and jumped off the wagon, holding back tears. Just then, she was accompanied by the tall knight who'd joined Asuna and Ronie in the previous night's recollection of memories in the tent. The woman's silver armor was stained with blood and dust, and there was a bandage around her forehead, but she did not seem to be badly wounded.

"Oh good, Sortiliena, you're all right," Asuna said.

The knight gave her an Underworld-style salute. "I'm glad you are well, too…But from what I overheard, the enemy general abducted Lady Alice…"

"Yes. I was just telling Ronie and Tiese: Emperor Vecta left his army behind and kidnapped Alice on his own. We didn't expect him to put himself at that much risk…"

"I…I can't believe it…," Sortiliena muttered, aghast.

Asuna reached out with her newly healed hand and squeezed the other woman's shoulder. "But it's not over yet. Bercouli's chasing after Vecta on the dragons. We're going to catch up to them before too long."

"All right."

Satisfied, the two rushed back to the main bulk of the Human Guardian Army's decoy force. The seven hundred guards were prepared to move out on Integrity Knight Renly's orders. The sacred arts healers were done with their task, and they and the supply team assumed the center position in the midst of the rows of troops.

When Renly came to announce they were all ready, Asuna said, "You're the only Integrity Knight left among the force, Renly. You're the commander; you give the order."

"R…right, I'll do it," the boy said, nodding nervously. He lifted his right arm and called out, "Lady Alice protected us in the battle at the gate! Now it is our turn to fight for her sake! Let us take her back from the enemy's grasp and return with her to the human realm!!"

The guards responded with a powerful shout. Renly swung his arm down. "All troops, depart!!"

At the head of the marching formation, Renly's dragon Kazenui began to run. Four hundred front guards followed on horse and on foot. After that came eight wagons with supplies and three hundred rear guards.

One unit, Integrity Knight Sheyta's dragon, did not move from its spot. They had no choice but to undo its reins, at which point the creature, scaled the same gray as its master's hair, trilled briefly and flew off in the opposite direction, heading for the battlefield at the ravine to the north, where Sheyta still fought.

In the wagon line, Asuna rode the same horse as Sortiliena and let her mind touch upon the situation.

Our only enemy is Emperor Vecta, no one else.

Like her, he was a real-world human, and his life here was temporary. So she would put an end to him, even if it meant they both had to die. She had to do it for the sake of Sheyta, who'd stayed behind in a deadly battle to prevent the red soldiers from pursuing, and for the one-eyed pugilist and his four thousand followers.

Some time later, the forest of dead trees gave way to a huge mortar-shaped sunken space ahead. A thin path led directly south through the craterlike deformity.

Going by RPG rules, any path would lead to a special location, like a town or dungeon. But supposedly, the southern portion of the Dark Territory did not feature any homeland for the non-human races. In other words, if this path led to anything, it could only be the World's End Altar, and somewhere along its length would be Emperor Vecta and Alice.

There was no sign of the emperor's dragon, nor of Bercouli's dragons in pursuit. But the dwindling army of seven hundred raced, footsteps rumbling, across the dusty earth with as much speed as they could muster.

They had crested the rim of the crater and rushed down the side and were heading into the center of the mortar-shaped space when something rumbled, low and heavy. It was a buzzing vibration, like the beating of insect wings.

"...?"

Asuna glanced up. Her head swiveled left and right. She turned to look over her shoulder.

Only when she faced forward again did she see what was causing the sound.

Thin red lines.

Strings of text in a small font, flickering on and off at random, descending to earth from the sky, hundreds at a time.

".........No........."

Her lips quavered.

No, it can't be. Not more. Not again.

But—

Zshaaaaa!!

A sound like a sudden downpour burst upon them. The red lines extended to the left and right, falling without end. They formed a high-density screen along the rim of the crater, completely trapping the armed formation in the middle.

Just minutes after swearing an oath that she'd never give in to fear, Asuna felt her legs going weak.

Where the lines fell, more of those vicious crimson soldiers appeared—the VRMMO players summoned here from the real world.

"N...no stopping!!" Renly commanded the rest of them. "Charge!! Chaaarge!!"

The rattled human army regained its poise and roared back, picking up its pace. The formation began to rush straight up the far slope of the crater.

But as though anticipating that eventuality, the new red troops were most densely clustered along the southern edge. There were at least a thousand soldiers directly blocking their way...if not two.

Should I risk logging out and use Stacia's terrain-alteration power one more time? If I'm not careful, it could end up blocking our army's path, too...

Asuna hesitated for a moment, but her thoughts were interrupted by a dragon's roar. At the front of the formation, Renly's mount, Kazenui, was charging ahead, flames flickering from the sides of its jaw.

"Ah...! Renly's going to sacrifice himself to tear the way open!" shrieked Sortiliena.

As if he heard her, Renly glanced back toward them. The boy's lips formed the words *The rest is up to you.*

He faced forward and removed the pair of beautiful boomerangs from his waist, holding them up.

Just before he could throw them, however, the sky directly over the crater abruptly changed color. The bloodred of the Dark Territory sky was split by a cross, revealing brilliant azure blue beyond it.

The mass of red soldiers preparing to charge from the crater rim, the rushing human army, even Renly at their lead—all looked up at the sky in unison.

It was an infinite blue. It seemed to reach out into space.

And from its vast reach came falling a bright, shining star.

No, a person. She was wearing armor the same blue as that sky

and a skirt as white as a cloud. The figure's short, wind-whipped hair was light blue. In her left hand was a massive longbow. But the shining was so bright that her face was not visible.

Who...? Who are you? Asuna wondered silently.

In answer, the descending figure raised the bow, which was as tall as she was, up to the sky as she fell.

Her right hand pulled on the string, which glowed faintly as well.

There was a brighter flash. Between the bow and the string appeared an arrow of fire that shone pure white.

Both the Human Guardian Army and the red infantry had come to a stop. In the resulting silence, Asuna heard Sortiliena whisper, "S...Solus...?"

Seemingly in response to her name being invoked, the brilliant arrow of light shot directly up into the sky.

Instantly, it split apart into many pieces that flew in all directions.

They curved and hurtled at tight angles, plunging down to the surface as blazing laser beams.

Sortiliena Serlut was only half-correct.

The figure who appeared in the air over the crater was indeed Super-Account 02, the Sun Goddess, Solus. But she was being played by a real-world human logging in to the system.

And the ability she'd been given was a Wide-Ranging Annihilation attack.

—◆◆◆—

Sinon, aka Shino Asada, viewed the absolute destruction she had caused with a thrill of horror and recalled the conversation she'd had with the engineer who called himself Higa.

"Okay, um, Sinon, this super-account is really strong, but it's not all-powerful. If you have to perform a major operation in the Underworld, it has to take a form that the residents of that world

will be able to process and understand. So your given abilities will reflect that."

"Um...meaning that I'm not actually a GM, I'm just a really, really strong player?"

Shino was resting inside an STL machine—which was as huge as some kind of first-generation experimental full-dive system—within the Roppongi office of a shady tech firm named Rath. Higa's voice was coming through the speakers. She heard the sound of him snapping his fingers.

"Yes, that's exactly right. So the Solus account I'm giving you isn't immune from the general principles that govern resource usage in the Underworld. To attack with your bow, you will have to expend spatial resources. You have an automatic recharging ability, so you'll never run out of power entirely during the day, but you basically can't shoot rapid-fire at will."

As Higa had said, the white bow in Sinon's left hand was noticeably duller after she executed the massive attack. The glowing effects were coming back to the tips of the bow, but it would probably take two or three minutes before she could use a max-power attack like that again.

Can't shoot it rapid-fire? Fine. I'm used to single-shot weapons more than automatics anyway.

She used this moment to survey the explosions she had caused on the ground below.

The crater was about two-thirds of a mile across, and along its rim, charred bodies were disintegrating back into light. This single attack had destroyed over five thousand of the enemy. Fortunately, those were not true residents of the Underworld, but American players who had logged in from the real world, just like Sinon had. They believed they were getting a free beta test and got burned to death the moment they logged in. They were all fuming back in the real world by now, she could only assume.

In the center of the crater, a group that was tiny in comparison to the red forces had begun forward progress again. There were well over ten thousand enemies left, but close to half were frozen in place, watching Sinon in the sky in preparation for another bombardment. They might actually be able to break the blockade.

Sinon narrowed her eyes and stared at the human army's formation. At once, she identified a brown-haired girl sitting on a white horse in the center of the formation, staring up at her.

Allowing a smile to creep over her features, Sinon attempted to control another of the unique powers gifted to the Solus account, Unlimited Flight. When Higa had told her that she could fly with the power of her imagination, it had sounded crazy to her, but once she tried it, there wasn't much difference from the "voluntary flight" of *ALO*. She flew straight downward, heading for the wagon just behind the girl.

When her ultramarine boots touched down on the canvas hood of the wagon, she held up her hand in greeting.

"Sorry it took so long, Asuna."

The girl in the pearl-gray dress-style armor looked up at her, wide eyes welling up with tears. Nimbly, she stood atop the running horse and leaped onto the hood, too.

"Shino-non...!!" she cried, wrenching the words out, her arms wide open. She enveloped Sinon in an embrace, and the girl patted Asuna's back and whispered, "You did so well. It's all right... I've got it from here."

With the slightly taller Asuna still clutching her, Sinon readied her bow, which was about 20 percent recharged, and pulled the string back.

The GM equipment given to the Solus account, a bow called Annihilation Ray, controlled its power by the force exerted on the string, and its attack range by the angle of the bow. By stopping her hand just four inches back, she produced a much smaller, thinner arrow of light. Sinon pointed it at the group of enemies in the path of the large dragon that led the pack.

It shot quietly and unassumingly, with the bow at a twenty-degree incline to the right. The light beam split apart, the pieces landing within a diameter of about ten yards from one another.

The resulting explosions would put a TOW missile to shame. Red armor blew sky-high and disintegrated. The dragon charged right through the space the blast created. It bowled over the other dozen-plus soldiers with its head and raked them with its claws. They didn't stand a chance.

At last, the rest of the soldiers had recovered from the shock of the laser attack and realized that their prey was in the process of getting away. They rushed along the slope of the crater, a red tsunami that howled and swore.

Sinon hung the bow on her arm and put her hands on Asuna's shoulders, pushing the girl away.

"Asuna. About three miles south of here, I saw something that looked like a historical ruin. This path runs right through the middle of it, and there are a bunch of huge statues on either side of it. I think we can fight the enemy off there without getting surrounded. Let's beat the rest of them from that spot."

Asuna was an experienced fighter herself, of course, and as she recognized the wisdom of this advice, her expression tightened up at once. She rubbed the tears away and opened her mouth. "All right, Shino-non...I mean, Sinon. America might have a lot of VRMMO players, but surely they can't get many more than this right away. If we can beat that ten-thousand-plus, the enemy won't have another move...I think."

"All right, let me handle this. Now...with that settled..."

Sinon glanced back to confirm that the very rear line of the human army had cleared the enemy blockade, then she continued in a quieter voice, "Is, er...is Kirito in this group?"

Asuna had to grimace at that. "Look, you don't need to ask me so awkwardly. Kirito's right in here," she said, pointing down at their feet to indicate the wagon they were standing on.

"Oh, he is? Then, um...I'll just go say hi to him."

Sinon cleared her throat and moved over to the rear edge of the canopy that covered the huge wagon, then she used her flight powers to easily slide into the interior of the vehicle. She waited for Asuna to come down next, then headed past the stacks of boxes.

The first thing that came into view was two girls wearing armor over what looked like school uniforms. They both looked back at Sinon with wide-eyed wonder.

"S…Solus…?"

Sinon glanced down at her fanciful outfit and shrugged. "Hello, it's nice to meet you. I might look like Solus, but not on the inside. My name is Sinon," she said with a forced smile.

The girls reacted with surprise, but when they looked over her shoulder at Asuna, they seemed to understand.

Sinon gave them a gentle nod and said, "That's right—I'm from the real world, like Asuna. And I am Kirito's…friend."

"Oh…I see," said the red-haired girl. But the one with dark-brown hair narrowed her eyes just a bit and murmured, "They're all women…"

Sinon had to smirk to herself—*I'm not even the last one.* She walked past the girls on her way to the back of the wagon space.

Sitting there in a simple wheelchair, clutching two longswords with just one arm, was a young man dressed in black.

Takeru Higa had described Kirito's condition to her already. But seeing him broken like this in person filled her chest with emotion and brought tears to her eyes.

"…Aa…"

His empty eyes could not focus directly on Sinon, but he did produce a slight croak when she came into view. Sinon took a knee before her one-time rival, then friend, then savior.

The swordsman's body, sunken into the back and armrest, was so skinny that she hesitated to touch him. Sinon placed her longbow on the floor of the wagon and reached out to gently enfold his shoulders with her hands.

Kirito's soul, his fluctlight, was deeply damaged down in the core of its being, his self-image. Higa had told her in hushed tones that they had not yet discovered a method of healing him. But Sinon just closed her eyes, sending the welling tears down her cheeks, and thought, *That's easy.*

Many people had countless irreplaceable memories of and

strong feelings for the young man named Kirito. They just needed to collect those feelings up, bit by bit, and return them to him.

There, can't you feel it? That's the you that exists in me. A sarcastic prankster, stubborn, naïve...and stronger and kinder than anyone I know.

For a moment, Sinon forgot that Asuna was there, and she turned to brush her lips against his cheek.

Shino Asada had no idea that, at that very moment, her fervent emotions were almost, *almost* encroaching on the one method that could actually heal Kazuto Kirigaya's soul. If Shino had known more about the nature of the Underworld and fluctlights, she might have landed upon the answer. But the advance knowledge she'd been given just before her dive covered only the current state of the world and the capabilities of the Solus account.

So when Kazuto's body twitched a little and rose in temperature after her lips brushed him, she did not think further of it.

Sinon let go of Kirito at once and stood to face the three behind her.

"It's all right. Kirito will be better before you know it. Just when we need him the most."

Asuna and the two girls nodded back tearfully.

"Well...I'm going to fly down to the ruins south of here to get an idea of the lay of the land. You take care of Kirito for the time being," Sinon said, turning toward the back exit of the wagon—only for Asuna to grab her shoulder.

Sinon held her breath when she saw the fierce look in the other girl's eyes. "A...Asuna, what is it...?"

For a moment, she was afraid that Asuna would be angry that she'd kissed Kirito, but that was not the case, of course.

"H-hey, Sinon, did you just mention flying?! Can...can you fly?!" she demanded.

"Um...yes," Sinon replied, startled. "It's a special feature of the Solus account. I heard it doesn't even have a time limit..."

"Then we're not the ones you should be saving! Go get Alice...
She was captured by the emperor!!"

Asuna went on to explain the situation in fuller detail; it was
more desperate than Sinon could have imagined. Emperor Vecta
was another super-account with a real-world player in it, and he
had abducted Alice the Integrity Knight, the key to everything.
Now he was flying far to the south with her on a dragon, and only
Commander Bercouli of the knights was giving direct chase.

"Even for the commander, facing a super-account alone is
too much of a burden. If we can't save Alice before the emperor
reaches the World's End Altar, he's going to destroy this entire
world. Please, Sinon...help Bercouli!"

Once she'd grasped the situation and had a description of Bercouli driven into her mind, Sinon jumped straight out of the
wagon into flight.

The seven-hundred-strong human army headed south, raising a trail of dust behind it. The army of red charging after them
from the north was at least twenty times their number.

*I'll head right back as soon as I get Alice. Just hold out until
then, Asuna.*

Sinon swung to the south and added as much acceleration to
her flight as her imagination could allow. She became a comet
with a white tail, splitting the red sky in two as she streaked
across it.

As she stared down at the landscape below, another thought
passed through her mind.

*Hang on...if she logged in at the same moment I did, then where
is Leafa?*

3

Renly the Integrity Knight led the human army, with the American players chasing furiously after them.

But far to the north, on the southern edge of the ravine Asuna created, Iskahn's pugilists guild and the Integrity Knight Sheyta were battling for their lives against the first red army, which was still over ten thousand in number.

Even farther north, at the plains outside the Eastern Gate, where the scars of battle were still fresh, one nonhuman stood deep in thought.

Steel armor covered his squat body. A leather cape trailed in the wind. Wide ears drooped at the sides of his round head, and a flat-ended nose jutted out of the front.

It was Lilpilin, the chief of the orcs.

With the mere three thousand remaining members of his tribe waiting, he walked alone to a place where he could see the Eastern Gate well. He did not allow a single bodyguard along with him, because he wanted no one to see him crawling along the ground.

After hours of digging through the gravel, Lilpilin finally found what he was looking for—a silver earring with a simple design carved into it.

He scooped it up into his palm. It had formerly been in the ear of Lenju, the princess who had led the orc troops into sacrifice for the massive dark art that the emperor had demanded.

That was the only item of hers he could find. Neither she nor the three thousand orc soldiers who'd died with her had left behind a body—or even a piece of armor. The horrific spell cast by the dark mages guild had converted the orcs' flesh and even their equipment into dark power, devouring them whole.

The chancellor of the guild, Dee Eye Ell, who'd carried out the cruel spell, and even the emperor, who'd ordered it, were no longer present.

Dee had perished in the deadly and beautiful wide-range counterattack of the Priestess of Light, and the emperor had flown south in pursuit of that priestess. He had not released Lilpilin from the order to stay put.

The three thousand surviving orcs could not defeat the Human Guardian Army and the Integrity Knights guarding the Eastern Gate. The desperate wish of the five races of darkness—the conquest of the fertile human realm—was over.

But in that case...why?

Why did Lilpilin's lifelong friend Lenju and the three thousand orcs who were sacrificed along with her...Why did the two thousand orcs who fought in the battle at the gate have to die? What glory had their death brought the Dark Territory?

The answer was "nothing." Not a single thing.

Five thousand of his people had died for an empty struggle. Just because they were uglier than humankind.

Lilpilin clutched the tiny earring to his chest and fell to his knees. Rage, helplessness, and overwhelming grief thrust through his heart, bubbling up in the form of tears and sobs...

Until there was a faint sound behind his back.

The orc chieftain leaped to his feet, spinning around to see a young human woman sprawled on her behind, grimacing with pain. Her hair was brilliant and golden, her skin was flawless, her armor shone, and her garments were the color of young shoots...

She was clearly a resident of the Human Empire, not the dark lands.

Lilpilin's initial reaction was not surprise at her sudden appearance, or anger at what humanity had done to him, but something closer to shame, a wish that she would not look at him.

She was just too beautiful for him to bear.

His first encounter with a young white Ium lady left him with a completely different impression than the tall, powerful, and darker-skinned women of the Dark Territory. Her body was so delicate that a mere touch might break off her limbs. Her hair shone brilliantly even in the weak sunlight, and the large eyes that gazed up at him in surprise were as pure as polished emeralds.

Lilpilin cursed his own senses, that he should find this small, fragile creature so beautiful that she made him quake and tremble. And he feared the recognition of disgust in those green pools.

"D...don't look!! Don't look at meeee!!" he screamed, covering his face with one fist and clenching the hilt of his sword with the other. *Cut off her head before you hear her scream with horror,* his instincts told him.

But in the moment that he went to lift his sword, he felt the earring in his left hand prick his palm. It felt to him that Lenju was telling him not to do it. And in that moment, he heard something he'd never expected to hear—not a scream, but words.

"Um...good afternoon. Or is it morning?"

The girl hopped to her feet, patted her short, flared trousers, and grinned at him. Lilpilin stared down at her from behind his concealing fist, blinking in disbelief.

There was no hatred in her eyes, nor disdain, nor even fear, it seemed. But to white Ium children, orcs from the Dark Territory were supposed to be people-eating monsters.

"Wh...why?" he stammered, at a loss. It was not the voice of one of the ten lords of darkness. "Why don't you wun away? Why don't you scweam? Aren't you human?"

Now it was the girl's turn to look startled and uncertain. "Why? I mean…"

In the manner of one pointing out such obvious facts as the earth being flat and the sky being red, she said, "Aren't *you* human?"

For some reason, a deep jolt ran through his spine. The demi-human chieftain struggled for words but kept his great-sword clenched tightly. "H…human? Me? Dat's widiculous, just look at me! I am an orc! Da being you white Iums call a pig-man!!"

"But you're still human," the girl repeated, putting her delicate hands to her waist. She spoke like a parent lecturing a child. "We're here talking to each other, aren't we? What more proof does there need to be?"

"What…? But………"

Lilpilin didn't know how to argue against that. The confident girl with the green eyes said things that just did not fit into his lifetime of experience as an orc chieftain drowning in hatred for humanity and his inferiority complex toward them.

…If I can talk to them, I'm human?

Was the definition of *human* really that simple? Because the goblins and ogres and giants could all speak the common tongue, too. And with the orcs included, the four races had always been known as demi-humans or humanoids, a class strictly separated from humanity.

Lilpilin stood there in shock and confusion, gasping and snorting for breath. But the girl just pushed all of that aside with a simple "More importantly" and spun around to survey the area.

"…Where are we?"

———

Suguha Kirigaya, better known as Leafa, surmised that she had dropped down at a location far off from the initial login coordinates. She stared up at the baleful red sky overhead.

When she'd heard that The Soul Translator she was being

given to use, STL #6, was still so new that they hadn't removed the plastic shrink-wrap yet, she'd had a bad feeling in the back of her mind. Suguha would never use a brand-new *shinai* in a kendo competition, and she didn't trust electronics when they were fresh out of the box. She had a very reliable streak of coming home with defective products.

Her login coordinates were supposed to be set to Asuna's present location, the same as Sinon's in STL #1 next to her. Given that they were nowhere to be seen, something must've gone wrong. But the blasted wasteland all around wasn't empty—there was a humanoid with a round body and a piglike face nearby: an orc.

According to the color marker that functioned for only a short period after the initial dive, this was an orc, and not one of the enemy American VRMMO players. It was an artificial fluctlight of the Underworld, a true bottom-up artificial intelligence, as Yui described it.

When she'd been given an explanation of what the Underworlders really were, Leafa had sworn to herself that unless it was absolutely, unavoidably necessary, she would never draw her sword to harm them.

It only made sense. She couldn't kill the people that her brother Kirito was trying to protect. If the artificial fluctlights died in this virtual world, their souls would be forever destroyed and never come back.

But now that she had a better look…

Leafa was used to playing in *ALO*, which boasted the finest graphics of any game found in The Seed Nexus, but the realism of the orc in her presence left her stunned. The movement and dampness of that large pink snout, the texture of the metal armor and leather cloak over its huge body, and most of all, the richness of expression and intelligence in its small black eyes—these things told her all she needed to know about the authenticity of the soul behind it all.

She tried asking the orc where they were, but for some reason, it looked away in seeming embarrassment and did not reply. Deciding that starting from a more formal position might be better, she switched to a different question.

—∿∿—

"Um…what's your name?"

The white Ium girl's second question was simple enough that despite the orc chieftain's extreme confusion, he answered it on instinct. Perhaps because, of all the things he'd been given in life, his name was the one thing he did not hate.

"I…I am Lilpilin."

Immediately, he regretted it. His introduction brought to mind the first time he visited Obsidia Palace and introduced himself to the human knights and mages, only to be laughed off.

But the girl just grinned innocently again and repeated his name. "Lilpilin…that's a wonderful name. I'm Leafa. It's nice to meet you, Lilpilin."

And once again, she gave him a shock: She extended her willowy arm in his direction.

He was familiar with handshakes, of course; orcs performed them on a daily basis. But he had never in his life heard of an orc and Ium formally shaking hands.

What in the world does this human want? Is it a trap? Or the work of some mage? Have I been placed under the effect of a bewitching art?

He stared hard at the little hand and growled. The girl waited for him for a good ten seconds before she finally lowered her arm in disappointment. He felt a prickle of pain in his chest at that, for some reason.

If he stood around talking to—or even just looking at—this girl, it was going to drive him crazy. Lilpilin had no desire to attack her anymore, so he clung to the simplest solution to this situation that did not involve violence instead.

"You…you awe a guard—no, a knight—of da human awmy.

I will take you pwisonah, den. I'll take you all da way to da empewah!"

She might appear young, but the girl's armor and the long blade at her side were clearly not ordinary army issue. The way it gleamed with brilliant detail was clearly a step above even Lilpilin's equipment.

But his threat did not seem to frighten the girl. She looked thoughtful and eventually tilted her shoulders to ask, "When you say 'Emperor,' you mean Vecta, the god of darkness, right?"

"D...dat's wight."

"All right. Then take me to the emperor," she said, sticking her hands out together. He was confused at first, until he recognized that she was motioning not for a handshake, but for him to chain her up.

I don't understand what she's thinking...

Lilpilin removed a decorative rope from his waist sash and roughly tied it around the girl's arms—though not very tight. Only after he held the other end and tugged on it did he recall that the emperor was no longer with the main body of the Dark Army.

If he stopped to take any further detail into account, his mind was going to catch on fire. If the emperor was absent, then that flippant dark knight who was his second-in-command, or Rengil, the head of the commerce guild, would be able to decide her fate.

He spun around and began to pull her along, not too roughly, but only got a few steps along when there was suddenly something like a black mist all around them. A nasty stench stung his nostrils. Soon Lilpilin could not even see, and he spun around in alarm.

"Wha...?!" came a yelp of alarm, which belonged to the girl named Leafa. Out of the corner of his eye, Lilpilin caught sight of an arm reaching through the thick darkness to grab Leafa's dangling hair and violently yank her upward.

Then the owner of the arm came tearing through the veil to reveal herself.

A woman who should have been dead—Dee Eye Ell, chancellor of the dark mages guild—stood there with a sadistic smile on her blue lips.

———∿∿———

Why can't I catch up?

Commander Bercouli of the Integrity Knights felt equal measures of impatience and alarm.

He'd been in pursuit with three dragons for over two hours now. They'd flown over the forest where the Human Guardian Army was camped, over the round crater to the south of it, over the ruins with their eerie, tall statues, and even farther into the south of the Dark Territory, but there was no indication that he'd gotten any closer to the enemy. The dragon bearing Emperor Vecta and Bercouli's prize pupil, Alice, was still just a tiny black dot on the horizon.

The emperor had the weight of two people dragging on a single dragon. But Bercouli had the trio of Hoshigami, Amayori, and Takiguri, which he rode in turns, minimizing the fatigue of the dragons. In theory, he ought to be catching up by now.

Why couldn't he get any closer? Could the emperor control the dragon's life by willpower alone?

That couldn't be possible. Directly manipulating life was the greatest of forbidden arts, something that even the late Administrator could not do.

And he couldn't possibly keep it flying indefinitely. The dragon would need to rest at least twice in order to reach the World's End Altar at the southernmost tip of the Dark Territory. The same was true of Bercouli's dragons. If they were going at the same speed, he would never close the gap.

Perhaps there was nothing to be done.

Bercouli could not use any ranged arts that could reach to the very horizon. If there was one thing that could break through this stalemate, it was…

The commander brushed the hilt of the sword on his left hip. It was cold, hard, and trusty. But he could sense that his sword was far from recovering all its life. The fatigue on the weapon from the Perfect Weapon Control art he'd used at the Eastern Gate was worse than he'd realized.

And the ultimate technique of the Time-Splitting Sword that Bercouli was considering would cost a vast amount of the weapon's life.

He could use it only once. It would have to be wielded with such accuracy that it could split the eye of a needle.

Bercouli patted Takiguri on the neck and leaped over to Hoshigami nearby. His longtime partner was so trustworthy he did not need to hold the reins to commune with the dragon. It carefully adjusted altitude automatically.

His aim was at a black dot on the distant horizon the size of a grain of sand. He wanted to aim at the emperor himself, but without being able to visually identify him, the threat of missing was too great. Instead, he focused his entire mind on the one detail he could just barely make out: the flapping wing of the black dragon.

Bercouli stood tall in the saddle. His right hand moved slowly and gracefully, pulling his longsword, which was entirely made of one material, from its well-used sheath.

He took a stance with his right side forward and extended the steel blade, which glowed with a faint light; he had activated its Memory Release art without a spoken command. The sword warped like a heat haze and left behind an unbroken afterimage as the dragon soared forward.

He spoke through gritted teeth, uttering a brief apology to the innocent dragon he was about to attack. Then his pale-blue eyes narrowed, and the oldest knight in the world uttered a brief but powerful command.

"Time-Splitting Sword—Uragiri!!"

He swung the blade downward, heavily but with tremendous speed. The blue afterimages traced the path of the sword, every bit of their length shining, before going out.

In the far distant sky, the left wing of the black dragon carrying Emperor Vecta silently separated from its shoulder joint.

—◦◦◦—

"The smell…This smell…! So strong, the sweet scent of life," croaked Dee Eye Ell as she lifted the human girl up by the hair.

He should have hated the dark mage more than hatred itself, but Lilpilin found himself utterly at a loss in this situation.

Her tanned skin, once gleaming with perfumed oils, and her thick, wavy black hair were both in a bedraggled state now. Wounds that oozed blood crossed every bit of her skin, like she'd been slashed with countless knives. With each movement, the lacerations pulled apart, sending more fresh blood spurting out. But the dark mist around the mage gathered around her wounds and began to plug them, hissing with an unpleasant stink.

The source of the mist was a small leather sack hanging from her waist. Every now and then, an insectoid creature popped its head out of the opening and belched out a healthy gout of the dark mist. This was clearly some dark art that was meant to minimize her loss of life.

Lilpilin's snout crinkled in disgust. Dee shot him a look, and the edges of her mouth curled upward. "This is quite a wonderful prize. You have done well, pig. I will reward you with a bit of entertainment," she croaked.

Dee stuck the clawlike fingers of her right hand down the collar of the hanging, anguished girl. Instantly, she ripped loose the silver armor and pale-green top she wore underneath it.

The girl squirmed even more as her blindingly pale skin was exposed. Dee's smile was sadistic, and she hissed with laughter.

"Is this your first time seeing the body of a human woman? Does a pig find this tempting? Well, the fun part is only getting started…"

Suddenly, her fingers wriggled as though the bones were gone. They were no longer fingers, in fact, but had the appearance of long wormlike things. Tiny mouths lined with sharp teeth opened at the ends of them, and they flopped and writhed in an unpleasant manner.

"Here we go…!!" shouted Dee.

The five worm things stretched and grew to dozens of times their length and wrapped around the girl's body. With her bound and immobile, the ends of the creatures reared back and jammed their heads into her flesh to bite down.

"Aaaah!!"

Blood squirted from the bites as the girl named Leafa shrieked, her green eyes bulging. She tried to brush off the worms, to yank them free, but her arms were tied down to her body, and Lilpilin's decorative rope was still tied around her wrists.

At first, it looked like the blood loss from the five bites was over in an instant. But Lilpilin intuited that the worm things connected to Dee's hand were actually drinking the blood instead.

The dark mage craned back her head and cried out, "System Call!! Transfer Human Unit Durability to Self!!"

A shining-blue glow appeared at the girl's injuries. It traveled through the long worms, marking the flow of blood, and made its way up into Dee's arm. The girl's anguish grew even more stark, and her delicate body thrashed backward so hard that it seemed ready to break in half.

"Ahhh…Incredible…It is incredible!! How rich…how sweet!!"

The screeching voice pierced Lilpilin's eardrums.

The pain of it caused the orc chieftain to return to his senses. He yelped, "Wh-what awe you doing?! Dat girl is my pwisonah!! I will take her to dah empewah!!"

"Silence, swine!!" shrieked Dee, her eyes bloodshot and mad. "Have you forgotten that His Majesty placed overall command in my hands?! My will is the emperor's will!! My orders are the emperor's orders!!"

The breath caught in Lilpilin's throat. He wanted to argue that the military operation had long ago failed to be; the words were right there. But the emperor had vanished without leaving any newer orders. So there was no evidence for Lilpilin to overturn Dee's claim that all orders were still valid and active.

As Lilpilin watched helplessly, the struggles of the human girl grew noticeably weaker. Dee's wounds, meanwhile, began to close and quickly heal.

"Guh…ggrh…," he grunted through gritted tusks. The sight of the girl with the life being sucked from her overlapped with the lasting image of the princess knight who'd given her life in sacrifice.

The light was going out of the girl's eyes. The paleness of her skin was turning sallow, and her arms dangled limply at her sides. But Dee's finger worms continued to wriggle and writhe, determined to suck out every last drop of blood.

She was going to die. His precious prisoner.

The very first human to look at him without fear or disdain.

Just then, Lilpilin's eyes bulged with shock. The ground…the blackened, sootlike earth of the Dark Territory, began to glow bright green beneath the dangling girl.

Soft, fresh shoots erupted from the ground—something that should have been possible only in extremely limited regions—and bloomed tiny flowers of many colors. Fragrant, healing scent exuded from them, and even the bloodred sunlight changed to a gentle, milky white.

The rich blooming of life from the little mound of grass swirled upward and into the body of the girl. Her pale skin began to flush with blood again, and her eyes went from dazed to bright.

The green on the ground then vanished, and the sun returned to its usual color, telling Lilpilin intuitively that the girl's life was fully restored. Strangely, relief flooded into his breast, though he shouldn't have felt anything like that.

The feeling was brief.

"Ohhh, yes…It is surging…Overflowing again!!" screamed Dee in her awful voice. She would've already been healed by now.

Dee let go of the girl's hair and turned the fingers of that hand into more of the hideous worm things.

With more wet smacks, the five new tentacles stabbed into the girl's skin.

"...Aaaah...!!"

Her cry was drowned out by a gale of Dee's laughter.

"Ah-ha-ha-ha-ha!! Aaaah-ha-ha-ha-ha-ha!! It's mine...!! This is all miiiine!!"

———

I have to endure.

Neither in real life nor in *ALO* had Leafa ever felt such mind-numbing pain. All she could do was repeat the mantra to herself.

She'd gotten an explanation of the unique abilities of Super-Account 03, Terraria, the Earth Goddess, before she dived. She had Unlimited Automatic Recovery, which absorbed energy from a wide range around the user automatically and could allow her to heal the durability of herself and other people and objects. With that ability, on top of her massive total of hit points, Higa assured her that it was virtually impossible for her to die by means of HP loss.

That was why Leafa prioritized encountering Emperor Vecta, even risking the danger of becoming a prisoner, and why she swore to herself that she would never draw her sword on the Underworlders.

The woman who was constricting Leafa and inflicting agony upon her, like Lilpilin, was an Underworlder—an artificial fluct-light. If she sliced the woman with her sword, her soul would be forever destroyed. She couldn't fight the woman without knowing why she was injured and why she wanted to be healed this way.

On the other hand...the pain of having her life sucked away was overwhelming, so much so that she didn't have room to feel the shame of most of her top being ripped away.

Was this really just a virtual sensation, with no relation to anything the real body felt?

―⁓―

"…Stop."

Lilpilin did not initially recognize that the word was coming from his own mouth.

But then the action repeated itself clearer, the movement of his mouth and vibration of his vocal cords unmistakable.

"Stop!"

Dee's pupils were contracted to the size of the eye of a needle. She glared at him balefully. The orc chieftain withstood the rising chill from deep in his gut and continued, "You have alweady wecovered all of yoah life. You have no need to continue sucking da life fwom dat Ium!"

"You dare…order *me*…?" Dee lilted, like an off-kilter lullaby. Her ten tentacles spasmed, squeezing the girl's flesh and continuing their blood feast. The dark mage's wounds were entirely healed now, and her skin was shiny and oily again. Even her hair was growing back with more fullness than before.

In fact, the excess of life flowing through her was dispersing out into the air in the form of blue lights. But Dee showed no sign of undoing her wicked bondage.

"I warned you, pig. This prisoner is mine now. I can suck as much life from her as I want. I can defile her right before your eyes or decide to gut her right here and now, and you have no say in the matter."

She chuckled, the laughter muffled deep in her throat.

"Hmm…but on the other hand, you *did* find her first. I suppose I could give you something in return…but only if you strip naked first."

"Wh…what do you mean…?"

"From the moment I first saw you, that fanciful armor and cloak of yours made me sick. What kind of a pig walks around like he's a person? Take it all off and run around snorting on all fours, and maybe I'll think about giving the girl back to you."

Zirnk.

Red light flickered on the right side of his vision. He felt a deep, deep pain in the middle of his head, like a steel needle had been jabbed all the way through his right eye.

What kind of a pig...

...like he's a person?

Dee's words repeated in his mind, only to be followed by the girl named Leafa's.

You're still human.

What more proof does there need to be?

He couldn't let Dee kill her. He didn't want Dee to kill her. And to do that...to prevent that...

Lilpilin's right hand moved to the clasp of his leather cloak. He ripped it loose from his shoulders.

The cloak fell to the ground, and he reached for his armor's leather straps next. But then came a faint voice:

"...Stop."

He looked up with a start, directly into Leafa's eyes.

Those emerald pools, tearful with pain, shook from side to side.

"I...I'm fine. Don't...do..."

She never finished. Dee leaned over and gave the girl's cheek a soft bite.

"If you spout any more of that nonsense, I'm going to chew off your sweet little face. Don't ruin our entertainment. And what are you doing, pig? Off with your armor. Or has the naked human form gotten you all excited?"

She cackled and giggled.

Lilpilin's hand shook on the armor's straps. The pain in his right eye was not going away at all. But it was nothing compared to the fury and humiliation that raged within his rib cage.

"I...I am...I am..."

Abruptly, he felt something burst from his eyes and drip down his cheeks. The droplets trickling down the left cheek were clear, but the ones on the right were crimson. His hand dropped from the armor strap to the sword at his left side.

"I am human!!" he shouted, right as the worst pain yet lanced through his eye, and the organ burst from the inside.

Through his reduced sight, Lilpilin kept a close watch on Dee. The mage's sadistic smile faded, and her jaw dropped in horror.

Lilpilin hurtled a quick-draw slash right at Dee's unguarded legs. But since he attacked in the moments just after he lost half of his eyesight, he failed to judge the distance correctly.

The tip of the sword only grazed Dee's right shin, and Lilpilin lost his balance, toppling shoulder-first into the ground. Through his upturned eye, he saw Dee Eye Ell's mouth curl into an expression of fury and disgust.

"You stinking hog…How dare you turn your sword on me…!"

She tossed the girl behind her and raised her hands. The ten appendages rang like metal and instantly went from tentacles to shining black blades.

"I'll carve you into chunks of meat, mix you with the hay, and feed you to the boars!!"

The orc chief waited for the array of blades to come down on him.

Tup.

Thump.

Two quiet sounds happened nearly simultaneously. Dee froze in place.

The mage's arms separated from her body just below the shoulders and fell heavily to the ground, a fact that Lilpilin only hazily registered.

Dee looked just as shocked as anyone else. Blood spurted and gushed from her shoulders as she slowly turned to look behind her.

Lilpilin saw the figure of Leafa shining brightly. Her body was so slender and fragile that none of it resembled muscle, but she was in the follow-through stance of swinging a truly massive and long sword. Her wrists were still bound together, but it was clear that she was the one who had severed Dee's arms.

The dark mage's head shook in utter disbelief. "A human…cutting a human…to save a pig…?" she rasped.

"No," Leafa explained. "I'm cutting evil to save a person." And with a smooth, practiced movement, she raised the long blade into a high position.

Shwip.

She slashed the woman from a distance that did not seem possible. It was…*beautiful.*

There was no excess effort anywhere from her fingers to her toes, but the speed of the strike was breathtaking. It was the ultimate demonstration of experienced precision.

Lilpilin's vision flooded with tears again, this time of joyful emotion, as the body of Dee Eye Ell, the greatest living dark mage and highest member of the remaining ten lords, split straight down the middle without a sound.

4

With its last bit of strength, the black dragon managed a soft landing with its one remaining wing and perished with a feeble cry. Gabriel Miller watched it die without emotion.

By the time he looked away from it, the dragon was completely purged from his memory and thoughts. He spun around to survey the area impassively.

They had crashed onto the top of a rock that stood in the center of a wide field of oddly cylindrical rock pillars. It appeared to be about a hundred yards tall and thirty yards across.

Perhaps just jumping down would be reckless. He had not nearly mastered the means of magic in this world, generating elements and wielding them to perform tasks. And of course, he was not going anywhere and leaving the still unconscious Priestess of Light behind.

Gabriel could easily rappel down a wall of this height in the real world if he had a sturdy rope, anchor, and carabiner, but there was no need to jump off this rock now. The enemy that had shot him down through unknown means was approaching from the north with a trio of dragons at this very moment. He could take care of the enemy, conquer a new dragon's AI, and resume the southward journey.

He looked straight overhead. The virtual sun in the red sky was already at a high angle. There was likely little time left before Critter resumed accelerating the time ratio. The only issue was whether the American "beta testers" could wipe out the Human Empire's army before the acceleration knocked them off the simulation. There were fifty thousand of them, however; it shouldn't be any issue for them to eliminate the less than one thousand remaining foes.

If there was an uncertain variable in the mix, it would be the Integrity Knights, who'd destroyed the Dark Army, which vastly outnumbered them, but he already had one in his possession, and whoever was pursuing him now would likely be a knight as well. There would be only one or two of them still fighting to the north.

Assuming that his problem would solve itself, Gabriel lastly gazed at the prone Integrity Knight, Alice.

She is simply beautiful.

Enough that it was hard to control the writhing anticipation deep in his core.

He wondered briefly if it would be better to remove all her equipment and tie her up before she woke. That would be the logical choice, certainly, but he did not like the idea of quickly and mechanically performing the task because an enemy was approaching.

This was something he wanted to savor. He wanted to take his time, once the acceleration rate increased again. Every last buckle of armor removed should be an act unto itself: graceful, solemn, symbolic.

"...Just rest peacefully there for now, Alice...Alicia," Gabriel said gently. He strode to the center of the table-like rock, preparing to greet his foe.

Although neither Gabriel Miller nor Critter was aware of it, it was not the simple dragon kick that knocked Alice, the strongest of Integrity Knights, unconscious for several hours, but a special ability belonging to Super-Account 04—Vecta, the god of darkness.

The four super-accounts in the Underworld were designed for the purpose of directly manipulating the world and its inhabitants in ways that were tantamount to the work of gods.

Stacia modified the world terrain.

Solus destroyed mobile units.

Terraria restored object durability.

And Vecta manipulated the residents—artificial fluctlights.

Technically, he overwrote their memories, altering the vector data in their fluctlights—the inspiration for his name—so that they could be placed in distant locations or given new families and still function.

Because this meant physically abducting the residents, that made the role unsuitable for worship, unlike the three other gods. Therefore, in addition to his top-priority gear and maximum life value, he had another layer of powerful protection: He could not be targeted with arts. The "lost children of Vecta," a kind of folklore myth in the Underworld, referred to those who had been moved elsewhere by Vecta's powers.

And the combination of the god of darkness's powers with Gabriel Miller's extreme sense of imagination—his ability to Incarnate—had a synergistic effect that even Rath's engineers could not have predicted.

He absorbed a person's will without using arts. Alice's fluctlight was temporarily rendered inactive, putting her into a kind of forced coma.

The way that he devoured Dark General Shasta's tremendous Incarnation was another feat of Vecta's and Gabriel's powers combined.

And now Shasta's longtime respected rival, Integrity Knight Commander Bercouli, was plunging headlong toward the same conclusion.

—◦◦◦—

Bercouli spotted the emperor's dragon crashing on top of a rocky growth that would leave him trapped for at least a little while. The use of that tremendous ability left him physically spent, but he swept the fatigue aside with sheer willpower.

"All right…One more burst of flight, Hoshigami, Amayori, Takiguri!!" he shouted, and the three mounts beat their wings harder to pick up speed. If the enemy was stationary now, the dragons could cross a distance of ten kilors in just a blink.

In the small amount of time he had before the fight, Bercouli engaged in a kind of meditative trance. The dream he'd had in the early hours of the morning flooded back into his mind, bright and vivid.

Have you ever sensed your own death? Administrator had said in his dream. Even after centuries of interaction with her, she was a mystery to the end.

When he was unfrozen, and Alice told him of the pontifex's death, he did not feel anything he would describe as shock. It was more of an appreciation for her long, long efforts. If anything, the real surprise to him was that Prime Senator Chudelkin was dead.

So he did not press Alice for details of the battle against Administrator or about how she died. Part of that was the sudden weight of protecting the human world now on his shoulders, but perhaps a part of him also didn't *want* to know. He did not want to know about the depth of that silver-haired, silver-eyed half goddess's desire, obsession, and karma.

To Bercouli, Administrator was a languid, fickle, and willful princess. He was obedient to her, but he did not worship her the way Chudelkin did.

And yet…his servitude to her was not something he hated doing.

"It's true…I hope you believe me on that point, at least," the oldest knight muttered to himself.

His eyes flashed open. He'd caught a glimpse of Alice's golden armor lying on the top of the rock—and Emperor Vecta looming before her like a standing shadow.

"Here we go…you three hover in the air!" Bercouli ordered the dragons. "If I fall, go back north and rejoin the group!"

With that, he leaped from Hoshigami's back out into open air.

With Sinon flying ahead and leaving a white trail behind her like a meteorite, the seven hundred members of the human army continued their desperate southern march. They were pulling away from the rumbling red army behind them, but the guards and the horses couldn't keep running like this forever.

Asuna stood on the canopy of the wagon carrying Kirito, Tiese, and Ronie and watched the sky to the south, praying.

After twenty minutes of progress, as Sinon had told them, a massive ruin that looked like a temple appeared on the horizon. There was no sign of large animals, including humans or demi-humans. It was a place of old, weathered stone, slumbering in silence.

On either side of the straight-line path sat long, flat temple buildings. They were about sixty feet tall, and over a thousand feet long. It was certainly a large enough obstacle to prevent the enemy from surrounding them on all sides.

The path continued right through the two temples and onward to the south. It had a ceremonial feel to it, thanks to the eerie giant statues lining it on both sides. The statues were not Eastern Buddhist style or classical European gods. If anything, they were more reminiscent of the ruins of South America, squat and blocky. Their faces had round eyes and gaping mouths, with short little hands joined in front of their chests.

Was that something that the Rath engineers designed personally when they were building the Underworld? Or did The Seed automatically generate it?

Or perhaps...the races that once lived here in the Dark Territory carved the stone from the mountains and brought them here. As giant gravestones dedicated to the dead...?

Asuna exhaled to push the ominous thought out of her mind. She called out to Renly, who was on his dragon at the head of the group. "Let's fight back against the enemy in the middle of that ceremonial path!"

He shouted back to indicate his understanding.

Within a few minutes, the army charged down the path between the temples without losing speed. The giant blocky gods stared down at them from the left and right. The ground underneath went from dirt to paving stones, making the horse hooves and marching boots louder.

Through the chilly air, Renly's handsome voice called out, "Lead group, branch off to the sides and halt! Let the wagons and rear group through!"

The eight wagons trundled past the split lead troops, and the rear troops made up mostly of priests followed them, taking position at the farther point down the road. A dry wind blew through the large gate, rustling Asuna's hair.

The silence lasted only a moment. The ominous rumbling of the army of American players reached the ruins, sending fine grains of sand spilling from the statues around them.

Asuna jumped off the wagon and spoke to the girls who peered out from the cargo space and the swordswoman who stood next to them.

"This is the final battle. I'm leaving Kirito in your care."

"Of course! We'll keep him safe, Miss Asuna!"

"He's under our protection!"

"Upon my life."

Asuna returned the salute of fist to chest that Ronie, Tiese, and Sortiliena gave her in turn, and then she grinned.

"Don't worry. We're not going to let them get this far."

It was as much for her own ears as it was for theirs. She waved her open hand and spun around.

At the lead of the troops, Renly was busy arranging the men-at-arms. The temple path was about twenty yards across, a little bit too wide to properly defend, but they had enough people that they could block it off and still rotate troops in and out.

The big question was whether or not they could grind down over ten thousand enemy troops, minimizing losses, while the

priests in the rear could still perform support magic. Fortunately, the red soldiers seemed to have no magic users of any kind
among them. It was probably because it would be impossible to
teach new players the complex command system of the Underworld's sacred arts in such a short amount of time. Whatever the
case, it was a welcome development.

And if need be, I will cut down the entire enemy army myself,
Asuna swore, inhaling deeply.

Given Stacia's vast life reserves and top-priority equipment, she
would not be defeated through numerical damage. The real question was whether or not she could stand the blinding pain that
came with each wound suffered. If she gave in to the pain, not
only would she be physically damaged, but she would find herself
cowering, unable to swing her sword back at the enemy.

Asuna closed her eyes and thought of Kirito, damaged and
broken. She thought of the pain he had suffered and the sadness
he still bore.

When she stepped forward again, there was no fear left in her.

The clash between armed forces, what promised to be the last
major battle in this war, started beneath the sun at its apex.

The first group of about twenty American players, seeking ultra-
realistic blood and screams as promised by the promotional site,
plunged down the path to the ruins. But they were not met in battle
by helpless NPCs designed for some sadistic pleasure-jaunt with
no board ratings. They were battling against true heroes who were
fighting to save the world and, more specifically, the golden Integrity Knight those people adored and worshipped. Their weapons
were ragged and chipped but shone with unyielding determination, blocking the enemy's blows and smashing their armor.

One figure observed the one-sided obliteration of the red-
armored players from above.

He wore tight-fitting black leather with almost no metal plating whatsoever, like a motorcycle riding suit. The smooth leather was instead studded with dull-silver rivets all over.

His only weapon, which hung from his left hip, was a huge dagger almost the size of a kitchen knife. His face was hidden; he wore a black leather poncho with a hood that he kept pulled down over his features. Where his lips were visible, they featured a smile twisted in the extreme.

Vassago Casals.

After logging back in to the Underworld, he deftly evaded Sinon's wide-ranging laser attack and snuck among the Americans chasing after the guardian army's decoy force. He chose not to take part in the first wave of attackers, instead climbing up the wall of the western temple building and perching atop one of the statues with a first-row view of the battlefield.

"Heh-heh, I see that part of her hasn't changed. She's ruthless when she snaps. Look at her kill!" he marveled, his shoulders rocking with mirth.

Far below, Asuna the Flash, the girl with chestnut-brown hair and pearly-white armor, jabbed and thrust her rapier with impossible speed, just as Vassago remembered from the distant past.

Now, as back then, Vassago hid and watched, unbeknownst to her. Deep inside, he swore to himself that he would finish her off before this world came to an end.

Along with the swordsman in black who fought even more ferociously than she did.

—∾∾—

When Bercouli jumped from the back of the dragon, there was nearly two hundred mels of space between his feet and the top of the rocky pillar. Even he could not withstand a collision of that much force if he simply let gravity do all the work.

Instead, the knight commander descended in a spiral, as though following an invisible staircase down the sky. As a matter of fact, he was generating wind elements under his feet with each step, setting them off and using the counterforce to slow his descent. He'd stolen the secret art of using feet as element control terminals from Chudelkin decades ago.

The oldest Integrity Knight leaped again and again, staying out of Emperor Vecta's sightlines on the artificial-looking rock pinnacle far below him. He put his hand on the hilt of his sword.

I'll settle it with the first strike.

Commander Bercouli had not fashioned a truly deadly Incarnation since he'd cut apart the dark general two generations before, 150 years ago. That was how long it had been since he'd faced an opponent that necessitated the summoning of such a feat.

When he'd battled the youngster named Eugeo in Central Cathedral, Bercouli had fought his hardest, but not with intent to kill. And on that note, he had never truly felt negative emotions like fury or hatred when he faced the dark generals who were his greatest rivals.

In other words, this was the first time in Bercouli's long, long life that he infused his beloved weapon with true anger.

He was furious. He burned with righteous wrath. And it was more than just for Alice's sake.

This outsider, from some place he called the real world, had swept in and driven the darklanders to war when there might have been a chance for peace. He'd caused tens of thousands of deaths for no purpose. And this was something that Bercouli could not forgive, after more than two centuries of dedication to the protection of the world.

I have no idea what makes you tick, Emperor Vecta. But I know from seeing that Asuna girl that not all the real-worlders are demons like you. It's your personal nature that's evil.

And you must pay a price.

You will know the weight of the lives of Dark General Shasta, of Integrity Knight Eldrie, of all the people who perished on the field of battle...with this blow!!

"Zeyaaah!!"

His last step came at a height of ten mels, at which point Commander Bercouli let himself plunge downward, bringing all the force he could muster into a swing at Emperor Vecta's defenseless skull.

The air seared and flashed. The light his blade produced was so bright that the world lost all color.

It was undoubtedly the most powerful single sword strike that had ever happened in the history of the Underworld. Its priority level in overwriting the Mnemonic Data of the Main Visualizer surpassed that of the system's commands themselves. It was a true automatic kill shot, nullifying any and all numerical stats that might oppose it.

Enough to deplete all the nearly infinite life of Super-Account 04, Vecta, the god of darkness.

As long as it hit.

Even in the instant that he noticed the lethal meteor plummeting at him from the heavens, Vecta's expression did not change.

The attack was so fast that the only thing he could do was look up at it. It was instantaneous, impossible to react or respond to.

And yet, Vecta's body in its obsidian armor simply slid to the side—in the only possible direction to avoid the blow, with only the minimum distance necessary to put him out of harm's way.

The only thing Bercouli's sword touched was his flapping red cloak. The hem of fur and thick fabric was obliterated into fine dust, and the top of the tough rock mountain split deep with a thunderous *kaboooom!!* The entire structure shook, and chunks of it split off and fell down to the ground below.

He...evaded that?

Bercouli's body did not stop moving for an instant, despite closing his eyes. He was long past the stage of experience when an unexpected action from the enemy paralyzed one's mind.

He kicked one last time in midair and landed around the flank of the emperor, instantly striking on a flat plane. He had missed on executing an all-consuming super-attack but transitioned to his next swing in less than half a second.

Vecta dodged that one, too.

Like smoke pushed by a breeze, he simply slid along the ground without any shift in momentum. The tip of the sword scraped the surface of his armor, sending up harmless sparks.

But this time, Bercouli was sure of his victory.

The first powerful blow from above had missed, but it wasn't gone. He'd activated the Perfect Weapon Control art of his weapon—the Time-Splitting Sword's Karagiri—the ability to cut the future. It was the skill that had caused Eugeo such pain in the cathedral, leaving the full power of the cut hanging in the air, such that anyone who touched that space received that slice courtesy of an invisible blade.

Emperor Vecta slid backward toward the space where the invisible slashes hovered.

First, his platinum-silver hair frayed and spread.

The crown over his forehead cracked and broke into pieces.

Vecta's arms rose high in a mockery of a pose of pleading for forgiveness.

Bercouli had a vivid vision of his tall black form splitting vertically.

Whap.

A dry smacking sound.

The emperor's palms clapping together, without so much as a glance behind him.

He trapped my Karagiri, the empty slice, between his bare hands? And with his back to it?

It was impossible. The secret technique of trapping a sword between the hands was known among the pugilists of the dark world, but it was possible only because of their incredibly tough fists, which were harder than tempered steel. And more importantly, the power of the Karagiri hanging in the air was beyond even what the chief of the pugilists could stop with his bare hands.

This understanding flashed through Bercouli's mind in an

instant, but at last, it caused him to stop moving. And therefore, he was caught flat-footed, only able to watch what happened in the next moment.

The slash that flickered in the air like a heat haze melded into the emperor's hands. His blue eyes began to swirl with darkness.

And within that pit of blackness flickered countless…stars…?

No.

They were souls. The souls of all the people he had absorbed, trapped within him. And among them were surely the souls of Dark General Shasta and the woman who'd served as his right hand…

"…So you can devour the Incarnations of others?" Bercouli muttered.

Vecta lowered his hands, the force of the Karagiri entirely absorbed now. "Incarnation? Some melding of mind and will, I suppose."

His voice was deathly cold, a human voice stripped of all living humanity. His thin lips moved into the shape typically recognized as a smile. "Your mind is like a wine of aged vintage. Rich, thick, heavy…with a lasting aftertaste. It is not to my taste…but as an opening act, it is a worthy flavor."

His pale hand moved to grab the hilt of the longsword at his side. He pulled the thin blade free from the sheath; it shone with a bluish-purple light. Vecta let the weapon dangle at his side as he smiled again.

"Now, let me drink more."

—◦∿◦—

A thick greatsword glanced off Asuna's left arm. It felt as though a searing hot poker had been pressed against the spot.

It doesn't hurt!! she told herself. And just as quickly, the wound on her skin simply vanished.

Already, though, her arm was a smoky blur, jabbing four consecutive times into the soldier across from her, from right shoulder to left flank. The man's face twisted, and he fell to the ground, but not before emitting a truly impressive string of vulgarities.

She'd long ago lost count of how many foes she'd defeated. In fact, she wasn't even sure how many minutes it had been since the battle at the ruins had commenced—or how many dozens of minutes. All she knew for certain was that the red soldiers pouring down the entrance to the temple path still seemed unlimited in number.

A battle of endurance like this is no big deal. It wasn't rare for the boss fights back in Aincrad to take three or four hours, Asuna recalled. She used her rapier to deflect an ax swing from a new enemy leaping over the body of his disintegrating comrade.

She thrust a quick, accurate strike into the heart of the unbalanced foe and used the opportunity to glance to either side of her.

To Asuna's right, Renly was hurling boomerangs with each hand and amassing a mountain of dead around him. Their power and accuracy were tremendous, and he seemed to be totally in control of his area.

The problem was on the left side. The captains of the men-at-arms were arranged there around Sortiliena, but it was clear that they were steadily getting pushed back.

"Left wing, shorten the intervals of your rotation! Focus more healing on the left side, please!"

"I can still fight, Miss Asuna!" Sortiliena shouted back. She activated the Two-Handed Sword skill Cyclone. Her sword glowed light green and made a rapid full rotation that sent three enemy soldiers flying, but she wound up down on a knee when it was done. From what Asuna had heard during their late-night sharing of memories, the swordsmen of noble birth were trained in one-on-one ceremonial battles, leaving them unfamiliar with a long, unpredictable melee like this.

As a matter of fact, Liena's combat was flowing and bold, but even Asuna, who'd been in this world for only a day, could see that it was *too* fair and square. She used big attacks with hardly any feints or tricks to unbalance foes, and the post-skill delay immobilized her long enough for the surviving enemies to land a few wild hits on her. Her armor was already chipped all over, and her purple guard's uniform was stained with blood in places.

"Step back and get healed, Liena! Trust in your companions!" Asuna commanded. Liena bit her lip but said "I'll be right back!" and retreated. Another head guard stepped in to fill the empty spot in the line she'd left, but there was already fatigue etched into his features.

There was one more thing that bothered Asuna besides the exhaustion of the left wing.

The soldiers in red armor they were fighting weren't human-oid monsters running on simple algorithms. They were veteran MMORPG players from America, the nation that had birthed the genre. They were used to PvP battle, and it wasn't a stretch to suggest that they would soon grow tired of simple charging and come up with a different strategy.

What would I do in their position? Asuna wondered as her rapier flashed and jabbed. The old faithful method would be a long-range attack from the rear. But the crimson army seemed to have no magic users. Even if there were, it was probably too much to expect them to use the Underworld's complex command strings without practice first.

That left only archers, but fortunately, it seemed that none of the enemy accounts were equipped with bows and arrows. They could also throw their weapons, perhaps, but nobody wanted to let go of their swords and axes and risk not being able to fight anymore.

So it seemed a safe assumption that the enemy side had no means of breaking through the stalemate.

That meant, as she'd initially surmised, that the only answer was to keep grinding until the ten-thousand-plus were gone.

But just as she told herself that, a dark shadow crossed the entrance to the temple road. The sun was blocked by a line of huge shields and a field of lances standing tall like flagpoles.

Heavy spearmen!

"Th-they're going to charge with spears!! Watch the points and avoid the first lunge!! Once you're inside their length, they can be beaten!!" Asuna called out to her comrades on the sides, right as the huge lances clanked into position.

""""Chaaaaaarge!!""""

The line of twenty lancers bellowed and began to rumble toward them. The men-at-arms grew antsy, sensing the pressure of a red tsunami approaching. *Just calm down, everyone!* Asuna prayed as she stared down those who were charging at her. The wicked, gleaming lances had lethal power, given the force behind them.

Wait until they're as close as possible...and parry!

The rapier slid along the side of the spear, spraying yellow sparks. The sharp point of the polearm passed just to the right of Asuna's face and continued behind her.

"...Haah!!" she screamed, thrusting the rapier up toward the gap in the enemy's armor, right near his throat. An ugly squelching sensation traveled back through her palm. Blood squirted from the bottom of the helmet.

But the screams that ensued were not only from the enemy forces. A number of men-at-arms on the left wing had been speared through.

"...!!"

Asuna gritted her teeth and ran to the left, leaving her station. She used the simple Linear Thrust to run through one enemy soldier who was trying to pull his lance free from a deceased guard. She then removed her bloodied weapon and took off the next enemy's arms with the two-part Parallel Sting skill.

The third enemy thrust his lance at her with an angry insult, and she jumped directly over it, landing on top of the spear and running along it until she put a foot on his shoulder, pulled off his helmet with her free hand, and jabbed her rapier deep into his exposed neck.

As the man sank without so much as a scream, Asuna stayed on his back and called out, "Take the wounded to the back!! They are the top healing priority!!"

Another glance at the battlefield told her that the twenty-lance charge had ended in failure thanks to the hard effort of Renly and the men-at-arms, but six of their number had taken a direct hit—and three of them would not likely survive.

If they repeat this strategy, our overwhelming disadvantage in numbers is going to be exposed when we don't have enough to maintain the line.

That horrible knowledge came true with another rumble. The next group of twenty lancers was charging through the entrance to the temple grounds. Asuna tore her gaze away from the oncoming lances and back to the center of the line, where she was supposed to be situated. A young man-at-arms there, practically still a boy, was holding his sword at the ready, knees knocking.

"Ah…!" she gasped, running to her right. She leaped for the spot between the lance charging from the left and the boy standing still on the right. She wouldn't be able to parry it in time with her rapier. The only thing she could do was try to grab the glinting lance head with her left hand.

If this were an ordinary VRMMO world, Asuna's block would be successful due to her incredible reaction speed and strength stat. But the Underworld had all kinds of parameters that games like *SAO* and *ALO* ignored.

The smooth steel lance slipped through her blood-slicked palm—and a dull shock jolted her body. Asuna looked down, voiceless, to see the chunk of metal jabbing deep into her side.

—∿∿—

Maximum efficiency with minimum movement.

That was how Commander Bercouli viewed Emperor Vecta's fighting style, which was different from anything he'd seen before.

For one thing, his feet hardly moved. When he dodged an attack, his feet just slid across the ground a tiny bit. He also had nearly no windup for any kind of attack. The sword would be limply held in his right hand, then slither forward to strike at the shortest possible range.

Therefore, it was essentially impossible to predict his movements. The emperor's attacks were not especially quick or powerful, but they kept the vastly more experienced Bercouli from countering, five consecutive times.

But five was enough.

Calling upon his vast past knowledge and instinct, Bercouli had a grasp of Vecta's attacks by that point and moved to counterattack on the sixth one at last.

"Sssh!" he hissed as quietly as possible, striking high before Vecta's swing could come. White sparks accompanied a piercing clash of metal.

Two swords connected in the air—and it was a battle of strength from here. The enemy's sword sank easily, without much resistance. Tall Vecta's knees bent, as if giving out to the pressure.

I sense victory!!

Bercouli poured all his finely honed Incarnation into his sword. The well-used steel blade began to give off light. The tip of the Time-Splitting Sword, which pushed Vecta's black longsword lower and lower, finally touched his shoulder and dug into the surface of his armor…

In that moment, Vecta's sword flashed eerily. The bluish-purple light moved like a living thing, wrapping around the Time-Splitting Sword. Suddenly, the rippling, powerful light of Bercouli's silver blade began to wilt and vanish.

What is this? In fact…

What was I…even trying…to do…?

With a sharp crack, Bercouli sensed a freezing chill in his left shoulder and snapped his eyes wide open. He leaped back, sucked in a deep breath, and collected himself.

What in the world was that? Did I just space out in the middle of a battle?!

Aghast, he shook his head, telling himself that it was not some careless accident.

It was as though his mind had been forcefully devoured by blankness, leaving him unable to explain why he was there or even who he was.

"You...you sucked my Incarnation straight from my sword?" growled Bercouli, deep in his throat.

The only answer he got was the faintest of smiles. Bercouli clicked his tongue and glanced at his shoulder. The wound was deeper than just a scratch.

"Hmph...well, you're proving to be a better opponent than I thought, Your Majesty. This will be a tough battle if I can't use my sword against yours." Bercouli grinned back.

That wiped the smile from Vecta's mouth. "Ah...That reminds me, I never tested it."

He stuck his sword out forward, but it was far from the proper range. The blade would never reach—

But from the tip in the air emerged a viscous blue-black light.

...*From long range?* Bercouli recognized, right at the moment that the light touched his chest.

His consciousness went dim, like the flickering of candle flames.

The knight commander stood there dumbly, watching as his opponent's sword slunk its way under his left arm.

Then it jumped upward, smoothly and easily.

Bercouli's thick arm split off from the shoulder with a wet, heavy squelch.

—⁓—

"Krh...aa...ahhh!!"

Asuna managed to hold the scream in her throat and keep it to a gurgle. This was not pain. It was an explosion of sensation that overwhelmed her capacity to feel at all, as if her stomach were pressed against a hot burner plate and unable to pull away.

This doesn't hurt.

I swear, this doesn't hurt!!

The dark lance pierced deep through her stomach on the left side. It had to be jutting at least three feet out of her back. She looked over her shoulder to see the boy guard behind her; his cheek had only been grazed by the lance. She summoned every last ounce of willpower she possessed to give the shaken, pale-faced boy a smile.

None of these virtual wounds mean anything...compared to the weight of that boy's life!!

"Aaaah!!"

She put all her strength into her left hand, which was still gripping the lance.

A horrible wet crunch sounded as the two-inch-thick piece of metal cracked in her palm. She reached around her back, grabbed the jutting end of the spear, and pulled on it.

Sparks flew in her eyes, and something like an electric shock ran from the top of her head to her toes. But Asuna never stopped, using the momentum of her strength to pull the lance out, then tossing it to the ground.

Blood gushed in astonishing amounts from both the gaping wound in her torso and her mouth, but Asuna did not stumble or sway. She lifted her free hand to wipe her lips and stared up at the stunned enemy soldier before her.

The big man holding the broken lance blinked several times. His eyes looked uncertain through the visor of his helmet.

"Oh, gosh," he stammered a few times. The English flowed from his mouth in rapid succession. "Geez, man...this game isn't fun at all. This sucks! I'm gonna log off."

Asuna obliged him by jabbing her rapier through his heart in one quick motion. His large body fell to the ground and was quickly surrounded by the visual disintegration effect.

For some reason, the tears that no pain could summon now burst from her eyes.

The pain and hatred that covered every inch of this battlefield did not need to exist.

There was no reason for the American players and the men-at-arms of the guardian army to do battle. These were people who could have easily gotten along under different circumstances—such as Asuna's.

This was not why virtual worlds—why VRMMOs—were created.

"H...el...p...," screamed a voice in Japanese, pulling Asuna out of her thoughts. She saw that a huge lance was being stabbed downward at a guard collapsed on the ground.

"Yaaaaah!!" roared Asuna, springing into motion. Her rapier darted forward. Light erupted from its tip, covering the entire weapon.

Her feet left the ground, and Asuna flew forward like a shining comet. It was the most powerful of charging skills in the fencing class, Flashing Penetrator.

The spearman trying to kill the guard was hurtled up into the air. The enemy behind him suffered the same fate, as did the one behind *him*.

The sword skill came to a stop only when a fourth body was laid at the feet of the holy statue. Asuna spun around, shoulders heaving with her breath. The second wave of charging lancers left at least another five dead in their wake. And a third wave of twenty was already forming up at the end of the path.

She pulled her rapier from the body already starting to vanish and shouted, "Everyone, protect your stations!! Renly, move over to the center!!"

The young knight paled when he saw the blood flowing from Asuna's stomach, so she gave him a reassuring grin and continued, "I'm going to jump forward into the enemy's position. Just worry about the ones I don't get first."

"M...Miss Asuna?!" Renly stammered. She raised a clenched left fist in answer to him and the other men-at-arms.

Then Asuna ran straight ahead.

—◈—

Bercouli faltered, his center of gravity thrown off. He stepped on his own left arm lying on the ground. It was the nasty, fleshy feedback he got from his foot that snapped him back to attention before the pain did.

"Grgh…!"

He jumped again, putting more distance between them. The blood spilling from the gaping wound on his left shoulder created a crimson arc on the light-colored rock.

How can this be?

Just by pointing his sword, he could cause the mind itself to stop working?

Bercouli placed two fingers on his right hand against the wound on his shoulder, still holding the Time-Splitting Sword, and thought rapidly. The healing arts he activated without a command glowed blue and stopped the bleeding. But there was not enough spatial sacred power on this desolate rock to regenerate the arm that had been lopped off.

How do I counteract this?

Karagiri, the empty slice of his Perfect Weapon Control art, would not work on Vecta again. He would just devour the Incarnate slash as it hung in the air.

The only skill remaining was Uragiri—his betrayal slice Memory Release attack. There were two major issues with using that, however. One, the enemy was not going to stand there and watch as he performed the lead-up motions. And two, it was nearly impossible to narrow down which specific place to strike…

Bercouli blinked to get the sweat from his forehead out of his eyes. In doing so, he came to a sudden realization:

I'm getting desperate. At some point, I lost all my composure. My back's against the wall.

This is the place where I may die. The very tipping point between life and death.

"…Heh!"

Bercouli Synthesis One, commander of the Integrity Knights,

smiled with the knowledge and certainty that he was was facing a true threat to his very existence. His gaze moved from the steadily approaching emperor to the form of the golden knight, Alice Synthesis Thirty, lying prone to the side of their battle.

Little Miss…I suppose I wasn't able to give you the thing you truly sought after—the love of a father. I don't remember my own parents at all.

But there's one thing I do know. A father is meant to die protecting his own children.

"I suppose that's something…you'll never understand as long as you live, monster!!" bellowed Bercouli.

And the oldest living knight charged, with no plan, no strategy, nothing but his trusty sword in hand.

———

"Gah…uh…"

As she panted, blood spilled from her mouth, pooling on the ground at her feet.

But Asuna stayed standing, using her rapier stuck point-first into the earth as support.

She had managed to cut down the third and fourth waves of heavy lancers, but she now bore over ten wounds in various places on her body. Her pearl-white top and skirt were ripped and tattered, stained red by blood belonging to both her and her victims.

The fact that her body could still move, despite the puncture wounds from the lances, was impossible to believe. In fact, it was just the brutal fact of her impossible hit point total that was keeping Asuna upright.

My body will give out when my mind does. And that means I will stay standing forever.

She could barely feel anything anymore. The only sensation from her nerves was burning heat that warped her vision.

When she caught sight of the fifth wave of spearmen through her dimming vision, she pulled the rapier loose from the ground.

She couldn't use nimble footwork to evade anymore. She could only block the lances with her body and hit back with sword skills.

The feather-light rapier was now as heavy as a leaden rod. She propped it up with both hands, her front half bent, and waited for the enemy.

"Go!!"

Twenty lancers began to charge, the earth pounding with their footsteps.

Dmm, dmm, dmp-dmp-dmp-dmp...

The steps accelerated. And yet, a high-pitched vibration was coming from somewhere.

Asuna found her gaze drawn upward.

There was a line stretching across the red sky. A very fine string of digital code.

Enemy...reinforcements...?

"......Oh no......"

There was, at last, the smallest bit of resignation in her voice.

But...this line was not the same red color as the previous kind she'd seen. It was a deep blue, like the color of sky just before the dawn.

She wasn't able to surmise what that might mean at this point. She just watched, wide-eyed, waiting to see the result.

The line coalesced about ten yards up, flashed momentarily, and turned into human form.

Vwom. The air buzzed, and the figure spun with blurred speed, then resumed descending, roaring and rotating like a tornado.

The twenty lancers beneath the lowering figure were all stock-still, too, watching it come down.

The dark-blue whirlwind descended lightly into their midst—and turned red.

It was blood. The tornado instantly severed the bodies of the soldiers, splattering their pieces all around it. They collapsed outward from the circle, and the spinning slowly stopped, returning the figure to human form.

There stood a tall, thin profile, facing the opposite direction.

Polished Japanese-style armor gleamed in the light of the sun. One hand was on a sheath, while the other was extended fully to the side, holding a tremendously long sword—a katana—in the follow-through of a swing.

Asuna had seen this attack before, in a different world.

It was a sword skill.

The heavy rotating katana skill, Tsumuji-guruma, meaning *spiral wheel*.

The figure straightened up again, lifted the long katana to his right shoulder, and inclined his head to the side. A stubbled face with a lopsided grin showed itself below a fancifully designed bandana.

"Sorry about the wait, Asuna."

"K…Klein…?" she rasped, though she never actually heard her own voice.

Everything was drowned out by the resonance of a multitude of vibrations filling the sky. It was the exact same sound that the American players had made when they appeared, but to Asuna, it sounded like a heavenly host of angels singing.

Thousands of lines of code came hurtling down out of the crimson sky like rain, glowing a vivid blue.

—∿∿—

Slash.

Mind fades.

Then awakens from the pain.

It was a pattern whose repetition he had lost count of by now.

Emperor Vecta refused to deliver a fatal blow, as though he was trying to extend the battle, but Bercouli was keenly aware that the blood he was losing from his countless wounds, his very life itself, was running perilously low.

But he had spent over two centuries hardening and focusing his willpower, and he used it to do just one thing at the expense of all thought and fear.

He counted.

Measuring time: Bercouli had the ability to sense time perfectly, and he used this measuring ability to do nothing but count the seconds in his mind. Even when the emperor's sword was muddling his thoughts, Bercouli's unconscious stayed dedicated to the task.

Four hundred eighty-seven.

Four hundred eighty-eight.

As he added up the seconds, Bercouli repeated simple, straightforward attacks. Occasionally, he added a provocation or two.

"…Looks like…your skill with the blade isn't much to write home about…Your Majesty."

Four hundred ninety-five.

"You keep hitting me, but you still can't bring me down. You're only second…no, third-rate."

Four hundred ninety-eight.

"Come on! I can keep going!!" he shouted, striking directly at his opponent.

Five hundred.

His sword brushed the bluish-purple light surrounding the emperor. It sucked up his Incarnation, causing his mind to grow faint.

The next thing he knew, he had a knee to the ground, and blood splattered onto the rock surface from a fresh wound on his left cheek.

Five hundred eight.

Almost there. Just a bit longer.

Bercouli stood slowly and turned around to face the emperor.

Vecta's face had never displayed any kind of emotion to this point, but now there was a faint whiff of disgust on it. Apparently, a drop of Bercouli's blood had flown over and landed on his pale cheek.

The emperor rubbed the red stain off with a finger and muttered, "I grow tired of this."

He stepped forward into a puddle of Bercouli's blood.

"Your soul is heavy. It is too thick. It clings to my tongue. And it is too simple. You think of nothing but killing me," he said, his tone flat. He took another step forward. "Begone."

Viscous light collected around his black sword as he raised it in silence.

Bercouli did not change his expression. He merely clenched his teeth the slightest bit.

Almost there. Thirty more seconds.

"Heh-heh...Don't get all huffy. I can still...keep going for a bit." Bercouli took a few wobbling steps in the wrong direction. He lifted his sword unsteadily. "Where...are you? Where did you go? Ah, over there...?"

The commander swung, his eyes empty and dull. The tip of the sword struck a spot well off the mark, and he stumbled.

"Huh...? Or was it this way...?"

Another swing that didn't even raise a breeze. But he kept moving, dragging one foot behind him. It seemed as though the loss of blood had robbed him of sight and was making his thoughts hazy and distant.

But this was, in fact, a master class in acting.

Beneath his half-closed lids, his gray-blue eyes focused on one thing only—footprints.

After ten minutes of fruitless attacking, Bercouli's blood was firmly splattered all around the rocky mountaintop, which was not very big to begin with. The emperor's boots and the knight commander's leather sandals left two very distinct sets of footprints when they tracked the blood.

In other words, they were creating a detailed record of how the two men were moving. And as he put on an act of being delirious, Bercouli was actually looking for the most darkened and dried of the emperor's footprints, from the moment he cut Bercouli's arm off, ten minutes earlier.

His unconscious timer started right after that moment. In other words, it would be the place where Emperor Vecta had been standing exactly ten minutes ago. His bloody footprints would tell the tale of which direction he'd moved after that.

Five hundred eighty-nine.

Five hundred ninety.

"Oh...I think...I found it...," Bercouli murmured weakly. He wobbled side to side and raised the Time-Splitting Sword for a strike at empty space.

It was, quite literally, intended to be his final blow.

There was little life left in either the weapon or its master.

Bercouli intended to consume all that was left to perform the Time-Splitting Sword's Memory Release art.

Uragiri, the art of the betrayal slice, was different from the future-slicing Karagiri, in that the ability to hold the slash's power in the air went into the past instead.

The Underworld's Main Visualizer kept a record of each human unit's movements for the previous six hundred seconds—ten minutes exactly.

The Time-Splitting Sword's Uragiri interfered with that log, confusing the system into thinking that the target's locational data from ten minutes ago was actually the *present* location.

As a result, a sword that appeared to cut through empty space would hit the body of the person who had once existed in that spot. It was unavoidable, unblockable, and a true betrayal of any and all technique and skill.

It was why Bercouli had resisted using Uragiri for years and years. Even in his battle against Eugeo, when he'd fallen to the Memory Release technique of the Blue Rose Sword, Bercouli had not used the move that would have given him victory. Even knowing that Prime Senator Chudelkin would have labeled this a betrayal of the Axiom Church.

But against Emperor Vecta, who used equally inhuman powers, he was not going to hesitate.

When Bercouli had struck down Vecta's dragon, he'd utilized the enemy's direct, unchanging flight direction to accurately estimate the coordinates of the enemy's position ten minutes earlier. But in the messy, chaotic battle up close, gauging those precise coordinates became remarkably harder.

Of course, he could pick a moment, memorize that spot, and wait ten minutes. But that method meant that if he was prevented from executing the move in any way, he would have to start counting to six hundred all over again.

Just like this moment.

"You're up to something."

Emperor Vecta slid over, and the waves of his darkened Incarnation extended from his sword toward Bercouli. He had to avoid their contact, and this required him to nimbly step out of the way. That ten-minute moment had passed, forever out of reach.

I failed to execute it, he lamented, rearranging his grip on the Time-Splitting Sword after he'd just been about to let loose with Memory Release.

He was totally out of ideas now.

Now that the emperor knew he had one final plan up his sleeve, he would ensure that Bercouli could never make use of any major technique. His longsword continued to extend that Incarnate light toward Bercouli.

But the commander persistently evaded the attacks for all he was worth.

He struggled.

He would struggle and struggle and fall in a miserable state. It was long in the past that he'd decided that would be how he eventually died.

Three times. Four times. Five times, Bercouli avoided the emperor's attacks.

But at last, the dark light brushed his body.

His mind went blank for a moment—and when he opened his eyes again, he saw Vecta's sword thrust deep into his own stomach.

When the blade pulled loose, the last of his life spurted outward as dark-red liquid.

As the commander slowly toppled backward, he caught sight of a dragon far overhead, tearing across the sky in a steep dive.

Hoshigami.

Come on, I told you to stay back and wait. You've never once disobeyed an order of mine before.

A jet of blue-white fire shot from the dragon's gaping maw. The blazing beam with the power to burn a hundred infantry at once descended upon Emperor Vecta, who easily took the brunt of it with his left hand.

The smooth black gauntlet deflected the blast without trouble. Flames bounced off and flickered away as they dissipated.

The emperor then unleashed the dark light from his sword and caught Hoshigami's forehead with it. He had used this trick to take control over the dark knighthood's dragon—but Bercouli's mount did not stop.

It plunged straight down for the emperor, its very life shining forth, dazzling, from its outstretched wings.

Vecta grimaced. He pulled back his sword, then thrust it toward Hoshigami's jaw, which rushed in to crush him. The blackened light tendrils squirmed and raged, sucking up the dragon's life as they sliced its massive body here and there.

Hoshigami's sacrifice bought only seven seconds of time—but Bercouli did not let it go to waste.

With the full sensory knowledge that the trusty dragon he'd spent so many years of his life with was breathing its last breath, the knight commander held the Time-Splitting Sword high, shining blue with its Memory Release power.

Using the method of memorizing just the enemy's location ten minutes ago, the chance to attack would arrive only once every ten minutes.

But if he etched that entire bloody footprint track into his memory, he could continually follow the enemy's progress of exactly ten minutes behind.

Bercouli unleashed his very best swing at the footprint in blood that indicated where Emperor Vecta had been just seven seconds *after* his prior failed target.

* * *

There was another feature of the Uragiri skill.

Because it interfered with the system itself, its power directly affected the life total of the target. It was impossible to block or defend against with Incarnation power.

So in this instant, even Emperor Vecta's ability to nullify and absorb all kinds of Incarnate attacks did not come into play.

First, Vecta's vast sum of life as designated by the system changed to zero.

As a result of that, the emperor's body split entirely in half from left shoulder to right hip.

Even as the two halves of his body slid apart, Emperor Vecta's expression never changed. His pale-blue eyes just gazed into space, as empty as glass marbles.

Just before his upper half made contact with the ground, pitch-black light erupted from the location of his heart and jutted high upward, like a grave marker.

When it subsided, there was nothing on the ground to indicate the existence of the emperor at all.

A few seconds later, a delicate sound from Bercouli's right hand indicated the final expiration of the Time-Splitting Sword, which crumbled into pieces.

—◦◦◦—

…It's so warm.

I want to stay here just a bit longer.

Alice the Integrity Knight smiled, adrift in the weightlessness of sleep just before proper awakening.

Wavering sunlight.

A large lap that supported her body.

Rough hands that gently caressed her hair.

………Father.

How many years had it been since she'd rested on his lap? It had been so very long since she had last known this feeling of security...of being protected, without a care in the world, knowing that all was right and well.

But...I need to wake up now.

And so Alice lifted her eyelashes.

She saw the face of an older swordsman, his face smiling and downcast, eyes closed.

There were countless old scars running along his thick neck and collarbones—and atop them, many fresh new blade wounds.

".........Uncle?"

Her mind was alert and working again.

That's right, I got caught by Emperor Vecta's dragon. How careless I was to let that happen. I was just running like mad, without being cautious of what was behind me.

But Uncle solved it. He saved me from the enemy leader. Everything's all right as long as he's with us.

She grinned again and sat up, only to realize that the commander's wounds were not limited to his face and chest. The breath caught in her throat.

His left arm was cut clean off his shoulder. The battle garb of the Eastern style that he liked to wear was red with blood. And peeking out from where the front first opened up, she could see a horrifically deep and gruesome wound.

"U...Uncle...!! Lord Bercouli!!" cried Alice, reaching out to him.

Her fingers brushed Commander Bercouli's cheek.

When she felt his skin, Alice learned that the oldest and greatest of Integrity Knights was already gone.

—∿∿—

...Now, now, don't cry, Little Miss.

You knew this moment was going to come sooner or later.

But the words that Integrity Knight Commander Bercouli

Synthesis One said to the golden-haired girl who clung sobbing to his corpse below did not reach the ground.

…You'll be fine, Little Miss. You can handle it on your own.

I know you can do it. Because you're my only pupil…and my daughter.

The sight below grew more and more distant. Bercouli gave his beloved golden knight girl one final smile and looked to the sky far to the north.

He sent a mental message to another knight who would be beneath that distant sky. He had no idea if his thoughts reached her, but all that he felt in this moment was a deep wonder and reflection that the end had finally come to his seemingly endless life. He had found his moment to die.

…Well, it wasn't a bad way to go.

"That's right. You've got plenty of people who will shed tears for you. Be appreciative of that," said a sudden voice. He spun around to see a girl floating nearby, her naked form covered only by long, flowing silver hair.

"…Oh. You're still alive?" Bercouli remarked.

Administrator blinked her silver eyes and chuckled. "Of course I'm not. This is the me that exists in your memory. The memories of Administrator you kept stored in your soul."

"Hmph. I don't really get it. But…at least it's good to know that the you I remember could smile like that." Bercouli grinned. He looked over and saw Hoshigami there, stretching its long neck closer to nuzzle him.

The commander gave the dragon's silvery neck a scratch, then leaped up onto its back. He reached down to help the pontifex into the seat in front of him.

The only master he'd ever served over the course of his long, long life craned her neck to look back at him. "Do you despise me? I trapped you in a prison of infinite time and stole your memories many times."

Bercouli thought the question over. "It was indeed an obnoxiously long time, but I have to admit that it was a fairly entertaining life. I would say that's true."

"...Oh."

He looked away from Administrator and gripped Hoshigami's reins.

The dragon spread translucent wings and flapped them serenely, heading to the infinite expanse of the sky.

—⁓—

Beneath the sky far to the north, on either side of the tremendous mass of rubble that was once the Eastern Gate, the ten thousand members of the Dark Territory's backup force and the four thousand members of the Human Guardian Army's main force glared at one another.

Emperor Vecta was no longer among the Dark Army, so it was not possible for his troops to attack of their own discretion, but the human realm's side did not know that and had to remain alert. They had been in a stalemate for quite a while.

A knight stood alone at the ruins of the gate, with nothing but the sound of the dry wind rustling past. It was Fanatio Synthesis Two, the Integrity Knight in charge of the guardian army's main force. She had instructed the men-at-arms and priests to rest in preparation of the next battle, but she herself was in no mood to sleep in her tent. So she went on a stroll out to the ruins of the Eastern Gate.

The dark of night was retreating already, and the light of Solus made the sky red on the Dark Territory side—and blue on the human half of the mountains.

Commander Bercouli and the decoy force had gone south into the Dark Territory from the gate over half a day ago at this point. It was clear that their mission was not going to be completed quickly or easily, but it was difficult to just stand around and wait.

The least she could do was put her hands together to pray to the three goddesses that the distant group returned safely.

Suddenly, Fanatio's eyes flew open.

She felt as though she heard the voice of the man she loved in her ear.

I'm sorry, Fanatio. Looks like we won't be seeing each other again.

The rest is up to you. Help them be happy…

They were the same words Bercouli had said to Fanatio when he'd left this place.

She lowered her gauntleted hands to brush her lower belly. It was three months ago that new life had begun to grow in her. For over a century, Bercouli had steadfastly refused to touch her. Perhaps his decision to break that personal vow was the result of a premonition: his own death.

Sensing that Commander Bercouli's long life had come to an end under distant skies, Fanatio slowly lowered her knees to the ground and covered her face with her hands. The sobs came tearing out of her, uncontrollable.

It was years and years ago that she'd heard why Bercouli distanced himself from any woman, whether her or another.

In the Human Empire, only a man and woman in an official marriage approved by an Axiom Church bishop could produce a child. Integrity Knights had the rank of bishop automatically, however, so no ceremonial marriage was needed. They could simply swear an oath of love and lie together to have a child.

But any child of parents who had received the life-freezing ritual would grow old and die before they did. And asking the pontifex to perform the same rite on the child would be cruel.

Bercouli only reciprocated how Fanatio felt about him after the pontifex's passing. He had made up his mind to watch over his child in the limited time they would have together. In which case…

"…Have no fear, Lord Bercouli. I will raise our child to be strong, brave, and proud—just like you," Fanatio announced, stifling another sob.

But for now…For now, allow me to grieve.

Fanatio flung herself to the ground and wept, clenching the dirt that Bercouli had trodden upon in his departure.

5

"I got no personal beef with you…"

Klein's voice echoed off the ancient ruins. He turned his katana toward the army outfitted in red.

"…But you've gotta pay for what you did to my friend. You'll get it back three times as bad…no, a *thousand*!!"

He charged at the enemy group. It was such a ridiculous and reckless move that Asuna actually forgot about her devastating pain due to exasperation. The next moment, however, another line of code rained down and formed a human figure next to Klein.

It was a large, burly man with chocolate-brown skin and a huge battle-ax.

"…Agil!!" she rasped.

The fighting merchant, who had assisted the *SAO* frontline group with both battle prowess and supplies, cracked a huge smile when he saw Asuna and gave her a thumbs-up. Then he turned and raced after Klein.

Already, the third and fourth people to arrive were on the scene.

One was a girl with short hair wearing a dark-red costume with a breastplate and a silver mace at her side. The other was a much smaller girl in a deep-blue tunic and skirt with her hair tied up at the sides.

"Liz!! Silica!!"

At last, Asuna's eyes filled with tears. All the tension went out of her body, leaving her just strong enough to stay standing. She stretched out her arms to her companions, with whom she shared such a powerful bond.

"You...you came..."

"Of course we came!"

"What else would we do?!"

The two newcomers' faces crinkled into smiles, Lisbeth taking Asuna's right hand and Silica squeezing her left. Their beaming expressions were soon tearful as well.

"Look at what you've done to yourself...all covered in injuries like this...You're pushing yourself too hard, Asuna."

"Let us handle the rest. Everyone showed up for you."

Just the presence of Lisbeth and Silica hugging her sides brought a warmth to the pain Asuna felt all over, and she felt her aches melting away.

"Thank...thank you..."

Through her overflowing tears, the rain of code fell on the entrance to the ruins. It led to hundreds of new warriors dressed in bright and varied colors.

"The red ones are the enemy!"

"Front line, charge! Push them back!"

"Rear line, pull back and check your spells!"

As soon as they landed, the new warriors traded calls in the language of the Underworld—Japanese—and prepared swords, axes, and spears to meet the oncoming enemy. It was clear from their impressive individual skill and orderly group coordination that these were all experienced VRMMO players.

That's what it is.

At last, Asuna had enough functioning brainpower to put it all together.

When the American players had joined the battle, it meant that the Underworld's time-acceleration rate was set to zero by the

ship's attackers. That meant that people from Japan could dive in with their AmuSpheres, too.

But the quality of the reinforcements' swords and armor made it clear that they weren't using default soldier loadouts.

They had converted their characters.

It was the only explanation. They'd moved the characters they'd spent so much time and effort into fashioning over to the Underworld.

Even though it wasn't clear at all if they could get them back to the normal VRMMO world they came from. In fact, considering the way the Underworld was designed, it was quite possible that every character would be permanently deleted the moment they died!

"I'm...I'm sorry...I'm so sorry," she said tearfully to her friends—and to all the fighters who came to help push back the enemy's front row.

"What do you mean, Asuna?" Lisbeth asked. Her voice was brimming with absolute determination. "Everything that I've worked hard at in *SAO* and *ALO* was meant to come into play right here—to protect what's important to me."

"Yeah...You're right.........Thank you........."

Asuna let her head drop toward the ground.

There was still something left she didn't understand. Who had told Liz and the rest about the Underworld's peril and recruited all these converted reinforcements? It was hard to imagine that Kikuoka and Higa, trapped in the sub-control room of the *Ocean Turtle*, would devise and carry out such a strategy.

"...Liz, Silica. Who actually brought everyone here...?" Asuna asked.

The girls shared a quick glance, then broke into grins. "Shouldn't that be obvious, Asuna?"

"It was Yui! Yui did her best to explain what was going on with the Underworld and the people living in it!"

The instant she heard these words, Asuna felt something wrench the muscles deep inside her. Tears flooded from her eyes.

Yui. The little top-down AI created in the old *SAO*—and Asuna and Kirito's daughter. Of course…it could only have been her. She'd sensed the plan of the attackers that Asuna and Kikuoka could never have foreseen, and she'd worked to counteract it.

"……Thank you, Yui," she whispered with all of her being. When she stood up again, her severed left arm was completely regenerated, and nearly all the wounds and scars across her body were gone.

From over her shoulder came a timid, hesitant voice.

"Um…Lady Asuna? Who are those people…and those knights…?"

It was Integrity Knight Renly, who looked stunned by this development. Behind him, the men-at-arms who'd just been saved were equally wide-eyed.

Asuna looked back and forth between Renly and the girls and gave him a smile. "They're my very good friends and companions. They've come from the real world to save us."

Renly blinked several times, then stared hard at Lisbeth and Silica. Eventually, his youthful face broke into an expression of relief.

"Oh, I see…I'm so glad…I was under the impression that aside from Lady Asuna, all the people from the outside world were fearsome warriors like the ones in red…"

"Hey! Of course that's not true!!" Lisbeth scolded, scandalized, but she gave him a warm smile and bopped him on the shoulder. "I'm Lisbeth. Nice to meet you, Sir Knight."

"Uh…th-thank you. And likewise. My name is Renly."

Asuna had been watching this unfold with a warm glow inside of her, but now there was something of a certainty within her: She would never forget this scene for the rest of her life.

Two people born in different worlds had met, exchanged words, and begun a personal relationship. It was a story that ought to last for a very, very long time, and she couldn't let it end in sadness.

She took a deep breath and asked Lisbeth firmly, "How many people converted in total, Liz?"

"Oh…right. I think it's just over two thousand. We tried our best…but obviously not everyone was going to join us in this…" Lisbeth bit her lip.

Asuna gave her friend a pat on the back. "It's more than enough. But…we don't want a battle of attrition, just in case there's a chance of reconverting. Focus on healing and don't spread the line too wide. Liz and Silica, you should take about two hundred to the rear to create a support battalion."

Focusing her mind on the battle ahead, Asuna gave quick orders to Renly and the guards behind him: "While I'm sure it's not your first choice, I'd like you to join the priests and use your healing arts. The real-world warriors are not used to sacred arts, so it would be good of you to help teach them the ways."

"Y-yes, Lady Asuna! You heard her, guards! We're going to support these reinforcement knights!" Renly cried out. Despite their deep fatigue after multiple battles, the men-at-arms answered fiercely.

"…And what are you going to do, Asuna?" Silica asked. Asuna gave her a wink.

"I'm going to fight at the front, of course."

This time, Asuna knew she wasn't going to give in.

She raced to the front line and shared firm looks of understanding with those familiar faces from *ALO* who had come to help—Sylphic Lady Sakuya, Lady Alicia of the cait siths, General Eugene of the salamanders.

In fact, they weren't all *ALO* converts. The ones assisting the swordsmen with extremely accurate crossbows were probably players from *Gun Gale Online*, like Sinon.

And there, in a tight-knit group and mowing down enemies like a storm, was the most powerful and experienced VRMMO guild of all, the Sleeping Knights. When Siune the mage spotted her, she smiled, and Asuna waved back, feeling the tears coming again.

They had all come to help, knowing that it could mean the loss

attle for the Underworld Status Map

nal Stress Test, Day Two

Eastern Gate

Integrity Knight Fanatio

Ravine Created by Asuna

Orc Battalion Chief Lilpilin

Earth Goddess Terraria, Leafa

Integrity Knight Deusolbert

Teaming Up   In Battle

Integrity Knight Sheyta

Pugilists Guild Champion Iskahn

American Players as Dark Knights

In Battle

Asuna

Ruins

American Players as Dark Knights

PoH

uman Army ecoy Force

Real-World Reinforcements: Klein, isbeth, Silica, Agil, etc.

Sun Goddess Solus, Sinon

tegrity Knight Renly

In Battle

Integrity Knight Bercouli

Student Ronie

Student Tiese

Dark God Vecta

Integrity Knight Alice

Kirito (Empty)

World's End Altar

of the avatars that were another part of themselves. As the only one protected by a super-account, she had to take the most risk and ensure that they suffered the fewest losses possible.

Asuna raced along the battlefield, giving orders to the new arrivals, instructing them to shrink the expanding line of combat, and rebuilding the semicircle of defense around the entrance to the temple ruins.

The two thousand converted warriors might have great stats and equipment, but there were over ten thousand American players still. In a war of attrition, the number of dead—those whose data was lost forever—would only rise.

There was one other worry she could not ignore.

The sensation of real pain, an unavoidable part of doing battle in the Underworld.

Unlike most of the Americans, who were already dead and logged out by the time they would actually feel much pain, the Japanese players were going to undergo a cycle of injury, retreat, and healing. Asuna had already experienced for herself how that kind of constant agony could break one's will over time.

Please, everyone, hang in there. Just hold out until we can finish off these ten thousand.

Then the attackers of the *Ocean Turtle* would truly be out of manpower to send into the Underworld. All that would remain would be catching up to Emperor Vecta, whom Commander Bercouli and Sinon were holding down, and taking back Alice.

Her rapier flashing at the front line of battle, Asuna cried out, "It's all right...We can win! We can win this working together!!"

―∽∽―

It was a bit late for the Japanese VRMMO player by the name of Takashi Hirono to be wondering what he was doing in this position.

He'd been awakened at five in the morning by a call from a friend. The reason that he'd logged in to *ALO* and converted his character out of nowhere wasn't because he had seen a cute girl desperately pleading her case or that he had found it to be a moving one.

If anything, the biggest reason was "just because."

He was also a little bit curious to see what a VRMMO built on a government budget would look like. There was a sense of abandon, too, because his first major test in high school was terrible, so they were going to take away his AmuSphere soon; he just knew it. And lastly, he had just a tiny premonition that there might actually be *something* to this place that he hadn't found in any other VRMMO he'd played.

Takashi converted the character he'd been working on for two years and logged in to a server he'd never heard of before. The first thing he saw was a huge man in red armor screaming in native English and swinging a halberd toward him.

He jumped back, his scream catching in his throat, but the point of the halberd hit his left leg armor, broke the plate, and dug a bit into his shin. He hadn't felt this kind of pain since the time he fell off his bike in elementary school and broke a bone.

You didn't say anything about this!! he wailed silently, doing his desperate best to dodge further halberd attacks, and used his ultra-rare longsword to defeat the large man somehow. He was about to throw up at the sight of real blood streaming from the wound on his leg when someone dragged him back to the rear, where the support battalion was located.

I hate this! I'm logging out! he screamed as his wound was attended to by a girl around his age wearing a light-blue frock, likely identifying her as a priestess class. Something about her struck him as very mysterious.

"I will heal you right away. Bear the pain just a bit longer, Sir Knight," she said weakly. She put her hands on the massive wound—by Takashi's standards, at least—and chanted a healing spell. At first, he thought she was an NPC.

But the diligence in her grayish-brown eyes, her winsome features neither Eastern nor Western in appearance, and the warmth of the light that she summoned to heal his wounds—all of them told Takashi that this was not an NPC, or a Japanese person role-playing, but a real human who lived in this virtual world.

Was that really possible? She spoke Japanese but wasn't ethnically Japanese, and she wasn't an NPC. So what did that make her?

Somehow, it wasn't the searing pain of the halberd hitting his leg, but feeling this girl heal that wound, that convinced Takashi he wasn't just taking part in some promotional event but was in the middle of something momentous and historic.

"There. You should be fine now, Sir Knight," said the girl in the robes, with just a bit of pride in her voice. When she removed her hands, the two-inch-long cut was completely sealed, with only the faintest light-brown scar in its place. He no longer felt any pain.

"Th…thank you…," he managed to stammer. He felt frustrated that he couldn't say something that fit the image of something a "Sir Knight" would say. His face grew hot, and his tongue was heavy in his mouth. The next thing he knew, to his great surprise, his arms were reaching out to grab the girl's slender body and pull her toward himself.

If this were a normal VRMMO world, Takashi's actions would be recognized as improper conduct toward an NPC, and he would be given a warning by the system.

But the priestess girl just seized up awkwardly in Takashi's arms and sucked in a startled breath. A few seconds later, Takashi felt her arms hesitantly circle his back and give him some small measure of pressure in return.

"It will be all right, Sir Knight from afar," she whispered into his ear. "Even as an apprentice sister, I am completing my duty, as meager as it is. You are fighting with many times more bravery than I can. Please remember…that you are swinging your sword to protect this world and its many people."

Then she brushed Takashi's back gently with her right hand.

It was the first time in Takashi's life that he'd ever hugged a girl, in either the real world or the virtual world. But he had the feeling that even if he got a girlfriend in the real world, he would never have a feeling that eclipsed what he felt right here and now.

The dreamlike moment passed, and they pulled apart. Takashi summoned his courage to ask, "Um...C-can you tell me your name?"

The apprentice priestess's white cheeks flushed just the slightest bit. "Yes...my name is Frenica. Frenica Cesky."

"Frenica..."

It had a strange sound to it, but it was perfectly suited to the girl across from him. Takashi introduced himself with uncharacteristic vigor—not his avatar's name of Verios, but the birth name he didn't particularly like.

"...My name is Takashi...Takashi Hirono. Ummm...when this war is over, do you think that I could see you again?"

Frenica's brows rose just a bit, but then her eyes narrowed warmly, and she nodded. "But of course, Sir Takashi. When the war is over and peace returns to the world, I would like that. I will pray to the three goddesses for your good fortune in battle."

She took Takashi's hand in both of hers and rose to her feet. As he watched Frenica spin around, blue robes swirling, and rush off to treat her next patient, Takashi felt a powerful compulsion—to fight bravely until the end, so that he might stand tall and proud when he saw her again. This world was not just some game. It was another plane of reality, as weighty and worthy as the real world Takashi had been born into.

Even if his hit points—his very life—should be depleted, kicking him out of this world, he would be forward-facing until the end and continue swinging his sword. No matter how much they wounded and hurt him. If he couldn't do that, he would never see Frenica again.

Takashi got to his feet, shouted to pump himself up, and began running for the front line of battle—not to complete a quest, but to fulfill his duty.

CHAPTER TWENTY-ONE

AWAKENING, JULY 7TH, 2026 AD / NOVEMBER 7TH, 380 HE

1

"I hope that was…in time…?"

Takeru Higa shook out his arms, which were cramped from overuse.

In less than an hour, he'd managed to convert the accounts of about two thousand characters sent to the *Ocean Turtle* from the Japanese Seed network to the Underworld. He could still feel the keys against his fingertips.

"It was in time. I guarantee it," said Dr. Rinko Koujiro, who handed him a sports drink. He took the bottle, struggled to twist off the cap with his exhausted wrists, and gulped it down. The liquid was lukewarm, but he felt it lubricating his insides pleasantly.

Once he was half done with the bottle, he exhaled and shook his head weakly. "Man…I can't believe how careless I was…"

When he'd been told that two teenage girls calling themselves Leafa and Sinon had shown up at Rath's Roppongi office and warned that the attackers were trying to get American VRMMO players to dive into the Underworld, Higa's mind had simply shut down for a good five seconds.

And he had to admit that he'd been caught blind when he'd learned that this threat had been detected by an existing model of AI connected to Asuna Yuuki's cell phone.

The high school girls, who'd claimed to be acquaintances of Lieutenant Colonel Kikuoka, had dived into the Underworld from Roppongi's Soul Translators using the remaining super-accounts. And after great effort, Higa had completed converting the two thousand players to allow them to drop on Asuna Yuuki's present location.

If they couldn't eliminate the much larger assortment of American players, Alice would almost certainly fall into the enemy's clutches. In fact, Lieutenant Colonel Kikuoka and Lieutenant Nakanishi had even discussed climbing up the outside hull of the *Ocean Turtle* to physically destroy the satellite antenna.

But to get outside would require unlocking the pressurized door splitting the Main Shaft into top and bottom sections for several minutes. If the attackers got wind of that, they would be able to commandeer the sub-control room, too, the worst of all outcomes.

So instead, Kikuoka and Higa had decided to place everything in their new allies' hands: the three teenage girls in the Underworld as the three goddesses of creation and the VRMMO players of Japan who'd agreed to come to their aid, at the risk of losing their characters forever.

The moment they'd been allowed to connect, the majority of the confidential secrets around Project Alicization had essentially become public knowledge. But that wasn't really the problem anymore.

Not compared to what would happen if the attackers, and the American military conglomerates that were most likely behind them, got their hands on Alice and seized complete control over the coming age of drone warfare.

"That's right," Higa mumbled at a volume no one else could hear as he slumped into his desk chair. "Alice isn't some control AI for UAVs. She's a new form of humanity, born in a different world from the rest of us...And you knew that way before any of us did. Isn't that right, Kirigaya...?"

He glanced from the main monitor window showing the situation in the southern Underworld to a smaller window displaying Kazuto Kirigaya's fluctlight status.

The gently radiating light contained a cold void at its center, as usual. That was his damaged, missing core…his self-image.

It hurt to see that window open all the time, so Higa finally grabbed the mouse so he could minimize it. But just before his finger clicked the left button, it stopped.

"Hmm…?"

He lifted his glasses and squinted at the rolling log graph for fluctlight activity. Just forty-five minutes ago, despite being essentially unmoving until then, there had been one sharp peak in the line chart. Higa squeezed the mouse and slid the log to the left. About ten hours earlier, there had been one even larger peak of activity.

"Um…come here and look at this, Miss Rinko."

"Don't call me that," Dr. Koujiro snapped. She looked at the main screen. "This is Kirigaya's fluctlight monitor, right? What's that fluctuation?"

"His lost consciousness broke into activity for just a moment… I suppose. But supposedly he's not supposed to be supposedly active now."

"Calm down—you're talking nonsense. Do you think he received some kind of powerful stimulation from an exterior source?"

"Well, any senses that might register such a stimulation are completely blocked off at the moment. Let's see, at this point here…"

Higa clicked the peak in the graph to bring up the time. But confirming that point in time couldn't actually tell them what was happening inside the Underworld at that moment.

And yet…

"Wait a moment," Dr. Koujiro said, her voice tense. "That time stamp. Both of these…are when the girls used the STL to dive in, aren't they? The first peak was Asuna, and the second one was for Sinon and Leafa from Roppongi…"

"Wow, really…? Wow, really!" Higa gasped. It was true; the two brief peaks on the line chart corresponded to the points in time when the young women had gone down into the Underworld.

"But wait, what does that mean…? Is it just that he had a stronger reaction when familiar people came close? But…the kind of damage he's suffered isn't going to heal itself with a fairy-tale explanation like that. There must be a reason…A physical, logical reason…"

Higa stood up from his mesh chair and walked around the front of the console. The movement caught the attention of Kikuoka, who was nodding off in a nearby chair. The other engineers slumping against the wall watched him with suspicion.

He didn't notice their attention, however. Higa was lost in thought.

"The self…The subject…The image that one has of oneself…Was there some kind of backup of that quantum pattern somewhere…? No, that's not possible…We never copied Kirito's fluctlight, and even if we had, it would be impossible to just cut his self-image out of that and overwrite his original…Is it some kind of living quantum pattern that can connect to his fluctlight…? But where… where…?"

"Hey. Hey…Higa."

He looked up only when he realized that someone had already called his name several times. "What is it?"

"You keep talking about the 'loss of the subject.' What exactly does that mean?"

"Um…it means…"

He stopped to arrange his thoughts for a few seconds before continuing rapidly, "That which sees—and thus knows…It's *you*, inside your head. In philosophical terms, the subjective, rather than the objective. The human being's main processor, which receives and sorts information from the senses."

"Uh-huh…So through the STL, you've combined materialism with dualism. That's fine. What I'm asking is, can you really separate the subject and object that clearly and easily?"

"…Huh?"

Higa blinked a few times, surprised. Kikuoka and the engineers maintained their silence, leaving the room quiet except for the low hum of the cooling fan and Dr. Koujiro's husky voice.

"That which observes: the subject. That which is observed: the object. These are simply philosophical concepts to explain the relationship of things. I don't think that they can be applied directly to the structure of the fluctlight, as a visible model of our individual consciousness. Humans are social creatures; we're not perfectly isolated individuals. The other people who exist in my mind, the me that exists in other people's minds...these things are connected into a kind of network. Do you agree with that?"

"The me...in other...minds..."

As soon as he put it in words, Higa recognized that the concept was one of the things he tried to avoid the most.

How do others see you? How do you compare?

How does Rinko Koujiro see you?

How do you compare to Akihiko Kayaba?

I see...

I barely even remember my own face. If I had to draw a self-portrait, it wouldn't really look like me. And it's because I've always tried to avoid facing myself—my exterior and interior, my existence that couldn't compare to Kayaba's in any way. That's the extent of my subjective sense anyway.

In fact, if you collected the Takeru Higa who exists within all the people around me, I feel like you'd be able to re-create me in every unflattering detail...

Higa was just snorting sardonically in his own self-hatred when at last, the intent of Rinko Koujiro's words sank in.

"...A backup self-image," he murmured, looking up with a start. The note of self-pitying loathing was totally gone from his face. "That's it...Then we *do* have something! We have the data that can complete the hole that was blown into his subjective self-image! It's right in the fluctlights of the people he's closest to...!!"

His pacing resumed, as fast as he could go short of running.

"But we'll need the STL to extract that data…and the level of re-creation's going to be weak coming from just one source. We'll want two…no, three…"

Higa paused with a deep breath.

Who would know Kazuto Kirigaya best and have the most detailed image of him stored in their soul? That would be Asuna Yuuki. And she was resting in the STL right next to Kazuto's.

Higa looked over to Lieutenant Colonel Kikuoka and said hoarsely, "Kiku, are the girls diving from Roppongi…connected to Kirigaya somehow?"

"…Yes, they are," Kikuoka replied, his black-rimmed glasses reflecting the light. "Sinon helped solve the Death Gun incident half a year ago with Kirito's help. And Leafa is Kirito's sister."

There was a brief silence. Higa's rounded glasses glinted in the same way.

"…Here we go. Here we go, then! We can do it…We might be able to restore Kirito's self-image! If we can extract the image of him that's stored in their fluctlights and connect it to the lost regions…then that data should be able to take to Kirigaya's fluctlight, activate, and repair the subjective sense that's supposed to be there…"

Driven by a fresh source of enthusiasm welling up from within, Higa smacked his hands together.

Exactly one second later, all that heat and excitement vanished, and his skin went cold.

"Oh…ohhh, no…It can't be…aaaah!"

"Wh-what? What's the matter, Higa?!" Rinko demanded.

He looked at her and mumbled absently, "The only place we can do that…is in the main control room…"

Heavy silence fell over the room again like ash, gathering on the floor of the sub-control room. Eventually, their commanding officer, Kikuoka, sighed heavily.

"That's right…Of *course* it's set up that way…Don't get down, though, Higa. Let's consider it a positive that we've shed some light on how to rehabilitate Kirito. We can perform the actual operation once this situation is over, and those people have been driven from the ship..."

"But...that's too late...," Higa said, cutting him off. "If the escort ship *Nagato* sends in a command team, and there's a major battle in the Main Shaft, the power's going to go down in Subcon. Hell, they might even damage the equipment in Maincon. Kirigaya's Soul Translator will shut down, and he'll be logged out of the Underworld, still unconscious. And my guess...is that he'll never be able to connect to the STL again. In his current state, he won't pass the initialization stage...Whatever we can do to heal him has to be done while he and those girls are in the Underworld."

As he spoke, Higa felt a kind of determination flood through him once again. What would he do in this situation? Not long ago, his subjective self would have answered, *I can't do anything. Who am I, Akihiko Kayaba?*

But that wasn't his real self-image. That was an escape. It was an excuse.

The Takeru Higa I know, the genius who crafted the STL and the Underworld, would say something like this:

"...I'll go, Kiku."

"Go...where?" grimaced the commander in his aloha shirt. Higa turned to him and sucked in a deep breath.

"I'm not sayin' I'm going to barge my way into the main control room, fists flying. Just listen...STL Room Two, where Kirigaya is now, and Maincon on the other side of the pressure-resistant isolation wall are connected by a cable duct that runs through the aft end of the *Ocean Turtle*'s Main Shaft. There should be one connector location on the cable for maintenance purposes. If we slip into the duct from STL Room Two and go down the ladder inside, we should be able to connect a laptop to the maintenance jack and manipulate Kirigaya's STL."

Kikuoka's eyes went wide behind the black-framed glasses when he first heard Higa's plan, but he soon returned to his usual stern look and argued, "But the maintenance connector's on the other side of the isolation wall that separates us from the attackers. In order to access that point, we need to briefly undo the lock on the wall of the cable duct. The duct is accessible from STL Room One on the Maincon side, so if they learn we've unlocked it and sniff out our plan, they could attack us from below."

"So we'll go with a decoy plan."

"A…decoy…?" Kikuoka repeated dangerously, eyes flashing.

Higa shook his head. "I'm not saying we're going to send valuable manpower to do it. If we undo the lock on the isolation wall, we can use the personnel stairs on the opposite side of the duct to send down…well, you know."

"Aha…you mean Ichiemon. Thankfully, it's in storage in the Upper Shaft. Will someone go and bring it over here?" Kikuoka ordered. Two of the staffers along the wall got up and trotted out of the room.

Dr. Koujiro, meanwhile, looked worried. "Look…if you're going to use Ichiemon as a decoy, all it can do is slowly go up and down stairs. There's no way it can draw the enemy's attention and then race back up."

Ichiemon, officially named Electroactive Muscled Operative Machine #1, was an experimental machine body meant to load an artificial fluctlight. It was, in essence, a humanoid robot with metal bones and polymer muscles. Because it was an experimental prototype, no effort was made to give it a pleasing exterior. It was all exposed mechanisms and wires, with no bulletproofing whatsoever.

Yesterday, Higa had asked Rinko to fine-tune Ichiemon's autonomous walking balancers. Despite a lot of grumbling, she took the job very seriously, so she would naturally have something to say about a plan to use Ichiemon as a decoy. Higa regretted the idea greatly, of course, but this wasn't the time to prioritize equipment over lives.

"…I feel bad for Ichiemon, but we need him to do this for us. And hey, given how he looks, the enemy might not shoot him right away, thinking that he might explode."

"...I suppose..."

While they spoke, the sliding door opened, and a large wheeled cart rolled through. Sitting atop it with arms around its legs was a blocky robotic body, its head equipped with three lenses.

Dr. Koujiro stared at Ichiemon with a conflicted expression, then turned away. "Well...with a look like this, it's certainly going to stick out, and it'll convince them that we're up to something ridiculous..."

"At the very least, they can't ignore it. While the enemy's reacting to Ichiemon, I'll sneak into the lower part of the cable duct and operate Kirigaya's STL through the maintenance connection. The only question is how many minutes this guy will buy me..."

Kikuoka waggled the wooden geta sandal hanging from the foot he had crossed over his other leg and said, "Can we throw Niemon in there, too?"

"I'm afraid we can't," Higa said definitively, shrugging. "Niemon's got better mechanical capabilities, but it's built entirely upon the premise of an onboard artificial fluctlight for control. Unlike Ichiemon, it has no autonomous balancing system. As soon as it starts to step down the stairs, it'll fall over."

"I see," the commander murmured.

Rinko turned away from him and focused her eyes on a spot on the floor with an odd expression. Then she snapped back to attention and said, "But, Higa, even if you're able to fool them about the lock on the isolation wall, that doesn't completely eliminate the chance of you being detected. Shouldn't you take someone along to guard you in the duct?"

"No...at this point, the military officers here are too valuable to risk that way. Besides, the only person with any mobility in that cramped duct will be me, the skinny short guy. I'll just zip down there and zip back up."

He answered in his usual cheery, aloof tone, but just imagining that experience made his heart rate jump a bit. If the enemy spotted him and shot from the bottom of the duct, there would be no escape. When the *Ocean Turtle* had been attacked, he'd only heard the guns firing and never even witnessed any of their attackers.

But…I—no, all of Rath owes Kirigaya too much not to do this, Takeru Higa thought, burning the words into the back of his mind.

Memories blocked or not, they had forced him into a dive that was three days in the real world, and ten years of internal time in the Underworld, giving the artificial fluctlights the crucial trigger they needed. There was no doubt that Kazuto was deeply involved with the birth of the breakthrough fluctlight Alice, from start to finish.

After that, they hooked him up to the STL with all its safety limitations off for the purpose of recuperation—and caused great damage to his fluctlight. And it happened because he was fighting a desperate, painful battle against the power structure of the Underworld in an attempt to save Alice, losing many friends in the process. As long as the possibility of healing him remained, they *had* to take every risk they could to tackle it. It was the only way to make it up to him.

Takeru Higa clenched his fists and started to motion to Kikuoka—when a fourth voice made its presence in the sub-control room known.

"Um…I would like to go with Chief Higa…"

They all turned to look at a Rath engineer who'd been sitting on a mattress along the wall the entire time.

He was just as small as Higa, but his hair was long and tied into a ponytail in the back. Despite his bold proclamation, the way he got to his feet was rather timid.

"As you can see, I'm quite skinny, too…but I might serve as a bullet sponge for you, Chief…Plus, I'm the one who's been maintaining the cables, so…"

Higa stared at the man with the quiet, mumbling voice. He was much older, probably past his mid-thirties. Even for having been on the *Ocean Turtle* for months, his skin was pale. Higa recalled

that this man had quit a major game developer before coming to join Rath.

He would be a vast downgrade from one of the military officers in a fight, but it felt better just knowing that *someone* was risking everything with him. Higa got up from the chair and bowed to the staffer.

"...To tell the truth, I'm not a hundred percent sure about the location of the maintenance connector. So I'd be grateful for your help, Mr. Yanai."

2

When he returned to the real world in STL Unit Two, Gabriel Miller's eyelids rose slowly.

Technically, it was less of a "return" than an unexpected exile. As the sensation of the gel bed he was lying on returned to him, Gabriel stewed over the faint taste of surprise on his tongue.

To think that he, of all people, would lose in a one-on-one virtual duel. And not to another human, but to an AI.

Gabriel spent valuable seconds considering the reason he'd lost to that knight. Was it strength of will? The bond of souls? Some power of love, tying people together...?

All bullshit.

A cold grin tugged at the corner of Gabriel's mouth. Whether in the real world or in the virtual world, there could be only one unseen strength out there—that of his own fate guiding him to his purpose.

It was thus inevitable that he lost. Perhaps it was necessary: Fate did not want him to fight in the borrowed avatar of Vecta, the god of darkness; it wanted him to fight as Gabriel. It demanded that he return to that world, in the proper way this time.

Then that was what he would do.

His considerations complete, Gabriel silently slipped out from under the sheet. He was surprised to see that in the other STL unit, his XO, Vassago Casals, was still in a dive. He'd thought the man had died and logged out long ago. He must have found something to seek out.

He can do as he likes. Gabriel shrugged and opened the door to the adjacent main control room. The bald team member facing the console looked up and said without much concern, "Welcome back, Captain. Got your ass kicked, huh?"

"Situation," Gabriel prompted.

Critter composed himself a bit more and reported, "Well, as you instructed, I inserted fifty thousand American players we scrounged up, in waves. Half of them have been wiped out already, but they should succeed at the job of eliminating the human realm's army. The uncertain variable in play is that Rath utilized similar means...There's been a large influx of connections from Japan. But only around two thousand, so it shouldn't make a big difference."

"Oh...?" Gabriel lifted an eyebrow and glanced at the main screen.

It displayed a terrain map of the southern part of the Underworld. The black line going directly south from the Eastern Gate until it ended in an X would be the movement path of Gabriel, as Vecta. It wasn't even half of the way to the system console at the very southern tip of the world, but Alice would still be around the location of the X.

There was also a thick white line, hugging the path of the black line. That would be the Human Empire's army. They were tightly packed and seemed to be stationary now.

A much larger army indicated in red was converging upon the white army. If those were the American VRMMO players, then the blue light between the white and red like a defensive wall must be the two thousand players connecting from Japan.

"Are the Japanese using default accounts on the human side?"

"That's what I assume. Why do you ask?"

"No reason..."

He lifted the bottle of mineral water Critter handed him to his lips and thought. Was it possible for the Japanese VRMMO addicts to have converted their characters to the Underworld? They were as devoted to those avatars as to their own lives, after all—if not even more so.

So no. That wasn't possible. Gabriel smiled coldly again.

He recalled the youngsters he'd faced and crushed in the VRMMO *Gun Gale Online*'s PvP tournament on the Japanese server half a month ago. They might connect to the Underworld out of sheer curiosity, but they would never convert their hard-earned characters if they'd risk losing them forever.

He briefly thought of the end of that event, when that sniper girl with the light-blue hair had refused to give up once in the clutches of his sleeper chokehold. The image passed, however, as he returned to his previous train of thought.

"I'm going to dive back in again. Convert this account to the Underworld," he said, writing down an ID and password on a piece of paper next to the control console and handing it to Critter.

"Oh? You too, Captain?"

"Too…?"

"Well, Vassago died once, too, the son of a bitch. But then he had me convert his account, and he happily dived back in."

"…Ahhh," Gabriel murmured, glancing at the piece of paper next to Critter. The three letters at the start of what was surely Vassago's ID stood out to him. "I see…I see."

Deep in his throat rumbled a rare, true chuckle. Critter looked even more confused, so he patted the man's shoulder and said, "Don't worry about it. Despite what you might think, that man has his own shackles that bind him…Go ahead and perform the process now."

Gabriel turned on his heel and headed back toward the STL room, a crooked smile on his lips.

———

At that very same moment, Vassago Casals wore a smile, too, visible under his dark hood, as he surveyed the battle below him.

From the top of one of the sacred statues lining the path through the temple ruins, he had a perfect view of American and Japanese players engaged in a bloody melee. But in fact, a melee would imply that it went both ways; this was more of an outright slaughter.

In the center of the entryway, two thousand Japanese players arranged in a wide circle were slicing through the rush of red-armored soldiers without suffering any losses at all. The difference in gear and teamwork was stark, but it was the system of backup from the rear that proved definitive. Injured players were instantly taken back to their makeshift camp deeper into the temple, where they got healing spells, and returned to the front line healthy.

Considering that the experience of the Underworld was just as painful as real life, their continuing morale was impressive. And the fact that two thousand players had chosen to convert their main characters to join this fight was damn near miraculous.

It was a situation that even Gabriel Miller did not think possible—but Vassago Casals had anticipated it all the way.

If it was possible to connect from America, it was possible for the other side to call for reinforcements from Japan. Vassago expected, too, that they would convert their characters over first.

When he noticed among the furiously battling Japanese players the familiar countenances of several more players than just Asuna the Flash, Vassago found himself in a state of utter elation. The game of death he'd thought he'd never experience again had come back in a different form.

Of course, this wasn't a literal death game, given that it wouldn't take away the real-world lives of those who were lost—but there was one thing here that the floating castle did not have and one thing that once existed but was no longer.

They were, respectively, pain and the Anti-Criminal Code.

That meant this would be a very enjoyable time. In fact, it might be even more thrilling than taking a life with his own hands.

"Heh-heh, heh-heh-heh, heh, heh, heh, heh…"

The quiet chuckles rose from Vassago's throat, uncontrollable.

―――

I didn't make it in time.

Sinon watched the crying knight in golden armor clinging to the scarred body of the older swordsman in silence. At the knight's side, two huge dragons hung their heads, apparently sharing in the grief.

She had raced through the air after Alice, the Priestess of Light, who would decide the fate of the world; her captor, Vecta, the god of darkness; and Knight Commander Bercouli, who was in hot pursuit of them. She'd made full use of the voluntary flight system she'd had to practice so hard in *ALO* and kept her bearing south at the maximum speed the system would allow—but by the time she caught up to them, the battle was already over.

Perhaps this was a moment where she ought to praise Bercouli's strength, instead. He had caught up to Vecta's dragon, which should have been impossible, and beaten the unbeatable super-account.

There was one great injustice in the situation, however.

With Bercouli's death, his soul was lost forever. But the destruction of the soul of Vecta, the god of darkness, was not the end of him.

Sinon needed to explain that the danger had not fully passed to Alice, who had cried all she could for now and so currently sat still and empty. But Sinon didn't know the right words to use.

Valuable minutes trickled away in silence, until at last it was Alice who spoke first. Despite the tears that reddened her face, Alice's stunning beauty left Sinon speechless. Her cobalt-blue eyes, shining like the surface of water, caught the sniper directly. Her pink lips opened to expel a voice as gentle and clear as a platinum bell.

"Did you…come from the real world, too?"

"Yes," Sinon admitted. "I am Sinon. I'm a friend to Asuna and

Kirito. I came here to rescue you and Bercouli from Vecta…I'm sorry that I wasn't able to make it in time."

Sinon knelt on the rocky top, which was scarred from the fierce battle, and bowed in apology to the other girl.

Alice just shook her head. "No…I was foolish. I paid no attention to my rear and was kidnapped as helplessly as a baby. It is my fault. Even though saving my life is nowhere near equal to losing the life of a great man like Unc…like the commander of the Integrity Knights."

The deep regret and self-admonishment in her voice robbed Sinon of the ability to speak. Alice looked up, fighting back tears, and asked, "What is happening in the battle?"

"…Asuna and the human army are managing to fight off the red army from the real world."

"Then I will return north to them," she said, getting unsteadily to her feet. She tried to head to one of the dragons, but Sinon stopped her.

"You can't, Alice. You need to continue south, to the World's End Altar. If you touch the console there…er, the crystal panel, the real-world side will summon you to them."

"Why? Emperor Vecta is already dead."

"…Because…because that's not true."

And then Sinon explained it all. About how if a real-worlder died in the Underworld, they did not truly lose their life. That the enemy who dwelled in Vecta's body was surely coming to attack again in a different form this time.

Alice reacted with tremendous fury, as though emotions she'd just barely been holding in check all exploded at once.

"So…the foe that Uncle gave his…his life to slay is not even dead?! He's only temporarily vanished and will return to life as though nothing ever happened…Is that what you are telling me?!" she shouted, her armor clanking as she closed in on Sinon. "That…that nonsense cannot be allowed to pass!! Then…why did Uncle…why did he have to die?! What is a duel when only one combatant is risking his life…but a folly, a farce…?"

Her blue eyes filled with tears again, and all Sinon could do was stare.

I have no right to argue with her. I've died countless times while fighting in GGO *and* ALO. *And like Vecta, I'm a god here who won't really die when I die...*

Still, Sinon took a deep breath and stared right back into Alice's gaze. "Then...would you say that Kirito's suffering is false, too, Alice?"

The golden knight inhaled sharply.

"Kirito is a real-worlder, too. If he dies here, he won't lose his true life. But the wounds he's suffered are real. The pain that he felt and the damage to his soul are real."

Sinon paused and took on the barest suggestion of a grin. "I'll be honest...I like Kirito. I love him. So does Asuna. There are many, many other people who do, too. They're all worried about him. They're praying, praying for him to get better. And though they can't say it, they're all wondering why Kirito had to go to these lengths."

She placed her hands on Alice's shoulders and said firmly, "Kirito was hurt because he was trying to save *you*, Alice. He went through all of what he did just for that purpose. Are you going to say that the way he felt was false...? And it's not just Kirito. The same goes for your commander. He suffered all these wounds and ultimately gave his life to create the opportunity to save you. He gave us this valuable time to escape from the enemy's clutches."

There was no answer right away. Alice simply stared down silently at the prone body of Bercouli.

Big tears began to fall from her eyes again—until the golden knight clenched them shut and raised her head, resisting some urge. In a hoarse voice, she asked, "Sinon, if I...if I leave through the World's End Altar to the real world, will I be able to return here? Will I be able to see my loved ones again...?"

Sadly, Sinon did not have the truthful answers to Alice's pressing questions. All she knew for certain was that if the enemy got Alice, the Underworld itself would be destroyed and deleted forever.

If they could protect the world and Alice, their hopes would come true. It was all that she could believe for now.

So Sinon nodded her head slowly. "Yes. As long as you...and the Underworld are safe."

"...Very well. Then I will continue south. I don't know what awaits at the World's End Altar, but if that is what Uncle and Kirito wished for me to do..."

Alice knelt, white skirt splaying outward, so that she could tenderly brush Bercouli's hair, and she placed her lips on his forehead. When she stood up again, the knight's body seemed surrounded by an aura of newfound purpose.

"Amayori, Takiguri, just a bit more work to do," she said to the dragons, then turned back to Sinon. "And...what will you do, Sinon?"

"Now it's my turn to use this life," she replied, grinning. "I think Vecta will come back to life on this spot. I'll find a way to beat him...or at least to buy you enough time to do what's necessary."

Alice tucked in her bottom lip and lowered her head.

"...Please do. I will be sure that your sentiments do not go to waste."

Sinon saw the two dragons off as they flew into the southern sky, then took the white longbow off her shoulder.

Apparently, it was highly likely that the people who attacked the *Ocean Turtle* were private military contractors working with the support of the American government. One of them used Super-Account 04, Vecta, the god of darkness, to attack Alice.

It was the kind of opponent that Sinon, just a normal teenage girl in the real world, could never deal with.

But here, in a one-on-one fight in a virtual world?

She would beat anyone who crossed her path.

With that oath in mind, Sinon waited and waited for the moment her enemy dived back in.

——✺——

He felt the dry sensation of the last bone breaking in his fist.

Iskahn, chief of the pugilists guild, looked away from the enemy, who toppled backward with limbs splayed out and a hole punched through the chest protector, and he stared silently at the hand that had inflicted it.

It was not the steel fist that crushed everything it touched any longer. It was a bag of swollen flesh, full of pulverized bones, lacerated meat, and loose blood.

His other fist had already been in that condition for a while. His legs were bloodied and bruised, such that he could no longer kick with them, nor even run.

"...You fought brilliantly, champion," rumbled his second-in-command, Dampa. Iskahn glanced over his shoulder.

The large man was sitting on the ground, both arms lost, and with many blade wounds on his face and body, indicating that he'd continued fighting with nothing more than head-butts and body charges. His eyes, which always glittered with aggression and intelligence, were now dull, making it clear that Dampa was at the end of his life.

Iskahn raised his broken fist to pay his respects to the brave warrior's soul and replied, "Well, I suppose this is one way to die that won't shame me when I visit the old generations in the afterlife."

He limped his way over to his aide, dragging his leg, and collapsed to a sitting position.

Over a long, furious battle, they had ground down the red army from over twenty thousand in number to maybe three thousand. The cost was that barely three hundred pugilists were still alive, all of them gravely wounded, unable to form a proper battle configuration, gathered in one big clump and waiting to be crushed for good.

The only reason the three thousand enemy soldiers weren't making one final charge to wipe them out at last was the presence of a single knight and dragon, visible ahead of Iskahn and Dampa, fighting as though possessed by demons.

—⁓—

The exhaustion of her body and mind were completely beyond their peak.

But through clouded vision, the Integrity Knight Sheyta Synthesis Twelve still detected the presence of enemies and lifted her arm, heavy as lead, to ready the Black Lily Sword.

Byew. Air whipped dully aside.

The ultrathin blade cut into the shoulder of the enemy's armor. The feedback sent needle stabs of pain all through her arm from wrist to elbow.

"Haaaaaaah!!"

She screamed a battle cry, her throat cracking, defying her epithet of "Silent." The sword managed to break through the thick plate and sliced right through the body beneath it. Then she pulled it free of the collapsing enemy, who screeched at her in words she did not understand.

Sheyta's breathing was labored. It was not just the near-infinite supply of enemies that had her so exhausted, but the odd hardiness of the red soldiers.

Her Incarnation was not working well. The weapons and armor of the enemy were far inferior to Sheyta's divine weapon, but there was a nasty resistance to the sensation of severing them. The same could be said of the enemy's attacks. They hurled their weapons at her in crude, unthinking ways, using nothing but strength to guide them, and yet, she found it strangely difficult to read them ahead of time.

It was like fighting against shadows. Projected against a wall was an army of shadows, who were, in fact, nowhere near her.

There was no enjoyment in fighting them. She lived to cut

things, but cutting these shadows left Sheyta with nothing but powerful disgust.

Why is it? Whether they are shadows or flesh, or even simple statues, I should be happy with anything that is hard to the touch. After all, I am a puppet who knows nothing but cutting...

The Black Lily Sword was a Divine Object whose narrow blade had the maximum priority level. It was a tool meant entirely for severing objects, and it was a kind of totem for Sheyta herself. If she stopped cutting, her entire reason for existing would be lost.

Administrator had taken the single black lily that Sheyta had brought back from one of the ancient battlefields in the dark lands and refashioned it into a sword. As she'd gifted it to Sheyta, she had said, *This sword is a representation of the curse carved upon your soul. The curse of homicidal urges created by a wavering in your genetic traits. Cut and cut and cut again. Only at the end of that bloody path will you find the key to undo your curse...perhaps.*

At the time, she'd not understood the pontifex's words.

Sheyta had done as she'd been told, and over almost countless months and years, she'd dedicated herself to slicing. At last, she'd met the perfect rival: a pugilist who was harder than any person or any thing she'd interacted with through her sword.

I want to fight him again. If I do, I might learn something about myself at last, she'd thought, a desire that had driven her to break off from the Human Guardian Army and stay here at this battlefield. But it did not seem as though she would have the chance for a rematch with that red-haired gladiator.

She drained the last mouthful of water she had left and tossed aside the empty waterskin, glancing over her shoulder as she did so.

Visible atop a distant rock was the chief pugilist, his body broken and bruised. He was staring right back at Sheyta, a note of sadness in his one remaining eye.

Suddenly, she felt a twinge in her chest.

What is this pain?

I just want to cut that man. I want to taste that battle again, to feel everything burning to its core, and to sever that fist, harder than diamond. That was my only desire, so what is it that makes me feel like…like my chest is being clenched in a vise…?

Suddenly, there was a faint cracking sound near her hand.

Sheyta lifted the Black Lily Sword and examined it. That ultra-black blade, which seemed to absorb all light that hit it, now had a single fissure running through it, finer than a spider's thread.

Oh…I see now.

She inhaled deeply and smiled.

All her doubts had been answered. At last, Sheyta understood the meaning of Administrator's words—and the nature of the curse.

A sudden rumbling drew her attention to the next enemy, charging at her with a crude war hammer raised high in the air. Sheyta smoothly sidestepped the initial swing and thrust her sword into the center of the red armor.

Her final attack was utterly silent. The Black Lily Sword slid directly into the man's heart, gracefully ending his life—and without any kind of sound whatsoever, it broke apart in the middle into a storm of black petals.

Sheyta lifted the hilt up to her mouth as it crumbled in her grasp, and she whispered longingly, "Thank you…for all of this time."

It even felt like there was a bit of flower fragrance in the air.

On her right, her longtime mount and partner, Yoiyobi, crushed an enemy soldier with a swing of its powerful tail. The beast's gray scales were dyed red with the blood from a plethora of wounds, and its claws and fangs were all chipped or missing. It had used up its heat breath, and its movements were sluggish.

Once she was sure the enemy's charge was done and the coast was clear, Sheyta walked over to her dragon and ran her hand along its neck.

"Thank you, too, Yoiyobi. You must be so tired…Let's rest now."

And so Sheyta and her dragon, each supporting the other, headed for the low hill where the remnants of the pugilists guild were gathered. Their chief was still sitting when she arrived, and he greeted her by raising a hand that was so swollen it looked about to burst at any moment.

"Sorry about that…I caused your precious sword to break," he offered, but she just shook her head.

"It's fine. I finally understand now. I know why I've been spending my life cutting everything…" She slumped to her knees and lifted her hands, pressing her fingers around the young warrior's face. "To find something I *don't* want to cut. I've fought and fought to find something I want to protect. That is you. I don't need the sword anymore."

To her surprise, the pugilist's left eye welled up with clear liquid. He gritted his teeth and grunted deep in his throat. "Yeah…damn it all. I wish I could have had a family with you. I'm sure we would have had powerful children. The greatest pugilist the world has ever seen, greater than my predecessors and greater than me…"

"No. Our child would be a knight."

They looked into each other's eyes and smiled. Under the warm gaze of the large man nearby, Sheyta and Iskahn shared a brief embrace, then sat side by side.

Three hundred pugilists, one Integrity Knight, and one dragon waited in silence for the steady approach of the red soldiers.

—◆◆◆—

"Looks like the battle is largely decided, by my estimation," said Klein as they returned from the front line to the rear of the group. Asuna murmured in the affirmative.

The Japanese players in magic-wielding classes set about casting their newly learned sacred arts to heal the wounds the two had suffered. They weren't able to utilize the same imagination-amplified boosts that the actual Underworldian priests could, but because high-level converted characters had an appropriately advanced arts-usage privilege level, they could get the job done.

"Thank you for coming to help us," Asuna said to the female player who was healing her. Then she said as much to Klein. "Thank you, too, Klein. I don't know how I can show my appreciation…"

The sight of Asuna at a loss for words made Klein rub the spot under his nose in apparent embarrassment. "C'mon, don't be like that. You know I owe you and that damn Kirito more than I can possibly repay with an act like this…He's in here, too, isn't he?" he said, lowering his voice.

Asuna nodded. "Yes. When the battle's over, you should go and see him. If you tell him one of your usual stupid jokes, I'm sure the urge to tell you off will snap him right awake again."

"Wow. That's just cruel," he said, his face crinkling into his familiar grin, but there was deep concern visible in his eyes. He already knew how deep the wounds to Kirito's soul were.

But maybe it's true.

Maybe, when everything's safely over, and the enemy is gone from the Underworld and the Ocean Turtle, and Sinon and Leafa and Klein and the rest of the ex-SAO gang, and Sakuya and Alicia and the ALO folks…and even Alice and Tiese and Ronie and Sortiliena all stand around him, Kirito won't have a choice but to wake up.

I have to keep fighting now, so that I can greet him with a smile when that moment comes.

As soon as her wounds were healed, Asuna thanked her healer again and got to her feet.

Like Klein had said, the outcome of the battle was essentially sealed at this point. The number of American players in red was about equal to the Japanese players now, and their attacks were growing desperate and simple, perhaps because their overall spirit had been broken.

But the battle here in these ruins was just the warm-up fight.

The real problem was Alice, the Priestess of Light, who'd been abducted by Emperor Vecta. While Commander Bercouli and

Sinon were holding him down, they had to rush after the emperor and take Alice back from him. They would select an elite team from the converted players, borrow the human army's horses, and race south at top speed.

If they could just catch up, then even the super-account wouldn't be able to handle the full force of an elite team of the nation's top players working together. Their power was so over-whelming that she felt utterly confident of that. The way they fought so bravely, swords and shields and armor glittering in the sun in every color of the rainbow, made them look like the einherjar, the heroes of Valhalla in Norse mythology...

Asuna wiped away her tears and turned from the front line to the very rear of their camp. The supply team's wagons had been brought forth from the back of the temple grounds to form a makeshift base. The sight of the wounded Japanese being healed by the sacred arts of the Underworlders felt like a blessed thing to her, something she couldn't describe in words.

"All right...It's all right. Everything will work out...I know it," she murmured to herself. Klein overheard and agreed firmly.

"You bet your ass. C'mon, we got one more round of work to do!"

"I know."

She turned to head back to the front line of battle—when something in the corner of her eye caught her attention, and she froze.

What was that? It was something dark...like a black smear...

She looked around, trying to capture the thing she'd seen, and at last, she spotted it.

Standing atop one of the huge holy statues that lined the path through the temple ruins, the closest one on the right-hand side, was a person.

It was hard to see against the glare of the sun. It was just a dark shadow, blurring into the red of the Dark Territory's sky. Was it one of the Americans who was taking refuge from the battle? Or one of the Japanese, using the opportunity to scout out the situation?

A closer examination revealed that the cause of the silhouette's flickering outline was a black half cloak that whipped in the wind. The cloak's hood was pulled low, keeping the face completely hidden. But...

"Klein, do you see that...?"

She tugged on Klein's sleeve before he could rush back into combat and gestured with her other hand.

"That person standing up there. Does that look familiar to you...?"

"Eh...? Whoa, someone's up there just scoping out the scene? Who the hell would do that...? I can't say they're familiar, because that cloak makes it impossible to see their...face..."

Klein trailed off. Then he turned his stubbled face to Asuna, white as paper.

"Hey, what's the matter? Do you remember them? Who is that person?"

"No...it can't be. There's just no way...Am I...looking at a ghost...?"

"Gh-ghost...? What do you mean, Klein?"

"I...I mean, that black cloak...That leather poncho...it's just like Laughing Coffin's..."

The instant she heard that name, Asuna felt the center of her head freeze, like it had just turned to ice.

Laughing Coffin. That was the almighty red guild, the group of murderous PKers who'd terrorized the old, deadly *SAO* from its mid-level to late-game sections.

Red-Eyed Xaxa. Johnny Black. Many legendary PKers had lurked in their midst. They'd claimed scores of players' lives... until ultimately, a major alliance of frontline players had teamed up to vanquish them and destroy the guild.

In the battle, virtually all the Laughing Coffin members either died or were apprehended and imprisoned, except for one who escaped alive. It was the guild leader, who was mysteriously absent from the guild's hideout: the one man who was responsible for directly and indirectly killing more *SAO* players than anyone else. He went by the name PoH.

He always wore a black poncho and did his bloody work with a huge dagger that was more like a meat cleaver than anything else. And now, two years later, that murderer was in the Underworld and watching Asuna and Klein from above.

"………It can't be," she whispered, her throat hoarse.

It's an illusion. I'm seeing a ghost.

Begone. Go away.

But the black silhouette flickering in the heat haze just mocked her prayer by raising its right hand. Then it wiggled it back and forth in a sarcastic greeting.

And what she saw next was worse than her nightmares.

Next to the figure of the man in the black poncho, a new figure appeared out of thin air. Then another. Then another.

An entire squad of red soldiers appeared on the roof of the massive temple ruins adjacent to the back of the statues. Another few dozen appeared atop the building on the left side of the path, too.

Please, no. Just stop, Asuna prayed. Her heart couldn't handle any more despair.

But the new red army continued to arrive, and continued, and continued. A thousand, five thousand, ten thousand.

When it had passed thirty thousand, Asuna stopped trying to estimate the number.

It was impossible.

They had just succeeded, at great cost, in removing all fifty thousand of the American players from the simulation. The other side couldn't possibly have arranged another such huge army in this short an amount of time. But they couldn't be Japanese, either. If there was a misleading recruitment effort on the Japanese Internet to get people to the Underworld, Klein and the others would have noticed it.

It was an illusion. They were all shadows without form, created by sacred arts.

Even the Japanese players on the front line of battle, their victory all but complete over the remaining American stragglers, stopped fighting and turned to watch. An eerie silence settled over the huge battlefield.

Then the murmuring began.

The rustling and activity of the red soldiers crowding the rooftops of the palatial temples reached Asuna's ears like a disquieting breeze.

With the voices all blended together, Asuna couldn't tell in the moment what language they were speaking. She concentrated hard and eventually heard a few voices speaking louder than the others.

"...*Bigeopan Ilbonin.*"
"...*Uri narareul jikida.*"
"...*Han zhong lianmeng.*"

It wasn't English. It wasn't Japanese.

At Asuna's side, Klein uttered a wordless groan from deep in his throat.

"Uhhh...that's not good...That's really not good...That army ain't from Japan or the US..."

Asuna felt a cold trickle of sweat run down her back as she waited for him to finish.

"......Those are Chinese and Koreans."

3

The VR bang in Cheongjin-dong of Jongno District of Seoul was fairly crowded, perhaps because the nearby university had just entered the summer vacation period.

Wol-Saeng Jo signed in at the front, filled a paper cup with cola at the drink bar, and sank into the reclining chair at a private booth with a heavy sigh.

It seemed like he was sighing a lot more lately. He knew the reason why—Wol-Saeng was a sophomore in college, twenty years old, and he would have to leave school next year for his two years of mandatory military service.

You could wait until thirty to serve, so he could put it off if he wanted, but young men who hadn't finished their duty while in school were at a major disadvantage when it came to the hiring season. Nearly all the sophomores around him were taking time off to enlist, and given that his parents were telling him to do the same, he didn't really have a choice.

He sipped the flat cola and sighed again.

Wol-Saeng wasn't the physical type, so he was worried about his ability to withstand the fierce training, and the possibility of being hazed by his troop, but what depressed him most of all was losing two years of the life he had now. Not his real life, exactly—it was a life in the virtual world that Wol-Saeng had become obsessed with ever since a friend invited him to try it out, shortly after college started. Two years of no full-diving would probably be harder than any training regimen.

"…If only they had these in the military…"

He picked up the AmuSphere full-dive interface off a rack on the desk. It was quite ragged and well used, being the property of a busy public VR bang, but to Wol-Saeng, it was as radiant as an angel's halo.

The device, which had gone on sale three years ago, in 2023, in Japan, had spread to the rest of the world the following year, and it had led to a new movement in South Korea, which had already been hugely into online gaming. The Internet cafés that had been known in Korea as PC bangs quickly became VR bangs, and young gamers across the nation became engrossed in Japanese and American VRMMORPGs.

Even Wol-Saeng's favorite game for the last year and a half, *Silla Empire*, was a Korean-localized edition of the Japanese game *Asuka Empire*. It wasn't just translated into Korean; the town design, avatars, and quest content were all modified to be based off the ancient Silla kingdom of Korean history. It had immediately become the most popular game of its kind in the country since its release.

Meanwhile, Korean players demanded purely domestic games tailored just for them, and more than a few developers got into the practice of building new VRMMOs using The Seed Package, an entirely free suite of tools. The package itself was Japanese in design, and it couldn't make full use of all its features without being connected to The Seed Nexus, a Japanese network—but virtually all the Japanese VRMMOs blocked connections from Korea and China. So no new games featured the quality of play that *Silla Empire* did, and the Korean gaming populace was more than a little frustrated.

I'd love to play a Korean-made game before I join the army, but I doubt it'll happen, he thought, sighing yet again. Wol-Saeng leaned back against the seat and placed the AmuSphere over his head.

"...Link Start!" he stated, using the English voice command that was shared across all countries of the world, and closed his eyes.

Wol-Saeng went through the rainbow-colored ring, entered the VR bang's user ID and password, and descended into the game launcher interface, where he looked for the icon of *Silla Empire*.

Before that, however, he noticed the social media window on the right side of the darkened space scrolling past at incredible speed. Apparently, several hundred of the accounts he followed were all sharing the same article.

"......What's this?" he wondered, craning his neck. He spun the launcher to the left to put the social window front and center, then tapped on the article and loaded it up. He read aloud the tweet that showed up.

"Let's see...A test server for a brand-new VRMMO created by a team of Korean, American, and Chinese players working together...got hacked by Japanese players, and the testers are being attacked...?! What the hell is this?!"

He couldn't really take it seriously. But there was a URL at the end of the tweet that seemed to point to a video, so he tapped it, still feeling skeptical.

A video player opened and a fierce voice boomed out of it: *"Front line, charge!!"*

Wol-Saeng had seen enough Japanese animation in his life to recognize that the language was Japanese. On the screen, players in silver equipment who he presumed were Japanese were attacking a group of players in dark-red gear and cutting them down. With each swing of a shining sword, buckets of blood flew outward, leaving behind only English shouts and screams.

There was no censorship of any kind on the brutal violence, which made it clear that this was from a test server. As the original tweet said, it seemed like the Japanese players were simply massacring the Americans.

When the thirty-second video finished, Wol-Saeng was left stunned. He'd heard of server attacks, where hackers tried to shut down servers with excess traffic or hack into websites, but diving into a VR world and literally attacking testers was a new one to him. If he was to believe the video was real, that was exactly what it seemed to be, but something still felt just a bit off about it.

Yes…going by the video, the Japanese players, who seemed to have better gear and stats, were exterminating the American testers. But it wasn't the Americans being attacked who seemed more desperate, it was the Japanese. A server raid was a kind of vandalism, a prank…but these people seemed to be fighting like their lives depended on it…

There was a high-pitched *ding-dong* sound effect, and Wol-Saeng flinched. One of his guildmates from *Silla* was giving him a voice call. He hit the button, bringing up a new window.

"Hey, Moonphase, did you see that tweet?!" an urgent voice said, calling him by his character name.

"Y-yeah, I was just watching the video…"

"What are you waiting for, then? Download that client, man!"

"C-client…?"

He glanced back at the social media window and read further in the tweet thread. According to this person, the call was going out to Korean VRMMO players to rescue the test players from the dastardly Japanese attackers. If anyone was interested in helping, they just had to download the client software to their AmuSphere and connect.

"Is this it…? Hey, Hwanung, do you think this is all real?"

"Of course it is—did you watch the video or not?! Our comrades are being slaughtered as we speak!!"

"I saw it…but on the video…," Wol-Saeng started, hoping to explain the odd feeling it gave him, but he couldn't finish his sentence.

"Just install the damn thing already! Myeongwang and Helix already dived in; I'll be waiting for you there!"

The voice-chat call ended, leaving his launcher space silent.

While he wasn't entirely gung ho about it, most of his guild-mates were already taking part, so he didn't want to get nasty comments later on if he ignored it. If he dived in, he'd probably get more information—and in fact, it seemed quite possible that this was all just some elaborate stealth marketing for the new game. In that case, it would be stupid not to at least try it out while he had the chance.

Wol-Saeng went ahead and pressed the download button to install the client on the AmuSphere. A new icon appeared on the screen. It had the English words HELP US written in black on a plain red background. He hit the icon and found his mind being sucked into a different world.

—◊—

Even after Critter finished guiding the Chinese and Korean connections into the Underworld, he had difficulty believing it.

As Vassago Casals had instructed him just before diving back in, he'd spread the connection client program for the Underworld to the Internet of the two countries just northwest of Japan, but he found the whole thing rather befuddling.

I mean, Japanese and Koreans are practically the same thing, right?

Many people in America didn't even know that Japan and South Korea didn't share a physical border. Some people just thought the two countries were a part of China. Critter wasn't that ignorant, of course, but he assumed that the three countries, being so similar, were on good terms—that it was similar to how the EU was all jumbled together.

So Critter didn't understand at all why Vassago told him to do what he did.

He didn't have time to build a new fake website, so he used social media to spread the message. The first tweet he wrote said, JAPAN IS ATTACKING A PRIVATE VRMMO SERVER SET UP BY AMERICANS, CHINESE, AND KOREANS!!

For the next one, he explained, JAPANESE HAVE HACKED THE SERVER, BECAUSE THEY WANT TO MONOPOLIZE THE SEED NEXUS,

AND THEY'RE GENERATING SUPERPOWERFUL CHARACTERS AND ATTACKING THE AMERICAN, CHINESE, AND KOREAN TESTERS. THE SERVER DOESN'T HAVE A PAIN BLOCKER OR MORAL PROTECTION CODE SET UP YET, SO OUR COMRADES ARE BEING SLAUGHTERED AND SUFFERING GREATLY, and attached a video recording of battle in the Underworld.

It depicted the knights and soldiers of the human army fighting back against the American players, but the Underworlders spoke Japanese, so there was no way to tell the difference. The impact of the video was clear, because the retweet numbers rocketed upward, and the download rate of the client program was far more rapid than it had been for the Americans.

Critter was stunned.

This kinda makes it seem like Japanese, Chinese, and Korean VRMMO players…don't get along very well?

---~~~---

In fact, you might even say they absolutely loathe each other.

Vassago Casals was back in the Underworld in the form of PoH, the character who once led the murderous Laughing Coffin guild. A smirk was lying across his lips, the only thing visible beneath his black hood.

He raised his right hand and spoke in Korean to the players in red behind him.

"Give those invaders a taste of their own medicine!! Make them feel pain! Slice them to pieces!! Make sure they never try to mess with our people again!!"

The huge mass of at least fifty thousand howled words of rage in two languages. In their eyes, surely, the Americans being killed by the Japanese players were testers from their *own* countries.

Vassago felt laughter bubbling up inside of him. He swung his hand downward.

With a noise like a tumbling avalanche, the crimson horde leaped down onto the Japanese below.

Now kill each other. Dance for me—so hideous, so pathetic, so comical.

———

"…Here he comes," Sinon muttered to herself.

She had spotted what looked like a black dotted line extending down from the red sky like a thread.

She wanted to charge her Annihilation Ray to maximum power and destroy the enemy as soon as he physically materialized. That way, he wouldn't be able to defend or evade.

But the actual thing for her to do right now was buy time. If the enemy could simply generate high-ranking accounts infinitely, for example, killing him was meaningless.

First, she would get him into a patient battle of attrition to see how he reacted. If he seemed to treasure his life, to play cautious, that would suggest that this was a precious account that could be used only once. Then she would attack with full power and destroy him so that he couldn't log in with the account again.

If this was a mass-production account, however, she couldn't go ahead and kill him. She needed to draw out the battle as long as possible, to give Alice enough time to travel to the World's End Altar.

So Sinon did not draw her bowstring. She hovered in the air and waited for the enemy to materialize. The black line of data descended upon the spot where Commander Bercouli's body had lain until a few minutes ago.

Alice had put his corpse over the saddle of one of the dragons. She said that she would have it taken back to another Integrity Knight waiting for him in the human realm—a woman.

"A love rival?" Sinon asked.

Alice just smiled and said, "You're my rival."

Good grief.

After that, there couldn't be any easy logging out of this place. She had to stay here in this world, no matter what it took, until the moment she saw Kirito awaken.

Newly determined, Sinon kept her eyes fixed on the rock top. The black line made contact with the center of the flat surface and pooled into a kind of sticky puddle. It was as dark and thick as a bottomless hole going down into hell.

The end of the line at last sank into the pool, and—*plish*.

A little ripple spread across its surface, and a moment later, a hand thrust through without a sound. When Sinon saw the five slender fingers wriggling and grasping at empty air, she felt a kind of revulsion run down her back.

She continued waiting, holding back the urge to burn whatever it was right this instant.

Slurd. A left hand appeared to join the right and grabbed the lip of the pool.

With a wet slosh, a man's head appeared.

It was a surprisingly unremarkable face. It certainly wasn't what she'd call attractive. His short blond hair seemed plastered to his head, his nose was narrow, and his lips were thin. It was a Caucasian face but oddly plain and underwhelming.

She almost started to doubt herself. Was this really the new form of the same person who was using the Vecta super-account earlier?

Then the man lifted his torso up out of the pool and looked around with empty eyes like blue marbles and caught sight of Sinon floating above.

As soon as she looked into them, she paused.

She'd seen those eyes before. They seemed to reflect everything and yet absorb it as well, all with an utter lack of emotion.

When they recognized Sinon, the eyes widened slightly. His lips twisted into the faintest suggestion of a smile.

I know it. I know him. I know those eyes…that face. And it was recent, too. Somewhere…

As she watched in a daze, the man pulled himself free from the pool all at once, making an unpleasant sucking sound.

His clothing was odd, too. There wasn't a single piece of fine metal armor anywhere on his body—it was most likely whatever gear had automatically been converted with his character. He wore a leather vest over a matching dark-gray top and bottoms and woven boots on his feet. It looked just like the kind of battle gear a soldier in the real world would have. He possessed a long-sword at his left side and a crossbow at his right.

The puddle of black water did not disappear when the man left it. To her shock, it pulled itself right off the ground and writhed like a living thing. In fact, it *was* alive. The part that separated from the ground stretched and thinned itself until it became a pair of wings that flapped rapidly.

It had a very strange shape, neither bird nor dragon. The body was round and flat like a basin, with four round eyeballs attached to the front. Batlike wings extended to the sides, and it had a long snake's tail in the rear.

The mysterious flying creature flapped its wings with the man standing atop it and rose until it was the same altitude in the air as Sinon. It hovered about a hundred feet away, and the man on its back smiled bloodlessly again.

He reached forward into empty air with his arms, for some reason. Sinon tensed, preparing for a spell or something of that nature, but that was not it. He curled his hands into a choking gesture and wrenched them together, simulating wringing her neck.

At last, and all at once, Sinon remembered. Her voice escaped from her lips, dry and hot.

".........Subtilizer........."

It was him. The American player in the fourth Bullet of Bullets tournament of *Gun Gale Online* just two weeks ago, who'd caught Sinon in a sleeper chokehold from behind during the grand final.

But why was he here?

Sinon was too stunned to remember to ready her bow. She just stared.

—〰—

Through the center of the pyramidal megafloat *Ocean Turtle* ran an extremely solid Main Shaft constructed of ultra-tough titanium alloy.

The cylindrical three-hundred-foot shaft housed at its very bottom, surrounded by multiple layers of protective walls, a pressurized water reactor. Above that nuclear reactor was the main control room, currently under enemy control, and STL Room One.

The core of the Underworld and of Project Alicization itself—the Lightcube Cluster—was located above that. All of this was known as the Lower Shaft.

Above the cluster was a horizontal pressure-resistant barrier that split the shaft in two. The Upper Shaft above the barrier contained massive cooling systems, the sub-control room, where Rath's staff was hiding, and STL Room Two, where Kazuto Kirigaya and Asuna Yuuki were using The Soul Translators.

It was nine o'clock on the morning of July 7th. A humanoid robot was walking down the staircase on the fore side of the Upper Shaft, all on its own. This was Ichiemon, Rath's prototype model. Three armed military officers followed its slow, plodding pace.

In the same moment, two small people were awkwardly making their way down a ladder inside the cable duct located on the aft side of the shaft.

I'm so glad I don't have claustrophobia, fear of heights, or fear of the dark, Takeru Higa thought, trying to bolster his spirits. But given the extreme circumstances, it didn't seem like the presence or absence of phobias was going to make a difference.

For one thing, the inside of the duct, which was lit by orange emergency lights, went on for forty yards below him. If his sweaty palms slipped on the rungs, or his shaking feet missed a step, he was going to have a very unpleasant time falling down to the pressure-resistant barrier that closed off the duct far below.

He should have had his fellow researcher Yanai go down first.

At least then he wouldn't have to keep staring down into that yawning vertical pit.

Also, he said he was going to protect me from gunfire. How will he do that if he tells me to go down first? Higa thought spitefully, glancing up at Yanai, who was a dozen or so feet above him on the ladder.

But when he saw the man's pale face looking even worse, and the way he desperately clung to the rungs, Higa couldn't blame him. It was laudable of him to have volunteered for this dangerous mission at all, and the presence of the automatic pistol tucked into his belt was reassuring, at least.

Higa looked back down and resumed climbing. A calm voice came through the earpiece on his left side.

"How is it going, Higa? Any problems?"

It was the voice of Dr. Koujiro, who was watching them from above, her face poking over the hatch into the duct.

Higa whispered back into the mic at his mouth. "W-we're managing. Should be down at the pressure barrier in about five minutes, I think."

"Got it. Once you're ready, I'll give the order to the Ichiemon team to send him in. You're going to open the wall up once the enemy notices Ichiemon and starts attacking."

"Roger. Whoa, I'm really getting that *Mission Impossible* vibe now."

"Let's shoot for Mission Possible, all right? I can't help but feel that the entire situation inside the Underworld depends on Kirito's revival. Please, Mr. Yanai, make sure my little friend can do his job."

Yanai gave the last part a quick affirmative in a tremulous voice. Higa couldn't help but snort.

I'm still just her "little friend."

He shook his head and, with palms whose sweat had dried up at some point, squeezed the next rung.

When he looked down, the barrier wall was much closer than he remembered it being.

Critter watched the players from China and Korea swarm on the monitor screen like a giant cloud, until an alarm out of nowhere jolted him to his feet.

"What was that…?!"

He glanced over the console and noticed that a single red alert was blinking on a sub-monitor off to the right side.

"Whoa…The lock on the pressure-resistant barrier's been undone! S-someone, go check out the corridor!!" he shouted. Before the sentence had even left his mouth, Hans the lanky assault trooper had grabbed an assault rifle and sprinted out to see.

"I had a good hand, dammit!" snarled the bearded Brigg, who tossed a number of similarly colored cards to the floor as he went after his partner.

Would Rath attempt a surprise kamikaze attack, knowing they don't stand a chance in a regular fight? Or is this some kind of strategy…?

Critter got up from the controls and headed to the Maincon door. The elevator had no power, so if anything was happening, it would be at the stairs. Hans and Brigg thought the same thing; he could hear their boots clanking on the metal steps.

Abruptly, however, the sound stopped, replaced by throaty bellows.

"Whoa!!"

"Are you kidding me?!"

It was quickly followed by rifle fire.

Higa already knew that the percussive *kata-ta-ta-ta* sound coming through the walls of the cable duct belonged to semiautomatic guns.

At this point, poor Ichiemon was on the opposite side of the Main Shaft, his body's muscle cylinders and titanium bone structure being pumped full of holes. But because his battery and control systems were on the back of his frame, he should have been able to keep walking for a time.

"Go ahead!" said Dr. Koujiro through the earpiece. "Open the barrier hatch!!"

Higa used all his strength to turn the handle of the hatch on the barrier that separated the duct into two parts. The air hissed out briefly as the hydraulic shock absorbers kicked in. The thick metal lid lifted upward.

Like the space above them, the duct in the Lower Shaft was lit with orange emergency lights. The sound of combat coming from the stairway area on the opposite side of the shaft grew noticeably louder.

Higa swallowed, adjusted the backpack with the little laptop inside, and made his way through the hatch, which was even narrower than the duct. He got his feet back on the ladder rungs and resumed descending.

"If this were an action movie, they'd be saying stuff like 'Go, go, go!!'" he whispered to himself—but it was directly into his little mic.

"Did you just say something?" Rinko asked through the comm.

"Er, n-nothing…I've got another thirty feet to get the connector for cable maintenance…Oh! There, I see it!"

A number of thick optic cables along the wall of the duct met at a black panel box. If he hooked up the laptop to the maintenance connector there, he should theoretically be able to perform direct operations on STL Units Three and Four in the nearby STL room—and on Five and Six in the Roppongi office.

Just you wait, Kirigaya. I'm gonna wake you up!

Higa continued down the ladder with renewed vigor, momentarily forgetting his fear.

Through his earpiece, he heard the voice say, "Well, I'll be back in Subcon monitoring Kirito's fluctlight signals. Good luck, Higa!!"

It was the same kind of encouragement Dr. Koujiro would

give him back in college, when he knew her as Miss Rinko. Higa couldn't help but glance up.

All he saw, however, was Yanai's face twisted with concentration and fear as he came down the ladder from above. Higa shook his head as he looked back to the approaching control box.

—◦◦◦—

The man in combat fatigues who appeared atop the scarred rock looked to the south. In a monotone voice, he said, "So Alice escaped...Very well. I'll catch her soon..."

Then he looked back at Sinon and smiled thinly at her.

"...I fought against you in a *Gun Gale Online* event, didn't I? Your name was...Sinon? To think we'd run into each other again here."

Sinon fought desperately to keep her hands from trembling as she listened to the vaguely inhuman voice of the man who was both Vecta, the god of darkness, and Subtilizer. But her fingers cramped, sweat greased her palms, and she knew that if she tried too hard to use Solus's bow now, she would drop it.

As he stood atop the round basin creature, Subtilizer spoke to her in smooth, fluent Japanese, holding a smile without warmth all the while.

"What does this mean, I wonder? I'd heard that there were STLs in Japan itself...Does this mean you're connected to Rath somehow? Or are you a mercenary, too, and flew out to this distant place?"

The voice that came through Sinon's cracked lips was hoarse.

"Subtilizer...why are *you* here?"

"I am here because it was inevitable, of course," he explained, barely able to contain his glee. He spread his arms wide, revealing gray sleeves. "This is fate. It is the power of the soul that brings us together."

His tone of voice was changing gradually. Even the temperature of his tone was dropping from moment to moment.

"That's right…I wanted you. And so we came into contact again. This will tell us so many things. I'll learn if I can suck up the souls of not just the artificial fluctlights, but real people in the real world, through The Soul Translator…And I will learn just how sweet your soul really is, since I didn't get the chance in *GGO*."

The bizarre words instantly brought back the thing this man had said to her at the end of the fourth Bullet of Bullets event.

"Your soul will be so sweet."

She felt her body going cold. Everything felt tense, and even her breathing went irregular.

"Now…come this way, Sinon. You must hand over everything to me."

Subtilizer's blue eyes shone coldly. The world shuddered and warped.

Air, sound, even light twisted—drawn and absorbed into Subtilizer's eyes.

"Wha……?"

What is this? But even the very thought was sucked out of her mind by an incredible magnetic force.

Oh no. I can't. I have to resist. I have to fight, cried a voice in the corner of her mind, but it was helplessly tiny.

Eventually, Sinon's blue-armor-clad body found itself being pulled toward the man's outstretched arms. She slid helplessly, silently through the air, bowstring still held between her numb fingers.

A few seconds later, with her wits fading, Sinon just barely sensed her body being slickly surrounded by the darkness that was Subtilizer.

His left hand went around her back. The fingers of his right hand brushed her cheek and swept away the hair over her ear. He brought his thin lips up to the exposed cartilage and sent a voice like cold black water directly into her head.

"Sinon. Have you ever thought about the meaning of the name Subtilizer?"

"…?"

In her powerless state, Sinon shook her head.

"Is it some wordplay, as Americans so often like to do, on the Japanese word *satori*, meaning 'enlightenment'? No, this is a purely English construction. Subtilizer means one who sharpens, one who renders, one who chooses…and one who steals."

Subtilizer's eyes flashed brighter, right before her own.

"I will steal you. I will steal your soul…"

—◆◆—

Wol-Saeng Jo descended onto a stone surface that was cracked and mossy. It was not natural, but carved. It looked like the roof of some massive, templelike building, in fact. The space around him was bristling and crowded with other Korean players, thousands of them…Perhaps as many as ten thousand.

There was no process for him to choose an avatar, so while the finer details and weapon types were different, everyone around him wore the same dark-red armor. Wol-Saeng glanced down at the red gauntlets on his hands before looking forward.

It was hard to see through the throng, but it did seem like the battle was still ongoing in a flat space in front of the temple. The reason that the other Koreans around him weren't moving was probably because the battle was practically won already. The colorful group that was presumably the Japanese players had finished exterminating the other group of red-armored soldiers and was now regrouping, but there was no cheering coming from their side.

Something *was* wrong. He just couldn't quite put it into words yet.

At the very least, this wasn't a promotional stunt for some new game, like he had imagined before he started the dive. The terrain, with its ugly red sky and featureless black earth, was too barren to be enticing, and there was no mention of any regulations or warnings before he dived. It couldn't possibly be an official event.

But still, he couldn't accept that tweet's claim at face value. For one thing, what possible meaning could there be in raiding a test server and killing testers within the game? You could inflict temporary pain and humiliation on them, but that wasn't going to delay or cancel the game's development, by any means.

Nearly half the Koreans around Wol-Saeng seemed a bit taken aback by the situation, too. He heard them asking questions like "What should we do?" and "Are they really Japanese?"

But just then, he heard a voice call in Korean from the right.

"My comrades!"

Wol-Saeng stretched and looked in that direction, but the crowd was too thick for him to identify the speaker. All he could see was a red marker reading LEADER hovering above the mass of humanity. The same voice came from that direction again.

"I am hugely grateful that you answered our summons! Sadly, the alpha testers have already been slaughtered by the Japanese intruders—no, invasion! But they've moved to a different test location to repeat the same thing!"

Wol-Saeng instantly sensed a bristling of anger, tangible among the crowd of thousands.

It was the word *invasion—chimnyak—*that set off the Korean players. It was clear within moments that whatever reservations or skepticism individual players might have felt soon burned away, leaving behind only fiery hostility.

"...*Bigeopan Ilbonin*!!" someone shouted—"Cowardly Japanese!!"—and the angry yells spread from there. When the wave died down, the leader addressed the crowd again.

"The Japanese hacked the server, so they can create as much high-level gear as they want! They stole admin access from us, so we only have default equipment now! But I know that your righteousness and patriotism will triumph over any sword or armor!"

He got a bellowed response.

"...*Uri narareul jikida*!!" ("Protect our country!!")

Next, far to the right, there was a fresh angry shout in a different language.

"*Han zhong lianmeng!!*"

Wol-Saeng didn't know what that meant, but he could tell that it was Mandarin. Apparently, there were as many Chinese players present as there were Koreans.

As the voltage of the gathering surged, Wol-Saeng still couldn't get over that lingering feeling. At the same time, his instinct told him that there was no stopping the momentum of the situation now.

On the other side of the throng, the "leader" raised a black-gloved fist.

"Go!!" he said in English, a command that players of both countries would understand. The furious red army roiled like one massive being and burst into motion.

"H-human forces! Supply team! Full speed ahead!!" cried Asuna, just before the swarm of red soldiers atop the roofs of the temple buildings could go into motion.

The Human Guardian Army's supply team was deployed at the entrance to the temple grounds. The palatial ruins extended out on either side of the path through the middle. In other words, the enemy was bristling with weapons, thousands upon thousands of them, just overhead.

"Abandon your supplies! Wagons and priests, start moving now!!" she instructed, but it wasn't going to be in time. The new connections, probably Chinese and Korean, were just about ready to leap over the heads of the holy statues lining the path to land right in the midst of the supply team.

Asuna gritted her teeth and raised her rapier.

She focused her imagination on the point of her weapon and swung it down hard. A rainbow aurora shot straight out of the end and slammed into the statues along the path.

A terrible, mind-bursting pain shot through her head, but she kept her imagination focused until the statues started rumbling into motion. Their square mouths opened, and they swung their short arms as they began to attack the players crowding the roofs of the temple.

The red soldiers in the front line leaped backward to get out of the way but collided with their own kind rushing up from behind, which started a domino-like chain reaction. While this was happening, the eight wagons and about two hundred priests that made up the supply team began moving.

Asuna could control the statues for only about thirty seconds—after that long, she fell to the ground in agony—but it did succeed in getting the weaker rear unit out of the danger zone, past the north end of the temple grounds and into the open wilderness. The surviving men-at-arms, less than five hundred in number, and two thousand Japanese players moved forward and enveloped the rear guard, preparing for battle.

But there was no real terrain to speak of here, and trying to fight tens of thousands of enemies would inevitably involve a desperate defense on all sides. They'd just barely defeated the American players and their numerical advantage by using the walls of the temple ruins to limit the size of the front line of combat and employing a thorough healing rotation system. If forty or fifty thousand Chinese and Korean players surrounded them now, it would only be a matter of time before their line crumbled.

"*Hng...*"

Asuna used what little willpower she had left to get to her feet and raised her rapier again. *We need a wall...Please, just let me make a wall that will protect everyone, right at the end*, she prayed, focusing her imagination once again.

Instead, however, she felt a tremendous jolt go through her, and she fell to the ground, gasping. Something rose to her throat and erupted outward. She looked down and saw a small puddle of blood on the ground.

"Don't press your luck, Asuna! Leave some of the glory for us!" Klein said bracingly.

"That's right, let us handle this!" Agil chimed in.

They stood before Asuna, katana and great ax at the ready—when the red army recovered from the chaos and began to leap from the roofs in earnest this time. It was a drop of at least sixty feet, so more than a few of them landed badly and suffered limb damage and mobility problems, but more of their fellows used the injured as cushions to land on the ground unharmed.

"*Dolgyeooooook!!*"

"*Tuuuujiiii!!*"

Asuna had never learned Korean or Chinese in school, but she naturally intuited that both of these words meant "charge."

The crimson wave fanned out to the left and right as it descended upon them, and it was Klein and Agil who struck back first.

"*Zeiryaaaaaaaa!!*"

"*Raaaaaahhh!!*"

With air-shattering bellows, they unleashed wide-spread katana and ax skills. White and blue light flashed together, and dozens of the enemy soldiers erupted with blood.

At their sides, the territorial lords and ladies of *ALO* and their followers, and the ferocious Sleeping Knights, opened battle with maximum strength. Metal thrust like machine guns. Heavy impacts sounded like explosions. Swords, axes, and spears roared, and with each colorful sword-skill blast, more red soldiers toppled over dead.

Air creaked as it compressed, and the massive army's charge briefly stopped.

But...it was no more meaningful than fighting back against the rush of a broken dam with one's bare hands.

Screams and shrieks of anger swirled over the battlefield, and above it all, a faint sound of high-pitched laughter that Asuna could barely hear from the ground where she hovered. She looked up through dazed wits and saw, atop the roof of the ruined building, the man in the black poncho practically dancing with glee.

—⁓—

Higa descended the ladder as quickly as he could manage with intermittent bursts of gunfire coming from the other side of the Main Shaft.

He reached the panel box that glowed dully in the orange light and opened the lid with cramping fingers. Inside, he was briefly disappointed to see that it was just a messy bunch of fiber-optic cables and had to rifle through them for a while before he found the connection port for maintenance purposes.

It was showtime.

He took a deep breath to calm his thoughts, then pulled a cable and his laptop from the backpack. He stuck one end of the cord into the connector and the other into the PC, then started up the STL operations program, praying nothing would go wrong.

A blank black window opened, containing nothing but a teasingly slow blinking cursor. After a while, it scrolled to the right, displaying status messages.

STL #3 CONNECTING.........OK.

STL #4 CONNECTING.........OK.

So the signals coming back from the units in STL Room Two next to the sub-control room were healthy. Next, he tried to establish a connection to Units Five and Six in Roppongi through the *Ocean Turtle*'s satellite signal.

"…Yes!"

It was successful. Now he could operate the four STLs housing Kazuto Kirigaya and the three girls.

Unfortunately, because the enemy was hijacking the lines from the main control room to the STL room and satellite antenna, he couldn't do anything about the other two Soul Translators. If he could, he'd be able to boot the two attackers currently using Unit One and Unit Two right out of the Underworld.

Higa caught himself before he thought too hard about that. He placed his hand on the laptop's tiny keyboard.

Here we go! he told himself, right as he heard a high-pitched wail overhead.

"……D-don't move!!"

It was Yanai's voice. What was he talking about?

Higa looked up, annoyed, and saw the muzzle of the pistol, gleaming and dark, just ten feet above him. Behind it, Yanai's little eyes were bloodshot and desperate. "Get your hands off the keyboard! Or I'll shoot!"

"……Huh?"

Higa's mind was blank for less than half a second.

Then it all instantly snapped into place, and he had his conjecture.

It was him!

Yanai. *He* was the spy who'd leaked information about Project Alicization to the Americans.

Sadly, he couldn't think of a counterplan. He asked a meaningless question with a parched tongue. "Why, Yanai…?"

The engineer's lips quivered, his pale forehead greasy with beaded sweat, and he wailed, "J-just so you know…you're wrong to treat me like a traitor."

"Treat" you like one? You are *one!!*

As if hearing that internal scream from Higa, Yanai added, "I've always been dedicated to my goal. I'm carrying on the boss's last will…That's why I worked my way in with Rath."

"The boss's…will? Who…are you talking about…?" Higa asked in a daze.

Yanai swept his hanging bangs out of the way with his free hand and gave him a smile with a hint of madness. "Someone you know very, very well…I mean Mr. Sugou."

"Wh……?"

Whaaaaat?!

It was a bigger shock to Higa than seeing the gun pointed at him.

Nobuyuki Sugou. The man who'd been in Touto Technical University's Shigemura Research Lab at the same time as Higa, Rinko Koujiro, and Akihiko Kayaba. He'd always burned with rival ambition over Kayaba's extreme genius but never surpassed

Main Shaft

Ship Aft

Takeru Higa

Yanai

**pper Shaft
ub-Control Room**

inko Koujiro

Seijirou Kikuoka

Cable Duct

**Lower Shaft
Main Control
Room**

Gabriel Miller

Vassago Casals

Critter

Ichiemon

Elevator

Ship Fore

Hans

the man's feats in the end. So for some reason, possibly related, he'd abducted a few hundred *SAO* players for inhumane experiments while they were still trapped.

With Kazuto Kirigaya's help, his misdeeds came to light, and he was arrested. His first trial ended in a jail sentence, but he appealed, and the case was still in dispute at the Tokyo High Court.

"...It's not like he's dead," Higa muttered, eliciting a high-pitched giggle from Yanai.

"He might as well be. He'll get a minimum of ten years. That's death for any researcher. It was a close call for me, too, but I blamed everything on one of his other followers and managed to escape scot-free."

"You mean...you were involved in Sugou's human experimentation, too...?"

"Involved? Oh, I was the one collecting the data. Ahhh, that was a fun bit of research...all that virtual tentacle groping..."

How did Lieutenant Kikuoka fail to vet this scumbag's background?! Higa wondered, incensed, but he realized just as quickly that it would have been impossible.

Rath was a group camouflaged as a tech start-up, an attempt to create a purely domestic military industry that did not rest upon the bedrock of the American defense-system monopoly. In other words, their existence would pose a threat to the market share and profit of the existing conglomerate manufacturers and defense companies.

That made it very difficult to put together their engineering department. They were getting almost no engagement from the major companies, so the chance to recruit Yanai, who was part of RCT's full-dive R&D department, was a huge opportunity they couldn't pass up.

Higa could see that Yanai's eyes were still glazed over with fond reminiscence, but that didn't last long. He aimed the pistol again, and the safety was clearly off on the left side of the frame. Kikuoka's comprehensive planning in making sure even the engineers got basic shooting training had backfired.

Fortunately, Yanai still had some things to get off his chest, so he wasn't pulling the trigger yet.

"…So the boss's life might be over now, but the line he set up is still alive. So it's up to me to pick up the slack and take over from where he left off."

"Um…what line is that?" Higa asked automatically.

Yanai made a show of weighing the question, then grinned and answered, "The American National Security Agency."

"Th-the *what*?!" he shouted, but on the inside, it was just confirming Higa's suspicions.

It was an open secret that the NSA was involved in wiretapping and signal intercepting inside of Japan. There was no way they wouldn't take an interest in Japan's lead in full-dive tech. So Yanai, Sugou's subordinate, had sent the NSA information on Project Alicization, and they'd chartered a navy sub to come and steal A.L.I.C.E. in return.

Yanai continued, "If the Americans below us manage to recover Alice properly, I'll get a stupid-fat bonus, and they'll guarantee me a position over there. That's the American dream that Mr. Sugou talked about."

And then the rest of the world will quake in fear at the Americans' high-powered unmanned weaponry, Higa thought. He had to stay cool, to find a way to keep this conversation going so that he could seize any chance that presented itself.

Please notice something's wrong, Rinko! he prayed. The laptop nearly slipped out of his hand, and he hastily readjusted his grip on it.

"D-don't move!!" screamed Yanai, pointing the gun at the side of the duct and pulling the trigger. There was a yellow flash of light as well as a powerful burst of air displacement that shook Higa's eardrums.

Sparks burst against the metal wall—and a sharp shock bit Higa's right shoulder.

"Huh?"

Yanai sounded surprised.

—◁∧▷—

In the center of the two blue eyes that gazed into hers, Sinon saw what vaguely looked like black whirlpools, black holes that rotated slowly, much like the dream she'd had that morning.

She had to do something. She thought she'd done something, but it was a dream, so of course she hadn't. A never-ending cycle of illusions.

Chilly fingers stroked her neck. She felt revulsion and fear, but even those emotions were sucked out of her mind, replaced by nothing but gray futility.

I can't.

This wasn't just some virtual-world event, a thing that wasn't really happening.

A red alarm light in some corner of her brain was flashing to alert her of that. She tried to grab on to that, to focus, but the sticky black liquid had swallowed her up to her waist now. There was nowhere to escape. She couldn't even struggle against it.

The man's face loomed closer. His thin lips puckered, sucking in air. Her emotions, her thoughts, her very soul was sucked away with that air.

Stop it. Don't steal them.

But even that wish was instantly stolen, leaving only dull paralysis.

"St...op......"

His lips approached hers...

Tzak!!

A sudden shock bolted Sinon's mind back into itself.

She opened her eyes wide and caught sight of a bright-silver spark leaping out from the collar of her top.

...It's so hot!!

A feeling of heat, almost like electrical discharge, briefly overcame the man's suction. With what little of her mind she'd just recovered, she jolted like a bullet's detonator, wringing a sudden burst of strength from her body and escaping from the man's arms.

With Solus's power of flight, she swept away to put distance between them.

"...*Eugh*...," she grunted, pulling the sparking object out from under her shirt. It was a light-colored metal plate hanging on a fine chain. The circular disc was less than an inch across, with a little puncture at one end for the chain to run through.

"Why...is this..."

...*here?*

Sinon was stunned. It was the necklace she wore around her neck as Shino Asada in the real world. It wasn't expensive. The chain was surgical stainless steel, and the trinket was just silver-plated aluminum.

But it was an object that held great importance to Sinon.

At the end of last year, she'd been a victim of the Death Gun incident. One of her classmates, a member of the criminal group, had tried to attack her with a high-pressure syringe full of deadly succinylcholine—but Kazuto Kirigaya had rushed to protect her and taken the syringe right to his chest.

What had saved him from the spread of the chemical was an electrode from his heart monitor, which he'd forgotten to remove.

Sinon had found the electrode on her floor after the incident, peeled off the tape, then fashioned the silver node into a pendant head. The fact that she wore this homemade necklace all the time was a secret from Kirito and Asuna, and when she'd dived in at the Roppongi office of Rath, she'd been fully clothed, so the man there named Hiraki wouldn't have seen it.

In other words, it was impossible for this necklace to exist in the Underworld as a physical object.

But...

Kirito *had* said that the virtual world created by the STL wasn't just a huge computer-modeled simulation, back when he'd explained all of this at Dicey Café. He'd said it was another reality created from memory and imagination.

In that case, this necklace was something Sinon's own mind had created.

She pressed the silver pendant to her lips and let it hang down under her top again.

Her mind was completely back in gear, and she turned it to concentrate on the black winged creature hovering in the sky a distance away.

Subtilizer stood on the creature's back, staring at his own hand. Sinon could see faint signs of smoke rising from his fingertips. He must have sensed her gaze, because he looked up then, traces of displeasure wrinkling the sides of his mouth.

Sinon stared the man in the face and said, "You are not God—or the devil. You're just a man."

Subtilizer's power was overwhelming, yes. The incredible toughness of his imagination must have been affecting Sinon's very mind—her fluctlight.

But I won't let him outdo me in imagination and focus. They were the tools of the trade for a sniper, after all.

She gripped the Annihilation Ray, Solus's GM weapon, and focused her gaze. The center of the shining white bow turned to a bluish-black color.

As the change in color spread, the bow's smooth curves shifted to straight angles. The long, dark, shining tube was a steel gun barrel. Then a muzzle appeared, then a grip, and a stock, and lastly, a huge scope attachment.

It was not a graceful, flowing longbow in Sinon's hands anymore.

This was a simple, ferocious, and stunningly beautiful .50-caliber antimateriel rifle, the Ultima Ratio Hecate II.

Sinon pulled the bolt handle of her eternal partner, and upon hearing its nasty slide, she grinned.

The bridge of Subtilizer's nose crinkled, and his lips twisted with anger.

It was only what you might call a "battle" for about seven minutes.

After that, there were three minutes of a defensive struggle, and then it turned to one-sided slaughter.

"Protect them…! Do whatever it takes to save the Underworlders!!" shouted Asuna, thrusting and swinging her rapier on the front line for all she was worth and trying to ignore the throbbing pain in the center of her skull.

But she couldn't hear any kind of hearty group response anymore.

All around her, other Japanese players in their colorful converted armor found themselves surrounded, one by one, by people from neighboring countries clad in red and succumbed to their onslaught of swords and spears. Raging, shrieks, and death screams filled the air.

Compared to this, at least the charging attacks of the American heavy lancers were a coordinated effort that could be strategized against.

This new army, either because it was made of people from two countries, or because they were driven by an abnormal rage, focused on nothing but obliteration, losses be damned. They would leap at a target's legs, several attackers all at once, and drag the victim to the ground and pile upon them. There was no possible strategy that could overcome a vastly larger army that fought like this.

The defensive circle made of two thousand was visibly eroding as the enemy consumed them. For her part, Asuna swung and thrust her rapier at the never-ending waves of adversaries, and in her mind, she repeated a plea she hadn't thought since she'd first dived into the Underworld last night.

Someone help.

Within the desperate, losing battle, one group fought relatively better than the rest: a team of warriors in green led by Sakuya, the lady of the sylphs in *ALfheim Online*.

The sylphs were highly agile and skilled at speedy combination tactics. It was a battle strategy devised to counteract the sala-manders and their heavy charges based on weight, and it worked fairly well here, too. The lightly armored swordsmen spun and rotated in and out with dizzying speed, preventing their foes from singling out a target or dragging down individual victims.

"We're going to break a hole through their line! Bellflower Team, Lily Team, push the fighting to the right!!" ordered Sakuya, in the midst of swinging her long, slender katana at the front line of combat.

They joined the salamanders who were fighting on the right wing, using their charging power to break through the enemy line. If they could help the supply team escape down the path toward the ruins again, and hold the fighting to the narrow entrance of the grounds, they might be able to whittle down the vast number of enemies the way they'd done against the Americans.

"Get ready! Prepare a synced sword skill!! Count off! Five, four, three…," Sakuya prompted—until a wail to their left dis-tracted her.

"Don't give up, everyone! Buy them as much time as you can!!"

Sakuya swallowed her words and glanced over to her left. A formation of Japanese players in yellow gear was collapsing just at that moment, swallowed by a wave of crimson. Right at the front, wearing metal combat claws on both hands and being pulled to the ground, was a small, familiar figure.

"Alicia!!" cried Sakuya. Instantly, she went from the cool, col-lected leader to a normal college student. "Stop!! Nooooo!!"

She ran off to the left on her own, sending enemies who blocked her path flying to the left and right, all in a rush to reach her dear friend.

Alicia Rue, leader of the cait siths, noticed Sakuya, swords through her chest and stomach, approaching steadily. She let out a bloodcurdling cry: "No, Sakuya! Go back! Lead your team!!"

And with that, the yellow hair and triangular ears of her friend vanished from Sakuya's view.

"Aliciaaaaaa!!" she screamed, charging straight into the swarm of enemies crushing the cait siths, all on her own. She unleashed sword skill after sword skill, spraying a rain of hot blood and shreds of flesh as she went. She was almost to the spot where her friend had fallen, almost...

Wham.

Something hit her body, and she looked down to see the head of a spear jutting out of the right side of her stomach. The first taste of severe virtual pain raced through her nerves and robbed her of strength.

She managed to still take four more steps, but then her avatar body fell out of her control and toppled forward.

A storm of hatred engulfed Sakuya: Her sword was ripped from her hand, half of her left arm was sliced off, and sharp metal pierced her body all over.

—◦◦◦—

Of the two thousand—and rapidly dropping—Japanese players in the battle, perhaps the one person most accurately assessing the state of the fight was the third-generation leader of the Sleeping Knights guild, Si-Eun Ahn, better known as Siune.

Her father was a South Korean resident of Japan, and her mother was Japanese. So Siune could speak two languages, and the scraps of information she gleaned from the angry shouts of some of the red soldiers gave her an idea of what had gotten them so riled up.

The schism between online users in Japan and Korea started in the early 2000s, before Siune was born—from what she understood. There were probably many reasons for this, and perhaps the development of the Internet itself only exacerbated the discord that already existed.

The rivalry between countries inevitably affected the online games that Siune and her friends played, too. As of 2026, in the international servers of VRMMOs, it wasn't unusual at all for Japanese, Koreans, and Chinese to squabble over hunting and harvesting areas. Most of the newer games simply shut out connections from outside the country, as *ALO* did, and that only increased the isolation and enmity between the neighboring nations.

Siune grew up in contact with both Korean and Japanese culture, and this development hurt to see. When she went into VR hospice, the members of the Sleeping Knights welcomed her and treated her the same as anyone else, even with her background. She hoped that, somehow, she could help bridge the gap that existed in the virtual world, for the betterment of everyone.

And yet...

Someone watching this battle from atop the ruins was cleverly manipulating the Korean and Chinese VRMMO players, whipping them into a furious frenzy, in an attempt to create the greatest outpouring of hatred and tragedy in the history of VRMMOs.

I...I have to do something. I'm probably the only one on our side who can actually speak Korean. Some things you just can't get across without confronting them. Isn't that right, Yuuki?

It was something their dearly departed previous leader liked to say; she had passed away three months ago. Siune turned to her four companions in the vicinity and shouted, "Please, you guys, create a break point for me!!"

Up ahead, where Jun was swinging his two-handed greatsword like some demon of battle, he shouted back, "Got it! Tecchi, Talken, Nori, let's sync up the big skills! Countdown! Two, one..."

High-powered single-attack skills went off in unison, creating an earth-shaking blast and knocking back dozens of enemies. In the ensuing moment of stillness, Siune rushed up to a large Korean player who seemed to be in charge of the area and caught his downward sword swing with her bare hand.

Her palm split, and blood gushed forth.

But this virtual pain was nothing next to the suffering of her bone marrow transplant for leukemia and the salvage therapy that followed. She merely grimaced the smallest bit, gazed right into the eyes of her attacker, and shouted in Korean, "Listen to me! You are being lied to!! This server belongs to a Japanese company! We are not hackers! We are connected legitimately!!"

Her voice boomed across the scene and managed to extend the silence of the crowd around her. The man whose sword she was stopping looked a bit intimidated but recovered and replied, "Liar! We saw you! You were slaughtering players who looked just like us earlier!!"

"Those were Americans, who were brought here under false pretenses, just like you! You're the ones who are being used as tools of sabotage!! Think it over closely—is that anger and hatred really yours?!" shouted Siune. The Koreans met her with confusion and silence.

The next voice to break the quiet came from the back of the crowd, harsh but questioning. "Is that story true?!"

That Korean player, who came rushing forward, looked just like any of the other soldiers in red. Siune tensed on instinct, but he lowered his sword and raised his helmet visor as he approached, to show he had no ill will.

"I'm Moonphase. Who are you?" he asked. Siune was taken aback by the question, but she could see from the look in his eyes that he was earnest.

She let go of the sword edge she was holding, clutched the hand bleeding virtual blood to her chest, and said, "I am Siune."

"All right, Siune. The truth is, I've been feeling that something was wrong about this," Moonphase said rapidly. Other Koreans around him objected angrily, but the young man silenced them by emphatically returning his sword to its sheath. He stepped forward.

"Do you have any means of proving what you've told us?"

"……Um…"

She held her breath.

The Underworld was a research-purpose VR world built by a Japanese company with the backing of the government, and its attackers were Americans trying to steal the new AI the experiment was meant to develop. That was what her friend Lisbeth had tearfully explained at the World Tree dome in *ALO*, and Siune had no intention of doubting her. But how to prove that to strangers was another question.

There was no "physical" evidence in a virtual world, of course. The only thing that might work would be a statement from someone, but nothing any Japanese person could say would work. As Siune struggled to find the right words, she could sense the suspicion and anger of the Korean players around her rekindling. What could she do…? Where would the answer be……?

"The Underworlders, Siune!" cried Nori from over Siune's left shoulder. "Show them the Underworlders who actually live here, and they'll see that they speak Japanese and that this is a Japanese server!"

"Oh……!"

True, that was a possibility. Siune's guild hadn't exchanged more than a few words with the Underworld soldiers at the center of their formation, but they'd felt a kind of soul-shaking shock at the way they were clearly neither real-world humans nor programmed NPCs. Even if they didn't speak the same language—or maybe even *because* of that—the Koreans might sense that feeling, too. If they could just interact, share a few words, and open their hearts…

She was about to translate what Nori said into Korean for Moonphase and the others, but a baleful red light glimmered behind them.

"Oh…watch ou…," she tried to warn, but wasn't in time. A short but thick blade dug deep into Moonphase's back and tossed him nearly ten yards through the air.

"Aaagh…," he groaned, writhing in pain. Now a new man stood before Siune: the one in the black poncho who'd been standing atop the palatial roof. In his hand was a dagger that looked more like a kitchen knife. He pointed it at Moonphase and shouted in Korean, "We don't need traitors in our midst!"

Then he spun around, pointing that dagger at the others. "Don't let these dirty Japanese fool you!!"

His voice was heavy, powerful, cold, and also mocking. Lastly, he pointed the knife at Siune, who stood rooted to the spot in disbelief. "If this is a Japanese server, and you're legitimate users, why are you guys the only ones with high-level gear? It's all shining like it's GM armor! You obviously just cheated and gave yourselves top-tier equipment!!"

Cheers of agreement rose up around him.

Siune raised a desperate defense. "You're wrong! The reason our equipment is different is because we converted our main characters over here!"

Immediately, the man in the poncho giggled. "Hah, what kind of an idiot would move their main character to a test server?! That's a lie! It's all lies!!"

"It's true! Believe us!! We came here at the risk of losing our charact..."

Something whipped through the air.

When Siune looked at the dagger sticking deep into her own shoulder, the pain registered less than the rush of despair. She couldn't understand the words the man who threw the weapon was screaming at her.

A small group of Chinese players had taken advantage of the brief stalemate to charge in from the right. The Korean leader called out to his group again and kicked Siune over.

She toppled to the ground and heard the footsteps of her companions rushing up to her, but she could not stand again.

—∽∾—

Why?

Integrity Knight Renly Synthesis Twenty-Seven could feel the depth and ferocity of the hatred hanging over the battle on his skin, and it left him repeating that simple question.

Why must they hate and kill each other with such passion, when they're both from the real world?

But perhaps, he realized, it wasn't right for him to ask that.

The people of the Underworld were split into those who lived in the human realm and those who lived in the dark realm, with a simmering, bloody war that had continued between the two for centuries. The amount of blood spilled in battle when the Eastern Gate fell just a few days ago was surely equal to what had been shed in this battle. Renly's own Double-Winged Blades, now hanging from his belt, had ended the lives of many, many goblins.

In fact, that was *why* he believed that the real world, this place somehow outside the Underworld, would be free of that kind of bloodshed and hatred.

Now it was clear that this was just a fantasy. Asuna and her friends from the real world spoke the same words that the Underworlders did, but the language of the new army of thousands and thousands was completely incomprehensible to Renly. If even the words they spoke were different, there could be no possibility of truce or peace negotiations.

Did it mean that warfare was simply humanity's basic nature?

Would the killing be endless here in this world, and outside in the real world, and in whatever world might exist beyond that one?

I won't accept that it's true! he thought, clenching his fists and fighting back tears.

Sheyta had stayed back in a situation that meant certain death so that she could protect the pugilists guild, their supposed enemy. Through the clash of sword and fist, she must have come to understand and sympathize with the darklanders. There must be hope at the end of this bloodstained road.

So now was the time to fight—not to stand around and be protected by others.

Renly headed for the front line of battle, where the real-worlders desperately continued their defensive fight. A small voice behind him said, "I will go, too, Sir Knight."

He turned around to see the red-haired girl from the supply team, Tiese. She had a smallish sword in her hand and a look of mournful desperation on her face.

"…No. You should stay and protect him…"

"Ronie will handle that duty. But the Eugeo I loved," Tiese said, maple-red eyes shining, "lost his life to protect what he truly cared about. I want to carry on his example."

"……Oh."

Renly bit his lip. Even he, an Integrity Knight, had no guarantee of surviving the battle. Tiese wasn't even a graduated warrior; it was impossible to think she'd make it through whole.

Then another voice joined the conversation. "I will go, too, Sir Knight."

This one, coming forward to stand by Tiese, was a tall chief guard with her brown hair tied into a ponytail. Her clothes and armor were dirty and dented from fierce combat, but her eyes were bright and full of purpose still.

"I, too, have yet to fulfill my promise to Kirito. I can't give up on the people and the world that he gave so much of himself to protect."

"Miss Sortiliena…," Tiese said in a trembling voice, and the young woman gave her a faint smile back.

They would fight not for pride or for honor, but to protect what needed to be protected. Renly could feel that desire seeping into himself and resonating.

He brushed his right hand against the divine weapon at his waist and bowed his head. "All right…In that case, I will protect you…as long as you make sure not to leave my side."

"Okay!"

"Thank you, Sir Knight!" Tiese and Sortiliena said, drawing their swords.

Renly removed both his weapons from his waist and thought, *Eldrie, Sheyta, and Commander Bercouli. I may have finally found the place for me to use my life, as you three did before me.*

And then, accompanied by two swordswomen, Renly the Integrity Knight rushed into the battlefield of screams and despair.

4

Rinko Koujiro rushed back to the sub-control room and lowered herself into the mesh-backed chair where Takeru Higa had sat minutes before.

Out of the many windows open on the big monitor before her, she focused on a small one near the bottom. It was the three-dimensional graph that represented Kazuto Kirigaya's fluctlight status. In the center of the graph, with its rainbow gradient spreading out from the center, was a yawning blackness that indicated his damaged sense of self.

Takeru Higa was currently performing operations on the four STLs, trying to repair Kazuto's fluctlight using the memories of the three girls who knew him best. To do so, he had to infiltrate the Lower Shaft under enemy control, all alone—well, maybe, as a lonely *pair*.

For the moment, the invaders were distracted fighting against Ichiemon, whom they'd sent down the stairs as a decoy. But even that metal robot wasn't going to last forever against assault rifle bullets. And once Ichiemon was destroyed, the enemy was going to wonder, what were those Japanese trying to do?

Hurry up, Higa! she prayed, right as the door slid open and a man in a Hawaiian shirt and wooden sandals clacked inside.

"H-how is Kirito doing?!"

"Higa just started his operation. How about our decoy?" she asked.

Seijirou Kikuoka inhaled and exhaled, his shoulders bobbing, and prodded his glasses back up the bridge of his nose. "I threw all the smoke grenades I had over Ichiemon's shoulder. There's probably a bit more we can do once they get the smoke out of the corridor, but it'll be dangerous not to lock the wall again as soon as that's over. We don't have much time."

"Higa said he could get it done in five minutes at the most...," Rinko said, going back to staring at the monitor.

Kazuto Kirigaya's fluctlight showed no change. She clenched her hands and thought of the proverb she'd learned in America: *A watched pot never boils*. It took force of will to pull her eyes away from the center of the monitor.

That part of the screen displayed what looked like a map of some fantasy world—which was exactly what it was, but it also was not. It was the terrain of the entire Underworld.

Outside the Human Empire's land, which she'd been shown not long after she'd first arrived at the *Ocean Turtle* a few days earlier, far to the south of the circular range of mountains, there were artificial markings, two squares in a row, that looked like ruins. There was a bright dot there indicating the location of Asuna Yuuki, along with a grouping of blue dots for the human army, and another group of white dots for all the Japanese reinforcements who had connected to the simulation, all bunched together.

And the vast swarm of red surrounding them represented the American players who'd been worked up into a lather by the invaders—yet, the group seemed too big. There were at least twenty, perhaps thirty of them for every single Japanese player.

Wondering if they were in danger, and where the other two girls aside from Asuna were, Rinko looked around the map until she found one dot, pale blue, far to the south of the ruins. That was probably Shino Asada, then.

So where was Suguha Kirigaya? Rinko squinted, glancing around the map, until she finally saw a light-green dot far, far to the north of the fighting. There was a collection of red enemies near her, too, but Higa claimed that he was helping them both dive on Asuna's location when they went in. So why…?

Then she noticed that nearly hidden by the brightness of Suguha's dot, there was another white one that was blinking.

"……?"

There couldn't be anyone from Rath using a Soul Translator other than them. So who did that dot represent? She scrolled the mouse cursor and carefully clicked the tiny dot, bringing up a new window, then squinted to read the small English font.

"Let's see…limit, opposition quotient…detection threshold… report? What is this…?"

She was about to inquire as to what she was looking at when Kikuoka abruptly yelped, "Wh-whaaat?!"

He'd been looking at Kazuto Kirigaya's graph when she read the words, and his outburst was so sudden that she nearly jumped. "Wh-what was that for?!" she snapped.

Kikuoka didn't reply. He grabbed the mouse and expanded the window Rinko had just opened. Then he leaned forward and muttered to himself. "My god…it is! It's a new kind of limit-breaking fluctlight…! But why now, why this moment?!"

He scratched his head furiously, thinking hard. Rinko stared at him in surprise. "What…? Do you mean there's a second A.L.I.C.E.?"

"Yes, exactly…No, wait a minute…This looks like…"

He scrolled rapidly through the text in the window and grunted again.

"Technically…this is not at Alice's level. It looks like the artificial fluctlight broke through the limits of its emotional circuits, rather than its logical circuits…But it's absolutely a valuable sample. I only hope that one stays calm and safe…Oh no! It's heading for the group of Americans just to the south!"

Kikuoka lifted his hands to his head in despair, so Rinko took the mouse back and examined the details log of the period when the fluctlight in question breached its theoretical limits.

"Hmm...yes, it looks like new nodes in the emotional field going off in chain reaction...Hmm? Hey, Mr. Kikuoka?"

"Wh-what is it?" he asked, craning his neck to look at the monitor while he writhed.

"What is this part here? The external order being inserted. It looks very odd to me, almost antagonistic...Like it's trying to prevent the generation of new circuits...," she said, following the fine text carefully. "Inserting simulated pain signal...to right ocular region? So whenever an artificial fluctlight is actually on the verge of surpassing its boundaries, this process is trying to kill that drive with pain. Why did you put this kind of limitation on the Underworlders?"

"Um...what? We didn't do that. Of course we wouldn't—it's completely contrary to the goals of the project...In fact, that would be outright sabotage."

"Yes...exactly. Also, this code is written differently than Higa's...Ahhh, there's a bit of text commented out here at the start of it...'Code Eight-Seven-One'? What is Eight-Seven-One?"

"Eight-Seven-One? I've never heard that number before...No, wait...Wait a minute—I swear that popped up not long ago..."

Kikuoka leaped up and rushed a few steps, wooden sandals clacking, and grabbed a filthy, faded lab coat from a nearby chair. He whipped it open sharply and stared at the inside of the collar.

"What is it? What are you looking for?" Rinko asked. Kikuoka's eyes were wide behind his black-framed glasses. He flipped the coat around and thrust the tag toward her. Written upon it in black marker ink was the number *871*.

"That coat belongs to the man who just left with Higa. I think his name was Yanai...," she mumbled, hearing her own voice trail off.

Yanai. *Ya-na-i.*

In the Japanese syllabary, where nearly every character could also be converted to one of the ten numerals, the three characters of *ya*, *na*, and *i* were...

"…Eight…seven…one?!"

Rinko and Kikuoka stood up straight in shock.

—⁂—

Through the fading vision of his remaining eye, Iskahn, the chief of the pugilists, watched the red army approaching.

The soldiers spoke to one another in their strange words and approached in a circle until they were just twenty mels away. When they were convinced the pugilists no longer meant to fight, they seemed satisfied.

Then they all shouted some fierce, unintelligible thing and stomped the earth together.

Iskahn squeezed the hand of the knight woman next to him with his shattered left hand. He could feel her giving pressure back, resulting in a pleasant kind of pain to his numbed hand. He started to close his eyes, ready to greet his end…

"……What's that…?" Sheyta said. He lifted his head.

From across the chasm to the north of the battle, a huge force was approaching, dust storms rising in their wake.

They had large, round bodies. Flat, protruding snouts. Hanging ears.

Orcs.

"…How come?" Iskahn mumbled in a daze. The orc army was supposed to be waiting far to the north near the Eastern Gate, as Emperor Vecta had ordered. Just because he had vanished didn't mean the orders no longer counted. As evidence of that, the surviving dark knights were standing around with foolish obedience just across the ravine, waiting for further orders.

Iskahn watched the orc army approach, baffled, until he noticed a small figure sprinting right at the front.

It was not an orc. It had greenish-golden hair, light-green garments, and blindingly white skin. That was a human—a young woman from the human lands.

But it almost looked as though that one frail little swordswoman was leading the entire force of orcs. The red soldiers surrounding the pugilists hesitated, noticing the oncoming army.

Then the girl at the head of the orcs charged out onto the stone bridge spanning the ravine. There was a bright flash; she had drawn a long silver blade from over her back.

In Iskahn's left hand, Sheyta's fingers twitched, reacting to something about this.

The human girl was about at the middle of the bridge when she raised the long blade high overhead. She was still over two hundred mels away from the red soldiers at that point.

But...

Suddenly, her arms blurred. Even Iskahn's sharp eyes couldn't make out the slashing motion. There was simply a glint of silver light—and then something much more terrible and wondrous.

A line of brilliant light ran across the blackened ground, and then suddenly, dozens of red soldiers standing in its path were dismembered, collapsing to the ground before they could even scream.

The sword in the girl's hands flipped back around, then jumped with chilling speed. The beam of light again split the red forces, slicing clean through the heavily outfitted soldiers, armor and all.

"......Incredible," Sheyta said in a barely audible whisper.

Sinon raised the Hecate II that had been Solus's bow moments ago without hesitation.

Subtilizer was maybe only fifty feet away. It was too close to snipe with an antimateriel rifle. At this distance, keeping a moving target within the high-zoom scope would be exceedingly difficult.

So Sinon, trying to finish the fight before Subtilizer could go on the move, pulled the trigger the instant that the finder lens of the scope went dark with its target.

There was a flash. An explosion.

Sinon was hit with incredible recoil force as she hovered in the air. Her body wanted to rotate on a diagonal, but she used all her will to contain it. If she was going to take this much blowback for every shot, consecutive firing would be all but impossible. But as long as this first shot landed, it wouldn't matter.

Once she was stable, Sinon caught Subtilizer in her view again.

Her eyes went wide with shock.

The man standing on the bizarre winged creature had his left arm raised and his fingers bent like talons. There was darkness and light pulsating violently in his palm, and in the center, shining brightly, was what could only be the bullet Sinon had fired.

So he could suck that up, just as he'd tried to do to her soul?

The .50-caliber antimateriel rifle bullet could penetrate an inch of steel plate.

Sinon felt an inkling of fear creep into her heart. Right on cue with that, the darkness exuding from Subtilizer's hand grew larger and more powerful.

"Don't give in," she muttered, not realizing that she was doing it. Then she shouted, "Don't give in, Hecate!!"

Zblurk.

The light split the darkness.

A huge hole appeared in Subtilizer's hand, spraying blood and flesh into a rearward vortex.

I can do this!!

Sinon inhaled deeply and pulled the Hecate II's bolt. The empty cartridge glittered and twirled as it fell through empty sky.

Subtilizer stared at his tattered left hand in silence. The inky blackness was filling the space the bullet had blasted there like liquid, but it was not the sort of wound that could simply be healed like that.

He looked up and stared at Sinon, no longer smiling. His other hand moved to his side, removing the crossbow there.

"…Hmph," Sinon snorted. There was no way that primitive thing could keep up with her antimateriel rifle……

Nyurp.

The crossbow suddenly warped. Its sideways-extending limbs folded inward, and it stretched to over twice its original length. The wooden frame took on a metallic shine.

In the span of a second, Subtilizer went from holding a crossbow to bearing a huge rifle nearly the size of the Hecate. She recognized it instantly.

A Barrett XM500.

It was a .50-caliber antimateriel rifle like the Hecate II but from a newer generation.

The twisted smile returned to Subtilizer's lips.

"...All right, then," Sinon muttered, steadying the butt of the Hecate against her shoulder.

⁓

"Whoa...a-are you okay?" Yanai stammered, as though he was actually concerned. It was enough to make Higa temporarily forget his pain.

"Y-you *shot* me! What do *you* think?!"

"Uh, I wasn't trying to hit you; I really wasn't. I'm not ready to be a murderer. What's the point of buying a nice condo on the west coast if I'm living my days terrified of catching a homicide charge?"

When he realized that Yanai was serious, Higa felt the tension drain out, along with his strength. He told himself to tighten up and gingerly checked on his shoulder.

The bullet had deflected off the side of the duct and hit him just below the collarbone. It wasn't pain he felt all along his right arm, but cold numbness. The underarm of his shirt was already dark red with blood; it was definitely more than just a scratch.

Fear of the present situation and future developments was finally starting to creep up from his stomach. Higa's breathing quickened. Above him, Yanai was still smirking over his advantage.

"The truth is that I was planning to mess with your work first, destroy the maintenance connector, then escape down to Main Control. I'm supposed to be hitching a ride with them on their sub. Since no one from Rath has died, as long as we get Alice all safely contained, that's a happy ending as far as I'm concerned."

"No one...has died...?" Higa repeated, feeling the pain vanish again. "If we don't take advantage of this chance to heal Kirigaya, his mind will never recover! *You'll* be the one who killed his soul, Yanai! And you claim you're not ready to be a murderer!"

"Oh. Ohhh...That guy..."

The expression was gone from Yanai's face. His stubbled cheeks twitched a few times in the orange emergency lighting.

"Yeah...That kid can die for all I care."

"Wha......?"

"I mean, he killed her. He killed my sweet Admi."

"Ad...mi...?" Higa repeated, perplexed.

Yanai exploded with indignation. "The pontifex of the Axiom Church! Her Holiness, Administrator! I had an agreement with her, you see. I was going to give her all the help she needed for complete control over the Underworld. I said that if the server ever got reinitialized, I'd make sure to save her on a lightcube."

Higa could scarcely believe what he was hearing.

The Axiom Church was the name of the organization created by the residents of the Underworld to rule over them. It enforced its control with unbelievably strict laws and a massive military might that the common people could not disobey.

The reason that Higa's team had known about their barrier-breaking fluctlight "Alice" and yet not taken control of her was because, in the time-accelerated Underworld, the Axiom Church had immediately arrested Alice and performed memory-altering routines on her fluctlight.

It was too fast, in fact. And too precisely performed.

Almost as if they'd known ahead of time exactly what an artificial fluctlight was.

And that, in fact, was true. The Axiom Church—or at least, the fluctlight who'd been its supreme leader, Administrator—had known exactly how the world worked.

"So *you* corrupted the Underworld...," Higa growled.

Yanai clicked his tongue. "Now, now, she was the one who made contact with me *first*. I was on duty, and I heard a girl's voice coming through the speaker, which was quite alarming... She managed to find the entire command list for the Underworld on her own and opened a connection back to the console. And if you want to assign blame, that's *your* fault for not eliminating the command to summon the list."

He chuckled and then, for some reason, got a dreamy look in his eyes.

"At first, I thought the Underworld in its current state was bound to be wiped sooner or later. If they were all going to get erased, then what was the harm? So I snuck into the STL to go see Admi. And let me tell you...I've never seen such a beautiful girl in my life. The girl Mr. Sugou had trapped in *ALO* was cute, but everything about Admi, from her personality, to her voice, to her mannerisms—all of it was my absolute ideal in a woman. So she made a promise to me. If I helped her, she would make me her number-one slave. And one day we'd rule the real world, too, and she'd make me a king..."

No...I take that back. He was the one who got corrupted.

The realization was a thrill of horror that put all of Higa's hair on end. Yanai was a fool and a traitor, but he wasn't a dunce. What kind of a being must this Administrator be to ensnare a man like Yanai and completely own him this way?

Suddenly, Yanai's look of reminiscence vanished. "But...now she's dead. She was killed...by that boy who ruined Mr. Sugou's experiment, too. I have to avenge her. My poor Admi..."

His bloodshot eyes bulged, and he pointed his gun at Higa again. The automatic pistol cocked the hammer after firing, so the pressure needed to pull the trigger was much lighter than the first time. If he squeezed his finger in at all, the gun was going to go off.

"That's right. I suppose it's true…I can't give her the true memorial she deserves unless I kill at least *one* person or so…"

The pupils in the middle of Yanai's bulging eyes were tiny and jittering.

…*Uh-oh. He's serious this time.*

Higa closed his eyes.

———

I won't make it.

Leafa knew that Asuna, Klein, Lisbeth, and the others were all in danger in the distance, and she bit her lip in frustration. But standing right before her were about thirty or so soldiers wearing red armor.

She had enlisted the help of Lilpilin, who seemed to be a leader of the orcs, and headed south to rescue Asuna and Kirito, but the first people they finally found did not belong to the Human Guardian Army she was looking for.

It was a few hundred men and women, apparently pugilists—a group belonging to the Dark Army with the orcs, according to Lilpilin—surrounded by an army that had dived in from the real world. Leafa cast aside her brief shred of hesitation and rushed to aid them.

"I'll attack the enemy force on my own. Lilpilin, you take your troops to the pugilists and only defeat those enemies who try to attack them," she ordered.

Lilpilin protested furiously. "We would wather fight with you!" But she stayed firm, shaking her head and grabbing his large orc hand to squeeze it.

"You can't. I don't want you to suffer any more losses than you already have. I'll be fine…I don't care how many thousands of them there are—I won't let them win."

She left him with a smile, then headed toward the red army alone.

Terraria's hit points had nearly infinite regenerative power, as she'd seen already. And she knew that the people ahead from the real world had expendable lives, like she did. Given that it didn't seem likely they'd reach Kirito's group in time anyway, Leafa couldn't stand the thought of letting the orcs die for no good reason.

She sliced up a few dozen enemies with a pair of ultra-long-range slashes and kept running, plunging straight into her foes' midst.

For whatever reason, her sword skills were expanded to several times the length of their *ALO* forms, and she unleashed them with abandon. With every colorful swing of Terraria's GM weapon, Verdurous Anima, blood sprayed and spattered.

The delay between sword skills had not disappeared, however, and in each interval, sharp blades came swinging for her. She was unable to evade them all and suffered many wounds, each one causing her to swoon with the burning pain. And yet...

"Eeeiii!!" she screamed, stomping the ground hard. A green glow wafted from beneath her feet, instantly healing all wounds. But while it healed her body, it could not stop the lingering memory of the pain, and Leafa had to keep swinging and fighting through it.

She would suffer a thousand wounds, if that was what it took to drive the enemies here back to the real world. If there was any role she was meant to play for having come down at unintended coordinates, it would have to be saving every last Underworlder she came across. The people whom Kirito loved and tried to protect.

"*She's such a boss!!*" shouted one of the enemies in English, thrusting his sword at her, which she blocked with her left arm.

"Seyaaaa!!"

Her return blow instantly ended the other man.

Leafa craned her neck to bite the sword that was still stuck in her arm and pulled it out, then spat it onto the ground with a fresh spill of blood.

The second shots were simultaneous.

The bullets from the two antimateriel rifles nearly touched as they passed, warping the paths and sending them both blazing off into nothingness.

Sinon did not lose her balance in miserable fashion this time; she kicked back against the air to control the recoil. She could see that Subtilizer kept his feet planted on the winged creature, which was frantically flapping its wings to stay stable.

This was an entirely new experience for Sinon, engaging in a shoot-out with antimateriel rifles in completely open space, both side to side and up and down. Obviously, it never happened in *GGO*, since the game didn't support player flight. Shooting the Hecate without a bipod to stabilize it the usual way was very different, and the kickback it had in midair was beyond anything she could have expected.

Whoever won this fight would do so because they could limit the recoil and get off the next shot first, Sinon thought as she expelled her empty. Subtilizer would be thinking along the same lines. When she tried to swing around him to the right, he went the other way, keeping them circling.

Eventually, they both launched into acrobatic maneuvers at the same moment, without any kind of signal. She made sharp turns in midair, as hard as she could without losing her balance, moving at random. As she kept the muzzle trained on the enemy, she was keenly aware that she, too, was within his sights.

Subtilizer's Barrett seemed to blur as it caught up to her movement and intercepted her path.

Here he comes!!

She gritted her teeth and opened her eyes wide in concentration.

Flames shot from the end of the Barrett.

Sinon twisted her body to the left as she traveled at maximum speed. The lethal bullet passed closely enough that it could have burned her chest. Her blue armor cracked audibly.

Dodged it!

It was her first and last chance. When Subtilizer came to a stop to stabilize the recoil, that was when she would shoot.

She lifted the Hecate, aiming it.

Battle for the Underworld Status Map
Final Stress Test, Day Two

Eastern Gate

Integrity Knight
Fanatio

Integrity Knight
Deusolbert

Ravine Created by Asuna

Teaming Up

Orc Battalion Chief Lilpilin

Integrity Knight Sheyta

Pugilists Guild Champion Iskahn

Earth Goddess Terraria, Leafa

In Battle

American Players as Dark Knights

In Battle

Asuna
Ruins

Chinese/Korean Players as Dark Knights

PoH

Human Army Decoy Force

Real-World Reinforcements: Klein, Lisbeth, Silica, Agil, etc.

Integrity Knight
Renly

Student
Ronie

Student
Tiese

Kirito
(Empty)

In Battle

Subtilizer

Sun Goddess Solus, Sinon

Integrity Knight
Alice

World's End Altar

Illustration: Tatsuya Kurusu

But a new bullet came flying straight at her.

Consecutive shots—how?!

Oh…oh no.

Unlike the Hecate, which had a bolt that needed to be slid for each shot, the Barrett was a semiautomatic rifle.

The recognition of that fact happened at the same moment that Sinon's left leg practically exploded off its base above the knee.

—∿∿—

The ones who fought the hardest against desperate circumstances and ended up standing on the battlefield at the very end were Asuna, who had the protection of her super-account; Renly the Integrity Knight, a resident of the Underworld; his dragon mount; Tiese the primary trainee, who fought bravely despite Renly's protection; and Sortiliena the swordswoman.

Through eyesight faded by extreme exhaustion and pain, Asuna watched Renly fight with a fervor that was positively demonic. Dozens of minutes ago, he'd appeared on the front line of battle, hurling a cross-shaped boomerang with a mind of its own that sliced the oncoming enemies in two with abandon. Its impact on the battle was so intense that it actually succeeded in pushing back the furious charge of the players from Japan's neighbors over the course of a few minutes. The burning breath of his gigantic dragon also frightened the enemy. It was more than enough evidence for them to accept that they were fighting a true dragon knight born and bred in the alternate land of the Underworld.

But eventually, they began to notice that while Renly was throwing and controlling the boomerang, he was essentially defenseless. After dozens of chances, the latest throw of Renly's weapon sweeping back the front line of red soldiers was accompanied by a hail of spears thrown from the rear. The strategy that Asuna had secretly feared seeing from the Americans was finally coming into play.

The spears came down from the red sky like black rain.

Renly's dragon swept in to protect its master with outstretched wings and body. Scales and blood sprayed into the air as the beast toppled sideways.

A fresh wave of spears came just as quickly. Renly looked up at the pointed heads as the missiles soared down, hissing. He immediately cradled Tiese, who was right behind him, hiding her beneath his body.

Two spears hit his back, and he fell forward, covering her. The cross-shaped boomerang lost its control and flashed, splitting in two and sticking into the dirt in the distance.

By that point, the fighting elsewhere on the battlefield was essentially over. The exhausted and fallen Japanese players were easy pickings for the red soldiers, who swarmed them, each eager to be the first to strike. Blood, flesh, brief screams, and whimpers emerged before the Japanese players quiet.

Many of them, too, suffered broken shields and armor and were bound and tied on the ground, helpless. Their tears of frustration looked just as painful as the tracks of red from their wounds.

The defensive line of two thousand converted players had been neutralized, and the army of the Human Empire that had been at the center was exposed at last. About four hundred of the human army's men-at-arms raised their swords and formed a circle around the unarmed supply team and priests. Their faces were filled with desperate determination, and they waited in silence for the right moment to make their doomed charge at the encroaching red wave.

"……Stop it……," Asuna heard her own voice say.

It was the sound of her heart breaking, not for the pain of the wounds she'd suffered, but out of despair and sadness.

"Please…don't do this…"

Her rapier fell to the ground. A little droplet that ran off her cheek splashed against its ragged, tarnished length. A red silhouette standing before her raised its doublehanded sword high overhead and screamed something furious.

But just at that moment, a voice like a clap of thunder paused the blade in its downward swing, as well as other fights happening all around them.

"*Stoppppp!!*"

It was the man in the black poncho who'd been watching the fighting from a distance. The ghost of PoH, leader of the murderous Laughing Coffin guild.

The players from the neighboring countries seemed to be taking their cues from the poncho man, viewing him as their leader, so they reluctantly lowered their weapons. The man who'd been about to cut Asuna in two clicked his tongue, pulled his sword back, and gave her a rough kick instead.

She fell helplessly to her back and struggled with limp arms to get up. A tall man was walking toward her, the ends of his black leather coat swaying. He said something in a low but clearly audible voice to the red players around him, but it was in Korean, so Asuna couldn't understand it.

All those closest to the man nodded and began to pass on the message to their fellows through the crowd. Out of nowhere, the man standing next to Asuna grabbed her by the hair and pulled her up. She shrieked, but he ignored her and dragged her roughly along.

Similar things were happening elsewhere. Apparently, they were going to bunch all the surviving Japanese players in one place.

The man in the black poncho strode right up to the men-at-arms of the human army, who still stood with their swords at the ready. Then he turned and waved, giving another direction to the man holding Asuna by the hair.

He kicked her in the back and sent her sprawling several yards forward into the dirt. More Japanese players toppled to the ground nearby. The number of survivors was already under two hundred.

Maximum HP value seemed to be linked to survival here, because many were high-level players. A quick glance confirmed the presence of the *ALO* territorial lords and the Sleeping Knights.

Everyone's armor was either shattered or ripped away, leaving them in nothing but tattered clothes. Exposed skin was covered in wounds, and many still had broken blades jutting from their flesh. All that she could see on their faces was deep futility and defeat.

She didn't want to see any more. She wanted to lie facedown in the dirt with her eyes closed as the final blow came.

Instead, however, Asuna watched through blurry tears, trying to burn into her mind the image of all these players who had converted to take part in the battle.

Another survey of the area led her to a female player on her knees some distance away, her shoulders trembling. The girl's pink hair was smeared with dirt and dust, and her dark-red outfit was torn here and there.

Asuna crawled over to the girl's back and put her arms around her friend's body. Lisbeth froze up for a moment, then rested her head against Asuna's chest. Her blood- and tear-stained cheeks twitched as she rasped, "They all...I couldn't...I was...They..."

"No...no, Liz!" Asuna told her sternly through her own tears. "It's not your fault. It's mine...If I had been thinking smarter, I would have seen this coming..."

"Asuna, I...I had no idea. I didn't know that fighting could be this scary...That losing could be this awful...I just didn't know..."

Asuna couldn't come up with an answer. She squeezed Lisbeth harder, cradling her friend. More tears flooded from her eyes and ran down her cheeks.

There was more quiet sobbing nearby, and Asuna saw that Agil was lying motionless on the ground, with Silica curled up and weeping next to him.

Agil was so horribly disfigured that it was a wonder he had any hit points left at all. He must have fought like a man possessed to protect Silica. Multiple broken swords and spears stuck out of his body, and his limbs looked like they'd all been crushed. His jaw was clenched, surely to fight back against unimaginably excruciating pain.

Nearby, Klein sat cross-legged with his head bowed. His left arm had been cut off from the shoulder. His trademark bandana was tied around the stump.

Essentially, all the survivors were in this sort of state.

The hooded man in the black poncho surveyed the crowd of two hundred whose weapons, armor, and even will to fight had all been taken away. He had a huge smile. Then he turned and started walking toward the men-at-arms of the human army.

Asuna waited in horror for him to raise his hand and give the command to slaughter them all.

But to her surprise, he addressed them in Japanese. "Throw down your weapons and surrender. If you do, we will not kill you or our prisoners over here."

The men-at-arms looked briefly startled, then deeply furious. Sortiliena the captain strode forward to stand face-to-face with the man in the poncho. She must have been fighting on the front line with Renly, because her sword was chipped, and blood ran down her forehead.

But Sortiliena was still beautiful in her defiance. "Slander!! After all of this, you think that our lives are so precious that we would—?"

"No! Listen to him!!" Asuna interrupted. She lifted her teary face, still cradling Lisbeth, and pleaded, "Please…you have to survive! Do whatever it takes, no matter how humiliating!! That's what…That's the only thing…It's our only…"

Hope.

The word caught in her chest.

Sortiliena and the other guards clamped their mouths shut, their faces contorting and trembling with emotion…until their shoulders dropped at last.

When they let their swords fall clanking to the ground, the rows and rows of players from the neighboring countries let out a victorious roar, which soon turned to chants of those countries' names.

The hooded man in black beckoned a few players over and gave them an order. They promptly obeyed and started running to the back of the circle, dividing up the surrendered members of the human army.

Before she had time to wonder what they were doing, the black-poncho man strode quickly over to stand right before Asuna. Even from this distance, she couldn't see through the darkness under his hood. The only details were a powerful lower jaw and black curls hanging around his neck.

That mouth of his formed a cruel smile, and he said, almost cheerfully, "Hey…long time no see, Flash."

Ah! It is him!!

Her breath caught in her throat. The words came unbidden from her chest. "You're…PoH…!"

"Ohhh, isn't that a nostalgic name? I'm so happy you remember it."

Klein had his hand on the ground and was leaning closer to them. Now he looked up at the hooded man with fire in his eyes.

"You…it's *you*. You're still alive…you murderous bastard!!"

Klein tried to grab him with his one remaining arm, but the man easily kicked him over with a boot.

Asuna gritted her teeth and growled, "Is this vengeance? Are you trying to get back at the frontline group for destroying Laughing Coffin…?"

"……"

PoH stared down at her without a word. Then she noticed that his shoulders were trembling. Within a few seconds, he was shaking with uncontrollable mirth. Under the poncho, his body twisted and writhed with laughter.

When the spasms finally stopped, PoH thrust a finger at her and said, "Uh, wait, wait…I'm forgetting how to say it in Japanese, since I've been in America for so long. I've forgotten all my slang."

He twirled his finger around and then snapped in realization. "Ah, that's right! Are you taking crazy pills? This is hilarious, man…"

He went down to one knee so he could stare Asuna in the face at eye level. The faint gleam of his eyes in the light was the only thing she could see in that hood.

"...I'll let you in on a little secret. Did you know that the one who told you people where to find the Laughing Coffin hideout was me?"

"Wha...?"

Asuna, Klein, and even nearly dead Agil were shocked.

"What...? Why would you...?"

"I mean, partly I just wanted to see you apes killing one another...but the biggest reason was this: I wanted to make all of *you* murderers, too. The great and mighty frontline conquerors, everyone's heroes. It was hard as hell to set that up...to time everything so that I warned Laughing Coffin ahead of time, but only just enough so that they could fight back, rather than abandoning the place and running."

So that's why we found evidence that our plan to ambush the hideout had leaked ahead of time, Asuna realized in shock.

Because of that, the superior frontline team—in both level and equipment—found themselves on the defensive and suffered a few casualties. It was Kirito's fierce fighting, as a solo player who was among the group, that turned the tide of battle. It was when he cut down one of the principal members of the gang that things turned for good...

"So you...*wanted* that to happen?" Asuna whispered. "You wanted Kirito...to have to PK someone...?"

"Yes, absolutely, yes," PoH said in English excitedly. "I was in hiding, watching the battle play out. In fact, I nearly lost my cover by busting out laughing when Master Black snapped and killed those two idiots. My plan was to paralyze him and you with poison and give you a nice long interview about that experience...but I wasn't counting on a premature ending at the seventy-fifth floor."

A sudden surge of anger made Asuna temporarily forget her pain. "D-do you have any idea...how much Kirito suffered and agonized over that?!"

"Oh, he did? That's nice to hear," PoH replied, but his voice was as cold as ice. "But I dunno if I totally buy that. If you *really* regretted it…then wouldn't you hate to even look at a VR game? You'd feel so guilty about the people you killed. I know he's in here, too. I can feel him. I dunno why he's locked up in a wagon… but I can ask him myself."

PoH gave the stunned Asuna a smirk and leaped back to his feet. Against the background of the still-simmering cheers of victory, his freezing voice said, "*It's showwwwtime.*"

That was his catchphase in *SAO* when he was up to his tricks. PoH raised his hand.

In the distance, the red soldiers violently pushed forward a wheelchair, with a girl in a gray uniform trying to keep up.

Oh…

No.

Anything but that.

The silent pleas filled Asuna's breast. Klein tried to jump to his feet, but the soldiers held him down at once.

PoH leaned over to stare down at the wheelchair being brought before him.

"……Hmm?" he grumbled, then tapped an emaciated leg hanging from the seat with his toe. "What's this…? Hey, Blackie, wake up. You hear me, Black Swordsman?"

Black Swordsman was an old nickname of Kirito's—but he did not react at all. His body rested against the back of the chair, painfully and visibly thin through his black shirt, and his face was downcast. His empty right sleeve swayed in the breeze, and the hand that clutched the two swords in his lap was bony.

Ronie got knocked to the ground at Asuna's side. Her eyes were red and swollen from crying. "During the battle," she whispered, "Kirito tried and tried to get up…and eventually he got quiet, like he was out of strength…But…his tears…his tears just kept coming…"

"Ronie…" Asuna reached out and hugged the sobbing girl.

Then Asuna lifted her face and snapped at PoH, "You can tell by now. He fought and fought and fought, and now he's damaged. So don't mess with him anymore! Just leave Kirito alone!!"

But the man in the black poncho ignored what Asuna had to say. He stared right into Kirito's face at point-blank range.

"Whoa, whoa, whoa! Are you kidding me? He's all slack-jawed! Hey, wake up! Stand up, dude! Good...*morning*?!" PoH said, placing his foot on the silver wheel and mercilessly kicking the chair over.

The wheelchair toppled with a tremendous clatter, throwing its helpless cargo onto the ground. Asuna and Klein made to get up, only to be stopped by enemy swords. Agil growled, deep in his throat, and Lisbeth, Silica, and Ronie all shrieked.

None of this had any effect on the aggressor, however. He walked over to Kirito and roughly turned him over with his toe. "The hell...? You really are busted, huh? So the great hero is a vegetable now?"

Kirito's left arm still clutched the two swords; PoH yanked the white scabbard away from him. He pulled the sword out until it revealed a blade pitifully broken in the middle.

PoH clicked his tongue in disappointment and made to discard the useless weapon. But...

"A...*aaah*..."

A tiny croak escaped Kirito's throat, and he reached weakly toward the white sword with his one arm.

"Oh?! You're moving?! What, you want this thing?" PoH said, teasingly waggling the sword. Then he dropped it, and when Kirito tried to go for it in the air, he grabbed the boy's arm and pulled him up.

"C'mon, say something!!" he said, smacking Kirito on the cheeks.

Asuna's vision started going red with rage. But before she could even get to her feet, Klein was screaming bloody murder.

"You son of a bitch!! Don't you dare touch hiiiiiim!!"

He tried to lunge for the man with his one arm, but a large, thick sword split his back and pinned him straight to the ground. Klein gagged and spit up a huge glob of blood, but he kept pulling upward, trying to rip his own body apart to keep moving.

"You…! You're the one…man…I'll…never…for……"

Whud!!

A second sword pierced Klein's back.

More tears flooded from Asuna's eyes. It was a wonder to her that she could have any left.

—⁂—

It was not the pain of losing her leg that got to Sinon; it was the fear of not being able to fly properly anymore.

To this point, she had learned to control the voluntary flight system by kicking her legs against the air. Her first attempt at a sharp evasive turn turned into an ugly tailspin instead.

"Ugh…"

She grunted and switched to the one bit of movement she knew she could manage: retreat straight backward. The stream of blood shooting from her left leg created a vivid red line in the air before her.

Sinon aimed at Subtilizer as she pushed backward at maximum possible speed and fired a third bullet. But her enemy, who pursued with confidence, fired a fourth bullet from his own rifle.

When the two bullets traveled the exact same path from opposite ends, they met with a horribly discordant twang, creating a shower of sparks and knocking each bullet off to the side to vanish into nothingness.

She pulled the bolt handle to expel both the empty cartridge and the growing fear in her lungs and then fired a fourth shot. Again, two thunderbolts overlapped. The collision of bullets in midair unleashed a massive amount of kinetic energy and sent them both spiraling away.

A fifth shot. Sixth.

The results were exactly the same. Subtilizer was intentionally shooting on Sinon's rhythm and hitting her shots in the air—that much was clear.

Obviously, in the real world, and even in *GGO*, this was

impossible. But imagination trumped all in this place. Because Subtilizer was intentionally doing this, and Sinon was anticipating that outcome, the impossible phenomenon of supersonic bullets striking one another became reality.

But despite this, there were only three actions Sinon could take: yank the bolt, take aim, pull the trigger.

The seventh bullet deflected off to the left with a mournful scream. Discharge. Aim.

Click.

Click, click. The striker did nothing beneath her finger.

A single magazine for the Hecate II was seven bullets. She had no backup.

But the Barrett XM500 could hold ten. He had two shots left.

Despite being over a hundred yards away from him in the air, Sinon could clearly make out Subtilizer's cold smile.

He pointed the black gun. It spat fire.

This time, it was Sinon's right leg that blew off from the base.

Now she couldn't even fly straight. Sinon's body began to plummet.

Subtilizer stifled his recoil and put his eye to the scope to aim his final shot. That blue marble eye, magnified by the other end of the lens, pierced Sinon right through the heart.

I'm sorry.

I'm sorry, Asuna. I'm sorry, Yui. I'm sorry...Kirito.

No sooner had Sinon mouthed the words than the XM500's tenth bullet emerged from its jaw. A spiral of red flames propelled it, tracing the route Subtilizer envisioned, until it shattered Sinon's blue armor, evaporated her shirt, and reached her skin—

Bzzat!!

There was another burst of sparks.

Her eyes went from half-closed in anticipation of the shot to wide open. The long, rapidly spinning bullet was grinding itself against a cheap little metal disc.

At the center of the spinning vortex of sparks, a piece of metal a fraction of an inch thick seemed to be shining with an unyielding will of its own. The sight caused tears to spring to Sinon's eyes.

I won't give up.

I'll never give up. I have to believe. In me. In the Hecate. And in the boy I'm connected to through this medal.

There was a brighter flash, and both the silver disc and the rifle bullet evaporated.

Sinon raised the Hecate II with purpose and put her finger against the trigger. The weapon might have been turned into a gun through the power of her imagination, but the system properties given to the weapon would still be maintained: the power of Solus's bow, the Annihilation Ray, which automatically absorbed resources from the space around it to charge up attacks.

She could fire it. The magazine might be out of bullets, but the Hecate would respond for her.

"Fiiiiire!!"

She pulled the trigger.

What the gun expelled was not an armor-piercing round encased in metal. Instead, it was unlimited energy, compressed into a beam of white light that shot out in a straight line, a rainbow halo radiating from the muzzle.

Subtilizer's smile vanished. He started to slide to the right to evade it, but the white beam hit the body of the Barrett. An orange fireball erupted from the gun, engulfing Subtilizer.

A boom. A blast.

Sinon felt a wave of heat on her skin as she fell like a rock, and a few seconds later, she slammed into the rocky ground below.

She certainly couldn't fly anymore; now she could hardly crawl. The pain from her blown-off legs was so intense it was difficult just to stay conscious. Still, she forced her eyes to stay open so she could confirm the outcome of her desperate attack.

The cloud of black smoke in the distant sky floated off with the wind.

And appearing from the center of it, still hovering, was Subtilizer.

But he was not unharmed. His right arm had been blown off in the rifle blast, and the raw wound on his shoulder was faintly smoking. The right side of his smooth face was charred, and blood trailed from his lip.

At last, there was true malice in his expression.

...All right. I'll face off against you as many times as it takes.

She drew upon all the strength she had left to raise the Hecate again.

A few seconds later, Subtilizer's gaze left her. The winged creature spun around, little trails of smoke rising from it, and flew straight to the south.

It was all Sinon could do just to hold the antimateriel rifle; she gently set it down. The moment it touched the earth, it returned to its original form, a white bow.

With her last bit of strength, Sinon raised her right hand to touch the broken piece of chain still resting on her upper chest.

"Kirito......"

A single tear ran down her cheek.

Leafa no longer had the wherewithal even to pull out the many blades stuck into her body.

All the pain of her body melted together, like her exposed nerves were being poked and prodded by needles. Several of the wounds clearly should have been fatal. The two swords penetrating her abdomen cut into her organs each time she moved, and the one going through her back and out her chest was clearly splitting her heart.

But Leafa did not stop.

"Aaaaaaah!!"

She screamed, blood flying everywhere, as she activated a sword skill for the hundredth time—if not twice that by now.

The long katana Verdurous Anima took on a green glow and cut through the air every which way. An arc of compressed light held its shape for a moment before expending it silently outward, countless enemies collapsing to pieces in its wake.

In the pause period after her massive attack, a number of enemies rushed in on her. She leaped out of the way in the nick of time, avoiding the majority of their attacks, but a long halberd did slice her left arm off.

Holding firm against the impulse to collapse from the shock, she screamed "*Zeyaaaa!!*" and sliced all three of the foes with a sideways swipe.

Leafa scooped up the arm that had fallen to the ground, pressed it against the stump of her shoulder, and stamped her foot on the earth. A green flash brought grass and flowers up from the dirt that vanished as soon as they arrived. Her hit points returned to their maximum value, and while the gruesome wound remained, her left arm was attached again.

In this situation, the unlimited regenerative ability that the Terraria account possessed was hardly what you would call a divine blessing. In fact, it was closer to a curse. No matter how wounded she was, how much agony she felt, she could not fall in battle. She was immortal but not invulnerable. It was unimaginable agony.

There was just one simple belief that kept Leafa upright.

Big Brother would never let himself fall from wounds like this.

So I won't fall, either. There are only three thousand of them; I'll cut them all down myself. Because I'm his...I'm Kirito the Black Swordsman's——

"—Little sisterrrrr!!"

The tip of the sword in her left hand blazed with crimson light. The blade thrust forward with a sound like heavy machinery, unleashing a massive spear of light that split the battlefield for a distance of over a hundred yards. *Bwashaaa!* The bodies of enemy soldiers flattened and disintegrated in its vicinity.

"...Haah...huff......"

The breath she expelled soon turned to a gout of fresh blood. Leafa wiped her mouth and straightened up unsteadily—only for a long spear to come hurtling toward her, ramming straight through her left eye and out the back of her head.

She stumbled a few steps backward...but Leafa did not fall.

Instead, she grabbed the hilt of the spear with her left hand and yanked it straight out. There was a very eerie sensation inside her head unrelated to physical pain.

"Aaah...aaaaaah!!"

She stomped the ground again to recover her hit points. The left side of her head realigned with a clicking noise, and she could see on that side again.

Somehow, now that she got a better look, the enemy was down to perhaps just a hundred in number. Leafa grinned, extended a bloody hand forward, raised her palm, and brought her fingers together.

The oncoming soldiers roared at her with one last desperate rush. She raised her long katana with a ponderous motion.

"Iyeeaaaaah!!"

A flash.

Blood flew, and Leafa threw herself amid the severed enemy group without fear.

Three minutes later, when the final enemy had fallen, the number of metal implements piercing Leafa's body had risen to ten.

The strength went from her limbs, and she toppled backward, but the swords and spears sticking through her back only propped her up before she could fall all the way.

With the sound of her name being shrieked, and the oncoming footsteps of Lilpilin and the orcs, Leafa let her eyelids close.

She mumbled, "Didn't I...give it everything I had...Big Brother.........?"

———

The muffled shout came through his in-ear speaker right as Yanai started to pull the trigger of the gun.

"Get out of the way, Higa!!"

Huh?

Get out of the way of...the bullet? he thought stupidly, when he caught the sound of something whistling through the air as it dropped from a considerable height.

Glonk!!

The sound was not the pistol firing. Something tossed down from the entrance to the cable duct far above them had landed right on Yanai's skull. The man's eyes rolled upward. The hand holding on to the rung slipped.

"Wait...whoa...!"

Higa forgot the pain in his shoulder and used that arm to clutch the ladder, pressing his body as tight to the side of the duct as he could.

The first thing to fall past was an enormous monkey wrench; he was baffled as to where it had come from. Next, he saw a small pistol hurtle by, smelling of gunpowder.

Lastly, Yanai's unconscious body wedged itself between Higa and the wall of the duct and came to a stop.

"Ah...aaah!"

Higa hunched his shoulders and pressed his back harder against the wall. Yanai's body gradually slid past, smearing pungent sweat on Higa's shirt.

"......Ah—," he uttered, right as the unconscious man squeezed through and plunged down the duct, which continued vertically for more than a hundred and fifty feet. There were several thumps as he struck the walls and ladder on the way down to a final, heavy impact at the bottom.

"......Hmm."

Is he...dead? I don't know. Seemed like maybe he just broke two or three bones...or five or six...

Higa's mental state was mostly dazed when a scream through the earpiece brought him back.

"Higa...Hey, Higa!! Are you all right?! Answer me, please!!"

".........I think I'm just a bit...shocked. I've...never heard you scream like that, Miss Rinko..."

"Is…is this really the time for that?! Are you hurt?! Did he shoot you?!"

"Ummm, well…"

Higa took a look at his shoulder. The loss of blood was starting to get gnarly. He could move his right arm, but there was no sensation in it, and it felt very cold. He could tell that his thoughts weren't as sharp as usual, either.

But he inhaled deeply, tensed his gut, and pushed out as lively a voice as he could manage. "Yeah, I'm totally fine! Just a scratch. I'll continue the operation. You keep monitoring Kirito's status, please!!"

"…You're certain you're all right? I'm going to take your word on it! If you're lying, you're in big trouble with me!!"

"Please…I'd appreciate your trust."

He craned his neck to look up at the hatch at least a hundred feet above and carefully waved at Rinko's protruding head. With the distance and darkness, she wouldn't be able to see how much blood he'd lost.

"Well…I'm going back to Subcon, then, but as soon as anything changes in the graph, I'll be right back here! Do your best, Higa!!"

The silhouette was starting to leave when Higa surprised himself by saying, "Uh…M-Miss Rinko."

"What? What is it?!"

"Oh…it's just, uh…"

Did you know that when we were students, it wasn't just Kayaba and that Sugou asshole who were head over heels for you?

It was a question he wanted to ask but didn't, because he felt that saying it out loud would dramatically decrease his chances of getting back alive. Instead, he came up with a substitute on the fly.

"When all of this nonsense is over, would you be open to getting dinner sometime?"

"Yeah, fine, I'll buy you whatever you want—hamburgers, beef bowl, anything. Just get it done!!"

And Dr. Koujiro vanished from view.

What a cheap date.

In fact, as far as trying to avoid "lines the doomed guy says," that wasn't much better.

Higa smirked to himself and looked back at the laptop. He set his numbed fingers over the keyboard and carefully began typing commands.

Connecting STL #3...to #4. Connecting #5...#6...

The font suddenly blurred and went double, probably due to blood loss. Higa shook his head.

All right, Kirito. It's time to wake up, buddy.

—⁓—

Through her veil of tears, Asuna stared at the figure of the man she loved, and she prayed.

Please, Kirito. You can have my heart, my life, my everything... Just open your eyes.

Kirito...

—⁓—

Kirito.

—⁓—

Big Brother.

—⁓—

.........Come on, now......Kirito......

5

Kirito.

It felt like someone was calling my name...and it pulled me out of a nap.

I lifted my eyelids and saw a multitude of ultrafine particles floating in orange light.

Slowly but surely, my hazy vision began to sharpen.

Wavering white fabric—curtains.

Silver window frame. Old, faded glass.

Rustling leaves. Sky colored by sun beginning to set. Slowly trailing jet streams.

I sat up, inhaling dusty air, and saw the back of someone in a high school uniform standing before a dark-green chalkboard. An eraser slid across its surface, smearing away white chalk words.

"...Um, Kirigaya?"

The mention of my name again drew my attention to the face of a different girl, who was standing over me, looking both hesitant and annoyed.

"I want to move that desk."

Apparently, I'd fallen asleep in homeroom, and now I was intruding on cleaning time.

"Oh...sorry," I mumbled, lifting the school bag that was hanging from the side of the desk and getting to my feet.

My head felt heavy.

I was exhausted, like I'd just finished watching some unfathomably long movie. I couldn't remember a single thing about the story, but the last remnants of bitter, powerful emotions stuck in my mind like cobwebs that I shook my head to disperse.

The girl was looking at me with suspicion now, but I turned away from her and began walking toward the door at the back of the classroom, muttering as I went.

"Oh…just a dream………"

(To be continued)

AFTERWORD

Thank you for reading *Sword Art Online 17: Alicization Awakening*.

(Fair warning: I will be discussing lots of spoilers for this book!)

I'm sorry that it took so long since the last volume, *Exploding*. The subtitle for this book, *Awakening*, probably made you wonder, Kirito's been asleep ever since Volume 15; is he finally going to wake up this time?! Well, I'm sorry, but for certain reasons I ended this book on an ambiguous "Is he awake...? Or still asleep...?" kind of scene, meant to carry us to the next volume. The truth is, I wanted to fit all of chapter 21 ("Awakening") into this volume, but that would unbalance things by making this volume *very* fat and the next one *very* thin, so I had to make the painful decision to do things this way. However, while I know it's not exactly an even trade, the follow-up should be right after the next book in my publication schedule, so you won't be left hanging for nearly as long. Just have a bit more patience...!

Now I'd like to talk about the content of the story for a bit. In this volume, Gabriel, Vassago, and Critter arrange an evil plot to bring a whole bunch of American, Korean, and Chinese VRMMO players into the Underworld to lead a fierce battle against the human realm's army and the Japanese players. When I originally wrote this story on my website about a decade ago, I was hoping that it would give pause to the general air of rejection and expulsion of foreign players from online games that was happening in Japan at that time. But because of my lack of writing ability, it ended up breeding more hostility instead, which was something I long felt ashamed of.

When it came time to expand and edit the story for the collected light novel publication, I considered changing this part of the plot entirely, but it felt like that would just be fleeing from my original choice...so in the end, I left the basic structure unchanged. In the *Progressive* series, you've seen the "agitating PKer" known as Vassago, or PoH, begin to leave his malicious mark. Wait until next volume to find out how Kirito brings an end to that malice.

This is the fifteenth year since the *SAO* series was born on a tiny little corner of the Internet, and I feel the satisfaction of realizing how long it's been. But there are also video games, a theatrical movie, and other projects in the works that will continue expanding the *SAO* world. I hope that if you're still interested, you'll come check it all out. Lastly, to my illustrator, abec, for the beautiful and bold depictions of Leafa, Sinon, and the others, and to my editor tackling a new challenge, Miki, thank you for making this happen!

Reki Kawahara—March 2016